The Mockingbird's Ballad

3-24-05

Doak M. Mansfield

The Mockingbird's Ballad

Doak M. Mansfield

illustrated by

Tyler Warren

The Mockingbird's Ballad

Published by Hats Off Books®
610 East Delano Street, Suite 104
Tucson, Arizona 85705 U.S.A.
www.hatsoffbooks.com

International Standard Book Number: 1-58736-383-6
Library of Congress Control Number: 2004112488

Contents

The Story

Perspective

History is a story written by the winner, boss, or owner: a vision of reality—the truth—from where they stand. Anyone who aspires to learn about the past, whether from an ancestor's journey or a nation's development, needs to be respectively attentive to a variety of sources.

The most available information is the winner's story. The honesty ethic requires the researcher or storyteller to seek out and listen to the story of the loser, the tenant, or the hired hand. These folk often don't have the resources or positions to record their version of events. Nevertheless, they have truths to tell. Their perspective is not as accessible as the winner's history, but if the researcher tries, the loser's history can be found. This acquisition depends on openness to unconventional sources—songs, myths, legends, oral traditions, subversive ideas, anti-social activities and attitudes, lawlessness, and counter-culture literature. At a personal level, an application of a form of the golden rule is helpful: "How would it appear or feel to me if I were … ? A phrase from my childhood comes in handy: "Imagine that!" Indeed, imagine that.

This story is not a conventional, traditional, or academic history. It is a historical novel. It is as factual as I could manage to discover from the works of serious scholars, and discern from the accounts by the real historical participants in my story.

Heroism, romance, dignity, and idealism are part of this story. Contemporary cynicism and our inherent, mostly subconscious, fear, estrangement, sloth, and selfishness hold those elements in contempt. Yet there are those "better angels of our nature" that Mr. Lincoln bore witness to, and which inspire many lives both yesterday and today. Thank goodness. Life is barren, hateful, and devoid of community without them.

Conflict, evil, compromise, and self-delusion are equally present in this story. If these elements are not harsh enough it might be because they are too often overemphasized for the sake of a counter-dependent need by some authors. I choose to hope rather than to despair.

The Mockingbird's Ballad is a story that blends my memories and unconscious impressions of my Tennessee ancestors, family, and friends. The names, qualities, and personalities of these characters are mixed composites of those I love and live connected to, and have lived, and are related still. Three generations of my blood and spirit are provided voices to describe their times, ideas, and feelings.

Is it true? Whose truth?

I believe it is real. That is a quality I value as an imperative. Besides, truth is subjective and inconclusive. I suggest to you that the story is a memoir and history of a time and people.

Thank yous are extended to the many folks who inform my life and sustain my living. They are blessed and bless.

Storytellers in the Brothers Grimm tradition begin their stories with "In the beginning..." Cherokee myth keepers begin their tales with "This is what the old ones told me..." So with respect of a unique heritage, "This is what the old ones..."

Balance and Harmony,
Doak M. Mansfield
in the Piney Woods
near Laurel, Mississippi

In Appreciation

- Tyler J. Warren, my illustrator, for his skill and vision. He is the artist I wanted to be at thirteen.
- Kathryn Anderson for her patience in transforming my very rough, handwritten, often untranslatable drafts into a workable, readable manuscript.
- Kathleen Fisher for her counseling on what I have said, what I might have meant to say, and what I could say.
- Melissa Beasley and Myers Brown, manager and curator at Joseph Wheeler's Pond Spring respectively, for their help with the biographical and historical elements of my story.
- Cynthia and Michael Schafer, artists of many media—especially the spirit—for their love and creative input.
- Peggy F. Owens-Mansfield for her love, forbearance, and countless gifts to my life—the foremost being her belief in me.
- A special acknowledgement to the folks at Hardee's, US 84 East, Laurel, Mississippi. Trish and the crew are good people and they tolerate me. It is the "office" where most of this book was written. Bill's Pool Room in Fayetteville, Tennessee, and Moonlight Chili in Batavia, Ohio, are my branch "offices." My table/desk at Hardee's faces the rising sun. I greet its light most every day

there. I've found this place to be a special oasis, for myself as well as a thousand other pilgrims on their many different journeys. I've seen many faces of life and overheard many testimonies: sad, loving, indifferent, mean, desperate, hateful, graceful, tired, disdainful, happy, kind—and some beyond parody. Buddha in ancient time counseled his disciples as he died to "stay awake." I find that to be a good way to live, honor life, and love the Creator Spirit and all creation.

The mistakes in this work are all mine. Any misuse or confused application of the contributions of others is regretted.

DMM

The Northern Mockingbird

Family: Mimidae,

Species: Mimus polyglottos

The mockingbird's scientific name—polyglottos—means "many tongued." This ten-inch gray/brown bird imitates dozens of other birds, as well as other animals, machinery, insects, and even musical instruments. The southern United States is considered the mockingbird's traditional home, despite the "Northern" part of their common name. They are very adaptable and are found in a wide range of habitats from the woods, fields, meadows, and gardens of the rural South to suburbs and cities, westward to dry cactus land, and even northward, particularly the Northeast.

The mockingbird perches in order to sing a variety of original and imitative songs. Their evening "whisper song" is especially significant in the calm nighttime. It often flutters skyward while singing, and then tumbles back to perch. It may sing well into the night or, on moonlit nights, until dawn.

Brave and tenuous with just a thirteen- to fifteen-inch wingspan and average-size songbird beak, it will attack larger birds and mammals that threaten its home and family. Males and females both defend their habitats. Mockingbirds are monogamous and solitary nesters. They are not dependent on flock participation.

Farrier

far·ri·er (far/e er)—noun
Chiefly British
BLACKSMITH. 1555–65; variation of ferrier
<Middle French, Old French Latin ferrarius =
Ferr(um) iron + -arius-ARY>

A good farrier must first be an accomplished blacksmith. But there is more than iron's manipulation involved, as they work also with flesh, bone, and blood—horses and mules, and even donkeys. The farrier by nature of this involvement learns and applies commonsense, life-learned veterinary medical skills. Their work is more than just shoeing animals.

For the cavalry in the American Civil War they could be considered as vital as the surgeon. All arms of service—infantry, artillery, medical, quartermaster, commissary, etc. depended on them and would do so until well into the twentieth century when the combustible engine mechanized the military.

A farrier and assistant were assigned in the organizational make-up of the cavalry to each company—two specialists for about eighty to one hundred troopers. The headquarters staff were also assigned a farrier unit. The stock they cared for could number as many as several hundred depending on the strength and functions of commands. As with any medical personnel or mechanic they went about their vocation wherever their skills were needed.

DMM

The Cavalry of CSA
in the West

War suits them," wrote Major General William T. Sherman, speaking of the Western Confederate cavalrymen, whom Joseph Wheeler commanded from October 3, 1862, to January 28, 1865. "The rascals are brave, fine riders, bold to the point of rashness and dangerous in every sense."

Quotes about Joseph Wheeler from friends:

"... one of the two ablest cavalry officers which the war developed."
                                                      —*Robert E. Lee*

"... a dash and activity, vigilance and consummate skill, which justly entitled him a prominent place on the roll of great cavalry leaders."
                                                      —*Jefferson Davis*

And from an old opponent:

"... in the event of war with a foreign country, 'Joe' Wheeler is the man to command the cavalry of our country."
                                                      —*William T. Sherman*

The Family •
• The Mocking

TIME
LINE

1800

1820

1840

1860

1880

1900

John *"Grand John L."*
Longstreet Fields

Joseph *"Joe T."*
Thomas
Mayberry

Mary Jane Fields
"Blue Cloud -
Sagonige Vlogilv"

John *"J.N."*
Norman Mayberry
"Red Hawk -
Gigaei Twodi"

John *"Johnny"*
Ross Fields
"Morning Star -
Sunali Noquise"

1798-1906
bird's Ballad·

Sarah Louise *Mama Bear* Cherokee Bear Clan
"Bear Woman - Yona Ageyv"

John *Nimen* Fields
"Quiet Crow -
Elowehi Gogv"

Nancy-Cherokee Bird Clan
"Lonesome Cedar -
Natsiya Atsima"

Alexander *Alex*
Auburn Fields
"Red Bird -
Dotsua"

Mary Louise
Bird Fields
"Mockingbird -
Skadagisgi"

Amos
Solon
Stevenson

Joseph *Joe*
Wheeler Stevenson
"Tall Hickory -
Galv ladi igadi Wanel"

James *Jim*
Taylor Stevenson
"White Oak -
Unega Adayahi"

Chapter 1
Fall 1862

The Sequatchie Valley,
Tennessee

T he candle was a poor second in illumination to the coal
fireplace. The coal grate sitting on the hearth offered a
warm glow and just enough heat to warm the small room.
Mary rocked slowly in her small cherry rocker. Its worn finish caught
the flickering light from the fireplace and gave off a golden glow
against dark red. Her nimble fingers, long and thin, worked the finger weave her mother had taught her more than thirty years back.
Her mind was somewhere other than this little room in this snug safe
cabin with her good man. It was in a dark place, a lonely place, a
place of dread and danger. The weaving came faithfully even with her
mind otherwise occupied. Her mind returned to the fireside of her
home, and she thought the woven coverlet she was making would be
ready for Mother's birthday in February. Joe T. was hunched over the
Nashville Dispatch with the candle a scant ten inches from his salt-
and-pepper hair. The flicker caught the reflection of his eyeglasses.

"Mary Jane, says here that Longstreet left Knoxville last week. Writer thinks he's headed for Chattanooga." He talked to his wife of nearly twenty-five years across the room without looking up. "Maybe old Bragg'll get straightened out. Lord, that man could argue with a stump. Looks like he fights with his generals more than the Yankees.

"Shame that 'Massa' Jeff Davis don't like our Frank Cheatham. He's got gumption. Word is, though, that brave Frank likes the sour mash a little too much and too often. But he does know how to lead men and fight! Bragg don't." Joe T. had made an avocation of following any paper he could come across that reported on Cheatham's Tennessee Division. J.N., his only son, was a sharpshooter with the Twenty-Fourth Tennessee Sharpshooter Battalion. "Lordy, Mary, Bragg can't back up all the way to Atlanta. Surely."

"No, Joe T., surely not," was Mary's distracted reply.

Joe T. responded, "Maybe those tough mongrel Texas boys of Hood and Longstreet's rough bunch will give Bragg some will, some fight." Scout, J.N.'s Indian yellow dog, asleep on the hooked rug near the fireplace, lifted his tan, yellow head and his pointed ears perked up. He sniffed and trotted quickly to the closed front door and stood there looking at it.

He looked back at Mary as if to say, "Open it, please ma'am."

She said, "Okay, Scout. I'm coming." Scout jerked his head back towards the door and growled as the hoof beats sounded on the river-gravel road that bordered the house's front yard. "Joe T., someone's out there! Get the shotgun, those bloody blue-bellies may be skulking around the valley again." Joe T. went to the corner of the room nearest the fireplace and picked up the shotgun, always loaded. Ready. Scout scratched the door.

"Easy back, Scout," Joe T. commanded in a low voice as he went past Mary to the door, cocking both barrels of his blued sixteen-gauge scattergun.

A muted "Hello in the place! Mother, it's me," came from the outside. She'd know that voice in a tornado. Mary nearly knocked Joe T. and his shotgun across the room as she bounded to the door, jerking it open. She and Scout raced through the door and into the dark night. The brightness from the opened door blinded J.N. for a moment, but he took the ten steps up to the porch two at a time. They were as familiar as his worn brogans.

His mother grabbed him, "Son, Son, Gigaei Twodi!"

"Yes, Mother, it's me. I'm home," he squeezed out. She smelled of lye soap and lilac powder. Mary Jane Fields Mayberry weighed 101 pounds and stood five-two. Her arms felt like steel belts around her twenty-three-year-old, 160-pound, six-foot son.

"Mother, the hand!" J.N. protested.

She let go, jumped back, "Brother, you hurt, hurt bad?"

"It's a busted hand," he said as he caught the smiling blue eyes of his father over the top of his mother's coal black hair. "I'll mend, no real damage," J.N. said reassuringly. Mary took J.N.'s good hand as gently as robbing an egg from under one of her laying hens. She turned, bumping into Joe T. as she escorted her son into the warm front room. Scout bounded in behind the two, cutting off Joe T. as he turned to follow his wife and son back into the house. Joe T. had an open smile on his freckled face.

Late supper was warmed corn bread and pinto beans with tart tomato relish on the side of his plain china plate. It was better than the feast for the prodigal. A bowl of Mama Bear's sweet butter sat in the middle of the worn poplar-plank kitchen table. The cold sweet milk Joe T. had brought in from the backyard springhouse was the best stuff J.N. had drunk since leaving home in the fall of '61. Taken all together, the homecoming and near-midnight supper almost brought tears to J.N.'s eyes.

His mother and father sat quietly while he ate, watching with soft smiles. Scout was asleep on his left boot toe. J.N. knew, as his folks knew, you eat first then talk. For working people, hunger's pain is to be sated before doing almost anything else.

"Well, Son, what happened?" Joe T. voiced as J.N. pushed the crumb-sprinkled plate forward.

"Still, Joe, let J.N. breathe a spell."

"It's okay, Mother." Joe thought for a second and began. "Sure glad I ain't shot.

"Fell out of a damned sycamore near Brotherton Road, up from Chickamauga Creek. Busted the blasted hand trying to break my fall. Dropped about fifteen feet into a damned heap of bramble bush. Got some bruises, but this hand took the weight. If it ain't broke, it's good busted."

"John Norman, you're home now, let go of that army language," Mary chided.

"Yes, home," J.N. thought as he took a long deep breath. His soul and belly shared a feeling he'd long forgotten was available. He smiled first into his mother's eyes and then his father's as he scratched Scout behind the ears.

"Cap'n said, 'Get home, corporal, before all hell breaks loose here 'bouts.' Mother, those were his words, now, not mine. 'You'll just be in the way with that busted firing hand. In the way and another hurt soldier I've got to find vittles for; go home. Heal up over the winter. S'pect we'll have a place for you come spring. Look for us down in South Kara-line or over in Tex-us!'"

Mary reached across the table and patted his unharmed right hand. "Good, Brother, good. Mama and I'll fix it good as new." J.N. drew his hand from under her warm patting after letting her briefly give him her gentle laying-on of hands. That simple unconscious act had been her blessing to him as long as he could remember. His now-freed hand went to his vest pocket. He brought out a beat-up pipe.

"Dad, you got any Burley stashed somewhere?"

Rummaging in his unbuttoned breast pocket, Joe T. said, "Always, boy, always." Mary hopped up and went to the shelf above the cast iron cooking stove to snatch a long locofoco from her supply in an old broken clay pot. She struck it on the side of the stove. Returning, shielding it from the quick movement, she offered it to her son's pipe. He craned his head forward like a robin taking its mother's offering and puffed a couple-three times. The dark brown, crushed tobacco fired and its aroma invoked benediction to his late meal. Wisps of gray smoke rose from the pipe's bowl; his grandfather, John L., had given him the briar when he left for war.

J.N. was ready to talk now. "There's something big going on over at that creek, really big! It's rough territory over there, and Blues everywhere. They keep coming into Chattanooga and have started to march south. I heard artillery fire day and night as I traveled down along the east side of the Lookout. I crossed the mountain the second morning, turned west and then north, and finally late that day I couldn't hear it anymore."

He suddenly leaned forward as he remembered the horse out front. "Daddy, you got some feed for that old bay? She brought me a good spell. Least I can do is give her a good feed after the meal I've just had." He winked at his mother as he stood up.

"Sit, Son, sit; talk to your mother. I'll take care of your mount," Joe said, getting up himself. "She got a name?"

"Artillery sergeant who loaned her to me just called her 'the bay,' but I've been calling her 'Sister,'" J.N. said cautiously. Being an only child, his remark about "Sister" might or might not have been hurtful to his folks. His parents smiled at one another and then at their son. He was glad to see they must have buried their shared grief, twice over, for his dead sisters up at the meetinghouse graveyard. Those twin girls had died fourteen years back. They had been three years old.

His father grabbed his broad-brimmed black felt hat and brown canvas coat from the peg beside the front door. He put them on and stepped out to the front porch. Scout stirred from his nap, looked at the front door closing, and went back to sleep under the kitchen table.

As J.N. settled back to the table, Mary took the dirty dishes to the sink counter and returned to the table and her son. Mary broke the quiet. "John Norman, Son, there's bad, bad news here, too." J.N. was suddenly alert, his relaxed thanksgiving ended. His mother did not use his whole name with that voice except at serious times. When he was little it was her warning of some childhood infraction to her family value.

"Mother, what is it, not Grand John L. or Mama Bear?"

"No, Son, they're fine, getting old with the trouble like all of us but feeding and sleeping in their own house." She paused, holding his eyes and his face in her shining eyes. "It's your Uncle Norman and his John Ross."

"It must be real bad!" J.N.'s mind shouted. It was ordinarily "Johnny," not "John Ross."

His mother's ruddy complexion turned as white as her prized china coffee cup. "They're dead, son, killed ten days ago." J.N.'s head went numb. He just stared at his stricken mother. He slammed his pipe down, knocking his smoke's fire across the worn, beaten table. Scout yelped when J.N. jumped up, nearly stepping on the dog. His mother caught his chair before it crashed backward. J.N. whirled and went to the wall, turning his head into the darkness there. His hand throbbed, his eyes watered, and his throat was trying to close up. He steadily patted his good hand against the wall just above his head. He said in a small, choking voice, "How? What happened, Mama?"

"Mama," his childhood name for this feisty tomboyish woman, had not crossed his lips since he was nine years old.

His mother's voice was steady and her sentences short and unembellished: "The Yankees out of Nashville, under Crittenden, your father says, moved through here after the mess at Tullahoma. They were after every horse, team of mules, hog, chicken, and sack of corn they could drive or tote off. They missed several other folks in this hollow, and us, but they come up on Johnny in their barn lot, eight of them. He had just put the mules in their stalls, about three in the afternoon, after lightning had stirred them up. The talking one of the gang told Johnny to bring those 'run-down Tennessee hybrid nags' out. He said he wanted to see if they were fit to pull good, strong South Bend wagons and haul loyal American supplies. Johnny cussed them and told them he'd send his stock to the hereafter before giving them over to Yankees or anyone, Rebels too. Three of them pulled their side arms and some their rifles. Johnny cussed them some more. As he moved across the lot with a halter rope, they shot him five times, head to gut." Her voice was cold and hard. "His daddy, Norman, was down at the foot log across the branch, shoring it up. It had washed out bad a while back."

Joe cleared his throat. He'd come into the house and hung his things up, and had walked over to the table without the two taking notice. He put his big hand on his little wife's thin shoulder, cold from the night chill. Mary looked up at him, then down at her lap.

After a struggle, she continued, "Brother came running, skirting toward their back porch. Your Uncle Norman must have been going for the shotgun. The soldiers shot him down, in the back, twenty feet from the back porch steps." J.N. blinked and blinked again. Mary stopped, taking a long breath, her cheeks wet with tears.

J.N. whispered, as if in prayer, "What about Alex, Lou, and Aunt Nancy?"

"The twins were in the back of the loft moving some hay. They saw it all through the front cracks. That's how we know what happened. They saw it, J.N., they saw it all. Thank the good Lord Alex had hold of Lou and kept her quiet or there would have been four buryings last Sunday." Mary stopped as though she had chopped a row of corn in the summer sun, exhausted.

"Aunt Nancy?" J.N. reminded her.

"She was up here with me working apples. I'm not sure whether that was a blessing or not."

Chapter 2

1842

He rode into the front yard on "Fog," the old gray horse; she was on the small sorrel mare, "Lady." The riders each had a lead rope tied to the back of their saddles. Norman trailed the studs and Nancy tended the jennies. He'd learned a life-changing lesson at the north Georgia gold mines: he was absolutely no miner. He had also learned life does bless one with luck sometimes, and in surprising ways. Now he was coming home with some wisdom, pride, possibilities, and a wife.

His home-leaving adventure was not a complicated or especially long story. He had gone away to strike it rich. With his dreams of gold and riches shattered in Dahlonega, he had come home within two months. A mean sore back, blistered hands, and trouble breathing in the dark, dusty holes had brought him to the realization that he required fresh air, nature's greenery, and home.

Being smarter than stubborn, Norman gave up his gold prospecting. Mad at himself and disgusted with his foolishness, he got drunk in a canvas-covered saloon on foul home brew. With eighteen dollars left (and in a hung-over stupor) he was drawn into a poker game that developed into a two-hour whirlwind of win some, lose more. In the last hand, the liquor was wearing off. He had lost all but his clothes, hat, brogans, worn leather satchel with a few necessities, and his rifle. He bet the Kentucky long gun in an all or nothing declaration. His father had given it to him for his sixteenth birthday. It was an old Kentucky rifle converted from cap and ball to percussion, but a prize—his only prize.

He was dealt three tens, a deuce, and a seven. He took two cards and won the pot with four tens, ace kicker. He was one happy eighteen-year-old pilgrim. His new estate included $37 in coin, $263 in dust, a broken gold pocket watch, fifty feet of good jute rope, three twenty-pound sacks of crushed corn, and five donkeys—three jacks and two jennies. The biggest loser, a donkey seller/muleteer, was a dried-up, wrinkled, brown man in funny clothes. Hailing from the Florida country, he had made his way somehow to the digs about a month ago. Norman figured out enough of his broken English to learn that he and his brother had brought fifteen mules through Savannah to Georgia's gold country. Ten had been sold. His older brother had been sick on the trail from the coast, got worse, and had died three days ago. He had buried his brother, said a prayer over his grave, and gotten drunk, playing cards off and on during his grief drunk. With a busted heart, and in his broken tongue, the beaten little foreigner patted the smallest donkey and said to Norman, "Go with God, senor. You be good-them. You find good horse mare, good

stud horse, breed them and make fine mules, good strong mules."
The former owner helped Norman make a lead line, communicating
with chopped words and acting out. He showed him how to secure
the donkeys in a line, one after another. The largest animal was in the
lead and one of the jennies in the rear.

Norman looked over his walking treasure, taking in his riches.
The donkeys were in good health with bright brown eyes. Scratching
his two-week beard he thought, "Better name 'em." His mother
Sarah Bear had taught him everything was something, everything signified, and a name established power and place in life. The biggest
male was "Ten," the dark brown one "Ace," and the smaller jack he
called "Lucky." The smaller matching jennies, reddish-brown and
slick, were "May" and "June." He learned as he tried to get them to
move that crushed corn worked better than cussing them or whipping them. He thought, after he stumbled onto that knowledge,
"Guess I'll make a muleteer after all, maybe."

After a greasy, fatty steak dinner at the make-shift gold camp
eatery, he went to the livery lot, haggled with the owner, and got
himself two horses and gear—an older gray horse and a small sorrel
mare. The stud was "Fog," and the sorrel was "Lady."

After five days of uneven riding and leading his mixed stock, he
arrived at the trading post on the Oconaluftee River in western
North Carolina. He picked up some supplies, then made his way up
a cove to his mother's brother's cabin. As he rode up the trail, his
uncle on his front porch stopped his whittling.

"It's me, Uncle. Elowehi Gogv. Norman, Sarah Bear's son,"
Norman called from astride Fog. He got off his horse, patted his
neck, and walked to his Uncle Samuel's front porch. Norman hand-

16

ed his boyhood mentor a little sack of store tobacco. "It is good to be here with you, Uncle," Norman said smiling. His eyes made quick contact with his favorite man besides his father, John L., then diverted to his uncle's moccasins.

After a chestnut-bread, fatback, cabbage, and fry-bread supper served by his Aunt Pearl, the quietest human he knew, uncle and nephew took pipes to the front porch. "Uncle, I have been fortunate." Over supper Norman had told him about his failed prospecting and life-changing poker game. Now on the porch, fed and relaxed in the soft falling of dark, he told his uncle what the story meant. "With my new stock and a bit of money, I can farm and make a living down from the folks' place. The living can be for a wife and family, too." Norman's green blue eyes were lowered as a sign of respect when his uncle looked at him. It was how the Principal People, Ani Yvwiya, the Cherokee, showed respect to one another. Direct eye-to-eye contact for them was a display of disrespect and arrogance. It was believed to be an assault, a threat to the spirit of the other.

The whites never understood that "eye to eye" was an act of aggression, not accord.

Uncle Samuel, oldest of his mother's two brothers, said, "That is good, Quiet Crow, Elowehi Gogv." And then, "You come for Nancy, Lonesome Cedar, Natsiya Atsima?" Cherokee mothers gave their children two names, an English one and an Indian one. Such had been the custom for generations since the white people had come to the Cherokee lands. William Norman was Quiet Crow, and Nancy was Lonesome Cedar.

"Yes, Uncle, I can be a husband to her now," Norman said in a lower voice to the porch floorboards at his feet. His uncle, mother, and father knew Nancy had been his choice of a wife since he was fourteen and she thirteen. During the last two fall return visits of Norman's family to the gathering celebration of the new moon, Norman and Nancy had come to know one another well.

"Quiet Crow, we will go to see Emily Long Hair tomorrow," confirmed Samuel. Emily was the Beloved Woman of the remnant of the Cherokee nation still in the Smokies. Before Nanna dual Tsunyi, the Trail Where They Cried, four years ago, the social structure of the Principal People had included an influential council of seven honored women of various ages. Emily and several hundred of the Cherokee people had escaped the removal of 1837-38 to the Land Toward the Dark, west of the Mississippi River. Some had taken small allotments of land to the northeast of the Cherokee nation in the years after the 1818 treaty. Others had eluded General Winfield Scott's blue soldiers, who came to round up those people still in the nation and send them into exile. Little William Thomas had bought up parts of the new government land in trust for his Cherokee neighbors, the original custodians of these coves, rivers, ridges, and mountains. Those Cherokee who remained struggled to sustain their traditions and life-ways in spite of the turmoil they endured. Emily Long Hair, Ani Gilahi, maintained her dignity and calling for the remnant Cherokees. Her people sustained her influence; her counsel on issues important to their society was sought. In the old days before the corruptions of the white soul, before thieves and land bandits led the Principal People to become ordinary people like them, the Beloved Woman had vast powers: blessing marriages, approving divorces,

welcoming children, giving pardon to captives in hostilities, and—
the most critical to the governance of the people—the removal of
unworthy or dishonorable male leaders, whether White Peace Chiefs
or Red War Chiefs.

After the grits and fatback breakfast with strong coffee, Norman
and Uncle Samuel went up the creek and over to the next cove to
Emily's home. Her herb garden greeted them with fragrance, strong
now in the drying season. Flowerpots along her front porch were covered in compost, and her rocker was draped with a bright, striped
shawl. She welcomed them, and Norman gifted her with a pouch of
store-bought tobacco in respect. He told her of his adventure and
ambitions.

Emily said to the nephew and uncle, "I'm glad you came, both of
you. Quiet Crow, Lonesome Cedar is a good woman." She knew the
purpose of their visit. To Samuel she announced, "Running Bear, you
have done a good job with you sister's son. He was a good boy and is
becoming a good man." Samuel blushed slightly, lowered his eyes,
pleased. Emily continued, "We will celebrate Quiet Crow and
Lonesome Cedar's togetherness in four days, sunrise on the waxing
moon. Quiet Crow, have you seen Lonesome Cedar?"

"No, Beloved Woman."

"Then go to her and her people. Tell them of my permission.
Now let's hope she'll have you," she giggled.

Lonesome Cedar and her mother and grandmother consented.
Lonesome Cedar's father was but a memory to her mother, Virginia
(Bright Leaves), and a shadow to their daughter. All she knew of him
was that he was short, thin, red-haired, and had come from Virginia
to these parts for deer hides and freedom. He had stayed three years,

fathering her with Bright Leaves. He left them after the summer of Lonesome Cedar's second year. His leaving was unseemly but accepted by them. There was little else they could do. He did not signify to them now, and the only evidence of his time here were his daughter's small build and pale blue eyes. Bright Leaves and her daughter had made a life with Bright Leaves' clan, Bird. Nancy and Norman would be married in the Cherokee tradition at sunrise in four days.

The radiance of the sun broke the ridgeline, and the power of the great light ordained the riverbank and the people standing near the cane break. The gray mist of the river offered softness to the occasion and enhanced its solemnity. Lonesome Cedar (Nancy Bird) and Quiet Crow (William Norman) stood facing the half circle of honored women. Emily Long Hair stood directly in front of the couple. Uncle Samuel stood behind Norman and was holding a haunch of fresh venison wrapped in tanned deer hide. He and his nephew had killed the big buck the afternoon before. Lonesome Cedar's mother stood behind her, holding a folded quilt of bright patches and designs made from leftover pieces of material bought over the years at Little Will's Trading Post. Quiet Crow's grandmother was holding three ears of corn.

At the cresting of the sun above the ridgeline, Samuel and Virginia placed the venison and corn in a basket before the couple. Then they unfolded the quilt and blanketed the couple over their shoulders, putting the edge of the quilt in each of the couple's hands.

Lonesome Cedar and Quiet Crow pulled the quilt snug around their shoulders, exchanged brief promises, and vowed to protect, provide for, and respect the family. Emily, placing her hand over theirs, conferred the blessing of their bond.

"You are now one, but also two. Care for one another, your people, and your home," was Emily's simple benediction.

Norman acted on the directives of the Spaniard. His father, John Longstreet—John L.—had read of the mule, the offspring of the donkey and horse. He had chuckled to himself as he read about mules in a pamphlet he had bought from a peddler. Seems George Washington had started mule breeding in the United States over fifty years ago. The penny pamphlet said the king of Spain had presented the general a large black jack, "Royal Gift," in 1785. Exportation of Spanish jacks was prohibited until 1813, and yet during the intervening years the breed had spread across most of the nation. People soon learned they were a cheaper and better choice than a horse for work and care. John L. had learned something new when he read about the odd breeding process it took to produce mules. A male donkey (jack stud) could sire a mule by a female horse (mare), and a male horse could sire a mule by a female donkey (jennet), but mules could not produce mules. The desired combination was jack-stud donkey with mare horse. It seemed the mule offspring were healthier, bigger, and less trouble than those of the opposite pairing.

John L.'s team of mare horses and Norman's two jack stud donkeys were the foundation stock of the Fields' future way of life. Having always been taught to respect life and its gifts, Norman and Nancy, John L. and his wife Sarah, and Norman's older sister, Mary Jane, became good and successful mule breeders and muleteers (trainers, handlers, drivers). New horse members for the breeding stock were added over the years, so the Fields' line of mules was strong and became sought after by farmers in the six counties of southeast Tennessee. They drove their sale stock to mule and horse auctions in Pikeville, Winchester, and Chattanooga. Norman and Nancy were quick students, and by the second generation their children, John Ross and the twins, Alexander Auburn and Mary Louise, had learned about mules, their ways, health needs and requirements, and the demands of training. A Fields' team of mules bought or traded at a county seat in the region became a sound investment for the farmer who came to town to find good work stock. The Fields family had a good life for nearly twenty years, but in 1862 trouble—bad trouble—was brought to their valley by strangers.

Chapter 3

The Twins

I'm going! I am going, J.N.!" Lou's face was flaming, her back ramrod straight, and she pressed her hands down hard on the kitchen table. She sat across from her cousin J.N. Her twin brother, Alex, sat to the right. At her emphatic declaration, J.N. hung his head, rocking it back and forth. Alex and Lou's mother, Nancy Bird Fields (Lonesome Cedar of the Bird Clan), who was J.N.'s aunt, the widow of William Norman, and the mother of John Ross, was sitting across the room by the fireplace, slowly rocking. Her eyes had an empty, hurt look. If she was aware or was listening to the discussion, she showed no sign of it.

"No, Lou. No! You can't go. It's foolish and damn dangerous! For God's sake, you're a girl not yet fifteen."

"I'll be fifteen next month, J.N. I'm nearly as big as you are and taller than Alex and Johnny! I know more about mules and horses than any of you. Daddy said how good a farrier I've become." Lou's brown eyes moistened, her tears struggling with her raw rage.

"You're a girl, Lou, a girl!" he said in frustration. "A mighty ugly girl, but still a girl." J.N. smiled, hoping his effort at humor would change the intensity of the argument or somehow distract Lou. Maybe she would focus on his jab rather than her determination to go to war. Lou did pause a second at the "ugly" remark.

"Yeah, I'm ugly! What does that have to do with anything? I can whip you and most anyone I've ever come across! Age and being a girl ain't nothing," the five-and-a-half-foot-tall fourteen-year-old asserted. Her hands were as big as J.N.'s, and bigger than those of most boys. Her hair was straight and her face was plain, with a light copper cast. Since she could walk, Lou's manner had always been rough and tumble. She had a collection of dogs, cats, and raccoons, even a bear cub the summer she was ten; she had roamed the creek, valley, coves, and ridges for years. Dolls and fancy things did not hold her attention. She liked to tinker, fix things, and be physically active, whether at the bellows, over her shoeing box, or turning somersaults to make her grandparents, John L. and Mama Bear, laugh.

J.N. had to admit she was not in any way dainty or fragile. She was strong, willful, and agile. "Lou, for a girl, could be a pretty good boy," J.N. thought. She had had her grandfather cut her hair like Alex's since she was seven. J.N. could not remember if she had ever had curls. Her hair hung straight and thick over her ears. It was cut below her ears and parted in the middle with the shine of a crow in sunshine.

"Well and good, Sister, but where do you, I mean we, go? General Wheeler can be anywhere from Knoxville to the Alabama Shoals." Alex had entered the argument so quietly, J.N. paused to take in his words.

"We get some supplies together and head down the valley toward Shellmound, we'll find him. Or some of his horse soldiers. They're all over around here and south, according to Jim up at Coop's Creek store," Lou explained, with confidence in Alex's loyalty.

J.N., the veteran soldier and oldest of the three, formerly four, cousins, leaned forward in the kitchen chair and patted the table in front of Lou with his good hand. "Listen, Lou, listen to me. You, too, Alex. I know how bad you want to go. I want to get back with my pards real bad. I did some damage in Tullahoma, got a fool officer on a big roan at near five hundred yards. Hell, I can't wait for this busted hand to mend. Mama Bear's salve and her tight wrap have taken the throbbing away." He lifted his hand from his canvas sling. It was wrapped and covered in a terribly smelly and greasy cotton bandage from elbow to fingertips. "Still, war is no place for a girl." When he looked deep into Lou's eyes, the light from the lamp and fireplace gave her normally calm brown eyes the flickering look of a wild thing, a mean thing—hard, black, and dangerous.

Alexander Auburn and Mary Louise Fields were twins of blood and birth, but different as night and day: Lou was night, and Alex was day. She was tall, dark, lean, and fine-featured, with heavy-laden brown eyes that looked nearly black. She weighed maybe 110 pounds. Alex was four inches shorter, tending toward fat, fair with pale blue eyes bright and sparkling. He could top 150 pounds. He had shape, but not Lou. She just had angles. Even with all their physical differences, they shared not just blood and birth, but a near mystical connection. She could nearly read his mind and soul—and he hers. Together no two or four of the valley boys could best them in "catch and grab," and they hadn't been able to since they were six.

She was the mechanic and he the artist. Alex was accomplished on the harmonica and Jew's harp. Tunes came to him, and he could copy on his mouth organ any fiddle or banjo music he'd ever heard. His truly special prize was a bull's horn he'd traded a one-blade pocketknife for when they were ten. He'd worked it with deer bone and river sand as his mother, Nancy Bird, had shown him, until it was smooth and shiny inside and out. The point had been filed away and the edges of the hole smoothed with a rock. The horn was nearly fourteen inches long and had a big opening of nearly four inches. Over the months after he'd gotten it, he had practiced and developed many calls for the mules, jacks, and horses, and he could even communicate with family when they were out in the fields, up in the cove, or on the ridge side. He had become the signal caller for his mother and father, sister and brother. Even his grandfather and grandmother had him call with his horn to family far away from the house or barn. Clear and true, Alex's bugling calls carried across the farm. A neighbor at the bottom of the hill, a half-mile away, said their stock perked up their ears when Alex blew his horn. Some laughed, others thought it was mighty handy and smart.

Lou fixed things, made things with iron and wit. Alex made music and found tunes and calls to paint pictures for others to see, hear, and feel.

The twins had seen the Yankees shoot down their brother and father at their own place not a month ago. In the barn loft during the raid Alex had held on to Lou as hard as he could and somehow restrained her during the killing and thieving. The Yankees had murdered their kin and stolen three teams of fine-trained mules and harnesses, along with six fifty-pound bags of feed. It was no real comfort, but the thieves had missed two good teams, three mares, and three jack studs. They were up at Joe T.'s place pastured with his two mares that were in heat. There would be a new generation of Fields-Mayberry mules come next fall, but breeding and training mules seemed a trifling matter now to Lou. She had a more urgent calling to be about now.

"I'm leaving tomorrow at sunrise, J.N. We're leaving," she looked at Alex with kindness. "You can come or stay, makes no difference," she announced slowly and strongly. Then, as if giving a report, "I'll be packing my tools and some necessities on Ben and I'll ride Tom. I'll go down the valley along the Huntsville stage road and find the general or somebody who knows where he and his troops are. Jim said there were over a thousand horse soldiers in this part of the valley. That many can't be hard to find. They'll take me. I'll make 'em. I'm as good a farrier as any they have." Even in her determination, she knew she wouldn't make a good soldier. J.N. was the marksman of the family. Besides, she was too fond of the creatures of her valley to shoot anything, man or animal.

She'd made up her mind to help those folks who could kill, work for those who were trying to rid the land of those murdering strangers who had cursed and destroyed her world. She'd tend to their mounts and they'd beat and kill the thieving murderers. Justice required it, she reasoned through her loss and anger.

J.N. could not really question her logic, and it didn't look as if he was going to shake her resolve. Alex had sat stone-faced staring at his sister, his eyes bright and shining, his mouth tight. He turned from her and looked at the wall beside the back door. His eyes latched onto his bullhorn hanging by its leather strap.

"Okay, Sister, okay," he confirmed. "If they take you as a farrier they'll take me as a bugler. I'm as good at that as you are with shoeing and doctoring stock. We go, both of us. I'll ride Bess and we'll take what we need on Ben and Tess. Bess likes me and she rides good." Pausing, he blew out breath hard, "Lord Almighty, we're going to war!"

"Damn, damn, damn and tarnation! You two are crazy fools. Kids, and one a girl, wanting to go to that hell," J.N. grieved.

"Not wanting, J.N., going," Lou said, as she looked J.N. in the eyes with a power he'd never seen before.

"Please, Lou. Please, Alex. You all listen to me! If you ain't cold and miserable, you're melting in the heat. And hungry, hungry most of the time and bone tired all the time. You're always dirty with your body aching in places you never knew were there," J.N. pleaded.

J.N. was conflicted about how his grandfather would respond to this madness. He pondered what would happen—their grandfather would be fitting to die when he learned of Lou's plans, that was for sure. Lou was the apple of that old man's eye. She'd walked thousands of miles in his shadow since she could waddle. She had been his attentive apprentice in life, soaking in his storied opinions and musings. Her mother, Nancy Bird, had been more like a companion and patient teacher of the domestic skills, for which Lou had little interest or talent. Her grandmother, Sarah Bear, "Mama Bear," had been her mentor in the healing medicine. Grand John L., her muse.

Their grandfather cared about all his grandchildren. He was stern but fair and generous of spirit. Lou was the special one—the only girl since J.N.'s twin sisters had died. The boys were his prizes, for sure, and he treated them as an extension of himself, but Lou had a different significance to him: she was the weekend, and they were the weekdays. The boy cousins didn't resent it; it was just the way it was.

J.N. thought, "He'll let her go. Damn, she has power over him and it's heart power, not head power. That's mighty strong. Maybe, just maybe, he won't give in to her. He hates this war so; maybe he'll stop her, maybe." They had to go see him, especially since Lou and Alex were leaving. It was not so much to get permission as to show the due respect. Blessing was impossible, knowing Grandfather's feeling about the war. But reporting the plan was necessary; they had to do right by their family elders. It would be hard to tell their grandparents and Mother what they were up to, but unthinkable to go without doing just that.

John Longstreet Fields had come to the valley in 1818 when he was twenty. He had been sixty-five years old in September 1863. His father, William, and mother, Hannah, had died when he was sixteen. He, an only child, had been on his own ever since. He said his father had come to America from north of Sherwood Forest, Robin Hood's country, in 1773. Lots of folks who heard his assertion easily accepted that his father, William, came to America in 1773, but doubted the Robin Hood part of his biography. His four grandchildren never doubted it. As kids, they'd liked the idea that their forebears had maybe been outlaws with Robin Hood. John L.'s mother was the orphaned daughter of a seaman, a pirate maybe, who came to Wilmington, North Carolina. William married her when she was seventeen and he nineteen. A pirate up the family tree was also an exciting notion for John L.'s grandchildren.

John L. had left the coastal area of southeast North Carolina when he was seventeen, hiring out as a field hand and learning the basics of blacksmithing and farrier work.

By 1817, John L. had made his way to the Cherokee country in central-western North Carolina. He was on his way to the Tennessee country around growing Nashville, but he did not make it. Smitten by a sixteen-year-old girl of the Principle People—Bear Woman, Sagonige Vlogilv, Sarah Bear—he had lingered in the Oconaluftee area long enough to court and marry her. They had pledged their togetherness one late spring morning in 1818, and left after a week for the Tennessee country. They made it on a young mare and an aging stud horse her uncle had given them. Their worldly goods were packed in deer hide wraps behind their Indian saddles. They had found the Sequatchie Valley, stopped, were awed by its rough beauty, and made it their home. Mama Bear had always said they knew the valley and the valley knew them. They cleared and claimed a parcel of land by the mouth of a small creek that emptied into the river. Here they built a cabin and made a life and family. John L. did a little blacksmithing, cleared new ground, and raised corn and tobacco. Sarah Bear tended a big garden and collected herbs and made medicine. Folks sought her out as a healer of minor ailments—and some major ones.

The audience went just about as J.N. figured it would. Grand John L. got sullen when Lou quietly but firmly announced what she intended. He and Mama Bear were on their front porch just before sunset. Grandfather was in his big rocker, Mama Bear was standing, taking in the sunset. The afternoon had become one of those special early fall days—clear, sunny and warm. The cool evening was not yet evident, but it would be soon by the smell and feel of the air. After the proper greetings, Lou told them the plan. John L. stopped his rocking when Lou began. When she'd completed her case, he tapped out his used-up pipe tobacco, refilled it, and started it up, looking at her with a hurt, then hard, look. He then walked to the corner of his porch, looking up for quite a spell toward the ridge and the streaks of clouds across the reddish-orange western sunset.

Talking to the ridge, he said, "Little Sister, when John Norman went to this damnable stupid war I told him he was a gold-plated fool." He paused, sighed, and continued as if awfully weary, "I told him to come back alive. He has and now you want to go off to it and take your brother. I guess, J.N., you're going back with them to that cursed foolishness."

J.N. hung his head with a guilty, "Yes, sir."

John L. returned to his chair and sat down. His grandchildren were sitting to his left along the porch on the other side of Mama Bear. His hurt and anger changed to one of disgust and indignation. "Folks just don't understand this war. It's all about arrogance. Those god-almighty planters in Mississippi, South Carolina, Georgia, and even west Tennessee want to keep Negroes in slavery. They want my children and grandchildren to fight for them so they can keep being the lords of the manor. Hell, I've been close to a slave to those sorts of folks and damn if I countenance fighting for them or my kin doing it."

He got his breath and looked to the sky as if putting together his thoughts. "My daddy never bowed his head and touched his hand to his forehead like a peasant to those highfalutin asses, and neither have I. How I despise those grand bottomland and tidewater lords. They've always suckered folks, and now they're sending them—you—to become cannon fodder. Lord almighty, deliver me and mine! Now some other suckers of some other lords from Boston, Philadelphia, or Chicago have come to our valley and shed my own blood on our land. Very well, very well," he paused, took a puff of his dead pipe, made a face, and began the process of making another smoke. Everybody sat quietly, not looking directly at their grandparents or anything in particular. When refired, John L. said in sad resignation, "You all go, go on, if that's what has to be. You're not going with my blessing, though, never." His face was hard and he looked as if he'd taken a hard hit. He said, "Sagonige Vlogilv and I'll be here." The grandchildren had very seldom if ever heard him speak Mama Bear's Cherokee name. "Mary Jane, Joe T., Nancy and we will make do. We'll be here when you come home. Great God, I surely hope it's alive."

"We'll be home, Grand," Alex promised. J.N. could not say anything. Lou was looking at the darkening western sky above the ridge crest as if far, far away.

It was about two hours before first light. Mama Bear tugged at Lou's quilted shoulder and said, "Up girl, we've got to talk."

From a hard sleep's lifting heaviness, Lou said, "Yes, Mama Bear. What is it?"

"Get dressed and don't wake the house. Come out to the porch," was the reply.

Lou tugged on her heavy coat as she quietly closed the front door. She put on her old hand-me-down felt hat and joined her grandmother on the porch's second step. Her mother sat in Grand's rocker behind Mama Bear.

"Good," Mama Bear began. "Your time of the moon came before your last birthday, in the fall?" was her question. Lou looked back at her mother, who nodded her head at her daughter.

"Yes, ma'am. October," Lou answered, a bit perplexed.

"You're not a child anymore. Haven't been since that day. Now you've gone and decided an adult thing. You go to be with warriors."

Mama Bear turned from looking at nothing in the darkened yard to gaze into the face of her only living woman grandchild, her legacy. "Take care with your moon-time out there. Take this." She handed Lou a small well-filled bag of leather. "At the beginning of your time, take two pinches in coffee or water each day of your moon days. It will help you during that time—less hurting. When you leave I'll have a larger bag of dried moss from the riverside live oak. Use it in your drawers with a woman cloth. Change it when it's soiled, and bury it." Her gaze returned to front, towards the river.

Lou looked at the side of her grandmother's serious, kind face. "Yes, Grandmother. I'll do as you say."

"Now we go up to the creek to the morning place."

Once on the bank side at a slow moving spot, grandmother, granddaughter, and mother sat without talking until the glow of the lighting eastern sky announced that sunrise would be there in a few minutes.

"Girl, take off your clothes and lay them here." She patted a place behind where Lou sat by her. "You need to take the waters and get the blessing of the Great Being, Uneque. It greets you as you welcome it. My people's spirit-way needs to be honored as you take the path you have chosen." She continued as Lou stood to undress. "Girl, you remember how I taught you to purify yourself going to the waters?"

"Yes, ma'am." She looked at her mother as if asking for permission, something Nancy Bird had never experienced from her tomboy daughter. Nancy smiled and said, "Yes, Mockingbird, Bear Woman is right."

Mama Bear looked at Lou's fourteen-year-old girl body as she undressed. It had a good start at being a woman's body, but had some ways to go. Her low hair was fine and sparse, and her breasts were just beginning to take form. Her nipples were small and dark brown. Her stature was slim but not skinny. She had good muscle tone and firm arms, calves, backsides, and thigh muscles. Her flesh was light reddish-brown. Mama Bear's childhood color had been nearly like her granddaughter's. In the sun it looked coppery. Lou hummed a chant Mama Bear had taught her years ago. She lifted up hands full of creek water and opened her hands over her head seven times, saying "Ah-Ho" each time. When she finished, she slowly walked out of the water to where she had sat by her grandmother and mother and, methodically, she dressed. Big chill bumps covered her from head to toe, and she gave a full body shiver as she sat down at her place.

Mama Bear began, "This is what the old ones told me when I was a child: before the whites came so close to our country, the people were strong and of great numbers. There was a powerful law among the seven clans. Lou, then we had no judges or laws like we have today in the white country. This law we lived by was written on all the people's hearts by the elders of each generation. If in an argument a person hurt or killed another person, the clan of the offended person had the right to give hurt or take the life of any member of the offender's clan." Mama Bear took a puff of her pipe, blew it out slowly, and continued, "You go now to avenge the murders of your father and brother. You go to carry out the blood law, the ancient way of justice. You may not kill with your own hands, but you help those who do kill. When this happens, always know it as a sacred thing— the making of justice with shed blood—a most sacred thing."

"I will, Mama Bear," Lou said to the shining creek. Her Mother, sitting on Lou's other side, took her hand and held it tight. She had not done that in an awfully long time.

Lou, her grandmother, and her mother sat for a few short minutes, then Mama Bear said, "Help me up, girl. We've got the morning meal to fix and supplies to sort out and get together."

When the three returned from the creek to Mama Bear's house, Nancy got busy rolling out biscuits on the table alongside the cook stove. Grand John L. sat stone-faced in his chair at the kitchen table. He looked only at his steaming gray coffee mug. The firebox of the stove was crackling, and soon the scents of bacon and biscuits blend-ed with the fragrance of burning hickory and coffee, filling the morning air. Lou rushed to the stove and stood with her back to it, not three feet from the firebox. Mama Bear started helping Nancy with breakfast, and Lou went for the plates and eating utensils.

In the yard as the three prepared to leave, Nancy Bird's strong hug was a strength Lou didn't know her mother had. The tiny woman's quiet voice spoke first into Alex's ear, "Redbird, Dotsuwa, come back to us safe, take care of Mockingbird," and then to Lou, "Sister take care of brother, and you'll come back to us safe."

The three riders and two pack mules left the place in single file: Lou on Ben in the lead with Bess's lead line attached to her saddle back, with Alex following astride Tom and leading Tess. J.N. rode at the tail with his hand resting on the pommel.

Headed south, they were determined to find "Fightin' Joe" Wheeler, his horse soldiers, and their war.

Chapter 4

"Fightin' Joe"

It was strange, most strange. He had not thought of his mother in a long time—years. Yet his awake dream was of his mother, her light blue eyes, soft hands, lavender scent, and sad face. She'd been dead over twenty years. His short life of twenty-eight years had been full of upheavals and travels. His mother was gone when he was six. He was sent to live with his aunts, Mary and Augusta Hull, in Connecticut, a thousand miles away from his Augusta, Georgia, home and his father, older two sisters, and brother, William. On his eighteenth birthday, September 10, 1854, he was in West Point, New York and had been a plebe at the U. S. Military Academy for three months. He'd been in New York City that spring. His uncle, Sterling Smith, his mother's brother-in-law, had wanted him to enter business with him, but the undersized Georgia teenager had other ideas. Through his persistence, his family relented and he got a five-year appointment, just extended from a four-year program, to the United States Military Academy at West Point. A distant relative, Congressman John Wheeler of New York, secured his place. Brevet

Colonel Robert E. Lee was in his first year as superintendent of the military academy in 1854 when Wheeler entered.

West Point did become a home of sorts where the small cadet was known as polite, aloof, and very serious. His sense of self would not allow him to be a little jester. He aspired to a dignified place in the scheme of things, short or not. That passage of training ended, and he was posted to the strange barren scenery of New Mexico. There he was christened by fire as a professional soldier and officer. The Apaches were very effective teachers.

Major General Joseph Wheeler, sitting aside his worn out mount, Jack, thought to himself about the words of a chaplain he'd heard conduct field services near Chickamauga: "We're all strangers in strange lands. Pilgrims looking for our real home."

"Amen," Wheeler said to himself.

Major General Joseph Wheeler, "Fightin' Joe," at twenty-eight years of age was the commander of the Army of Tennessee's cavalry and had been for over a year. In the moonlight darkness of October 8, 1863, on the riverbank, he sat erect in his saddle. His gaze was fixed on his dog-tired troopers fording the Tennessee River near Caladonia Plantation, just northeast of Courtland, Alabama. It was nearly midnight and his 2,500-member command was well deserving of a few days of "rest and rearming." He thought, "Rest maybe; rearming doubtful."

A few days earlier, over a hundred and fifty miles to the northeast in Sequatchie Valley, Tennessee, Wheeler's cavalry had destroyed over a thousand of General William S. Rosecrans's Union supply wagons filled with needed supplies. The Union occupiers of

Chattanooga faced starvation with this lifeline disrupted. The rich prize was seized just twenty miles from its destination of Chattanooga, on the Anderson Turnpike at Walden's Ridge. The corridor of destruction created by Wheeler's raid of this vital supply wagon train stretched over ten miles back towards Nashville. Saved from the torch and explosives were enough supplies to benefit his command for a month. Scores of the best mules and horses were spared. They became desperately needed fresh stock for the troopers and teamsters. General Braxton Bragg had sent Wheeler and his rough and ragged boys from every Confederate state—and some undisclosed places—to come around Rosecrans's rear and do as much mischief as they could stir up.

It had been a good fortnight for Wheeler's cavalry and Bragg's Army of Tennessee. The Confederate forces—infantry, artillery and cavalry—under General Braxton Bragg had stopped General William S. Rosecrans's Army of the Cumberland cold at Chickamauga Creek in north Georgia on September 21. The Union Army was stymied in Chattanooga with a short supply of food and desperate need for the most necessary items—clothing, medicine, and ammunition.

Now Wheeler's cavalry, three quarters of Bragg's horse soldiers, were retiring into north Alabama three days ahead of the pursuing U. S. Cavalry led by General George H. Crook. Once across the Tennessee River, they were in friendly territory. Crook wouldn't come after them without infantry support, and Rosecrans had none to send. Wheeler's scouts had located a good site for the trooper's encampment. By daybreak, the recently victorious and successful cavalry of the Army of Tennessee would be in camp, their stock fed and in temporary corrals, the cook fires burning, arms stacked, and their bodies and souls prostrate from fatigue.

The commanding general had sent his senior staff officer, Major A. S. Stevenson, to the owner of the land Wheeler had chosen for the cavalry's temporary camp. The crusty major, a career field officer with seventeen years in uniform, felt old enough to be his young general's father.

"General Wheeler presents his compliments," Major Stevenson announced when presented to Colonel Richard Jones, the third largest landowner in all of Alabama. Jones's twenty-two-year-old widowed daughter—Daniella Jones Sherrod—was standing beside her father.

After the necessary pleasantries, and after her father had welcomed the Confederate soldiers to his domain, she spoke up. "Major, is that General Wheeler, 'Fightin' Joe'?"

"Yes, ma'am," Major Stevenson confirmed.

"I'd like to see him," Mrs. Sherrod responded.

"Well, madam," the Major said with a little smile, "you won't see much when you do."

General Joseph Wheeler, West Point Class of '59, stood 5 feet 5 inches erect, which was his straight, natural posture. He weighed 120 pounds at his heaviest. He was certainly less than that after two and a half years of army vittles. He'd earned his nickname, "Fightin' Joe,"

while stationed in the New Mexico territory before the War Between the States. Assigned to the Mounted Rifles, U.S. Army, at Fort Craig, he, a teamster, and a surgeon were assigned escort duty for a new mother and baby en route from Hannibal, Missouri to Fort Craig. A small band of marauding Apaches attacked them in the slow army ambulance. The wagon train it was trailing had moved several miles ahead. Halting the ambulance, Wheeler ordered the driver to keep firing at the raiders. The new Second Lieutenant Wheeler, twenty-three years old, shot down one of the attackers and then, on horseback, charged the remaining half dozen, screaming a wild yell and blasting away with his Colt pistol. The surprised hostiles took flight. After the muleskinner and physician had told of the actions of Joseph Wheeler, he became "Fightin' Joe" and would be known by that nickname for the remainder of his life.

Joseph Wheeler was born in Augusta, Georgia, on September 10, 1836, and was the youngest of the four children of Joseph Wheeler, a transplanted Connecticut Yankee merchant and planter, and Julia Hull Wheeler, the daughter of General William Hull, a veteran of the Revolutionary War and the War of 1812. When his mother died in 1842, the six-year-old, diminutive boy went to live with aunts in Connecticut and New York. He went to school there until entering West Point in the summer of 1854. He was seventeen, barely over 5 feet 2 inches tall, and weighed only 105 pounds when he walked up the hill from the Hudson River landing to the thirty-year-old United States Military Academy.

"Fightin' Joe" resigned from the U.S. Army and joined the Confederate Army. His older brother, William, helped him get a commission as First Lieutenant in the Georgia forces in February of

1861. He won favorable attention at his initial posting at Pensacola, Florida, from General Braxton Bragg and General Leroy Pope, a Confederate politician and secretary of war. He was made a full colonel at age twenty-five, and was given command of the 19th Alabama Infantry Regiment. He and they distinguished themselves at the Battle of Shiloh in west Tennessee on April 6-7, 1862. Given also the 25th and 26th Alabama and the 4th Mississippi, he conducted rear guard operations during the Confederate retreat from Shiloh to Corinth, and then to Tupelo, Mississippi. He received praise for that activity. Colonel Wheeler, after this noticeable and daring leadership, was assigned by Bragg to command three cavalry regiments in late August 1862.

Leading cavalry raids into Tennessee and Kentucky in late 1862, he gained a good reputation for very effective duties: covering the front and flanks of the infantry and artillery, intelligence gathering, raiding from surprise, and delaying actions against enemy advances. Nathan Bedford Forrest and John Hunt Morgan were in his command. He had less success in keeping these two, especially maverick Bedford Forrest, in his chain of command. After graduation, Wheeler had chosen to attend additional instruction at the Army's cavalry school in Carlisle Barracks, Pennsylvania.

The cavalry student had come a long way since those grueling classes four years ago. Little "Fightin' Joe" was very quickly becoming the real thing—an excellent commander, attentive subordinate officer, and an energetic, resourceful warrior. His troops were rough, unruly, and ragtag. Not the best disciplined crowd—and maybe the worst; they fought and fought hard for their bantam chief.

A creative tactician, his tree-felling to delay Union advances gained he and his men the designation "the Lumberjack Cavalry." He also further developed the use of the lighter-armed—with short carbines and pistols and limited use of sword—more flexible mounted infantry. Wheeler was the first to use it extensively in the United States. He was appointed Brigadier General and Chief of Cavalry for the Army of Mississippi in October of 1862, and would later assume that position in a reorganized army structure for the Army of Tennessee. His troopers earned another nickname, "the Horse Marines," for their destruction of a Union gunboat and four transports on the Cumberland River north of Nashville, Tennessee, in February 1863. He was promoted to Major General in May 1863. Wheeler, that summer, published a manual entitled *Cavalry Tactics*, which proved very valuable in simplifying and systematizing cavalry operations. It was widely adopted by cavalry commanders.

The General sat in the parlor of the Jones's plantation mansion. He was served scarce English tea in an elegant china cup. It was obvious that his host had connections with blockade runners on the coast—Charleston or Savannah. Mrs. Daniella Jones Sherrod sat in a richly upholstered chair to the right of her aristocratic father, Richard Jones.

"General, I've heard the most amazing story about you," Mrs. Sherrod said.

"Ma'am?" Joseph said. His cup was midway to his mouth. "And what could that be, Mrs. Sherrod?"

"Well, it seems they say that when you were up in Shelbyville, back in October last year, you escaped a whole regiment of Yankee soldiers by jumping on horseback fifty feet into the Duck River. My goodness, sir, that is quite a feat!"

"Mrs. Sherrod, I assure you it was not fifty feet—more like twenty—and my horse did the real work," Joseph said with a straight face and a prankster's twinkle in his dark green blue eyes.

Wheeler's Jump

Chapter 5

Becoming Horse/Mule Soldiers

I t was about three hours past sundown. The full moon was a quarter way up in the night sky.

"Hold up there! Who the hell are you, pilgrim?" a rough throaty belligerent voice called from the trees beside the narrow road, just west of Decatur, Alabama.

"Same as you, neighbor! A wandering Reb looking for some messmates and hot food," J.N. responded lightly to the phantom voice, raising his good hand slowly above his head. "Don't shoot. We're friends, trooper."

"Advance and be recognized," the picket ordered. The three riders and two pack mules slowly moved towards the veiled voice. The moonlight was bright, and they could now see one another in the middle of the road.

"Rebels, huh, you all with what unit?" the Confederate corporal said to the three, his musket at his shoulder with its sights trained on

J.N.'s chest. Two other Confederate soldiers with muskets aimed at Alex and Lou emerged from the tree line.

"24th Tennessee Sharpshooters, Sergeant. Who are you folks? Wheeler's boys, I sure hope," J.N. answered.

"Hell, I ain't no sergeant. I'm a working soldier. 24th, you say, then why you ain't over at Chickamauga Creek stuck with Bragg? You near two hundred miles from his happy command," the guard responded.

J.N. raised his busted hand, only lightly wrapped now, but the salve was fragrant. He had taken off his sling three days ago. "Busted hand got me sent home near three weeks ago to heal up. It's not all the way mended, but I can hold a rifle or pistol. We just rode a long way to find you all. Awful quiet and boring at home sleeping in a feather bed and eating real food, don't you know." J.N. smirked.

"Well, ain't you the Tennessee terror," the guard grunted.

Later, at the guard station, the officer of the day, a fresh fish from Mississippi, questioned J.N. and determined he was who he said he was. J.N. lied and said he'd brought his nearly eighteen-year-old twin cousins to join up. He said to the officer, "Sir, Yankee raiders killed my uncle—their father and big brother—last month. They had to come, sir. They couldn't do nothing else." J.N.'s face was somber, his eyes hard. The second lieutenant looked as if he credited his story.

Every morning on the trail, J.N. had rubbed dirt on Lou's face and hands and told her to keep her battered wide-brimmed hat down on her head. He'd ordered her to keep her collar up and not to wash her face, ever. "Just rub it off every day, no water!" Her guise seemed to have worked.

"Lou there, Lieutenant, the tall skinny one, is a fine farrier and Alex, the pleasantly plump one, has the makings of a bugler." J.N. paused and changed to a more serious tone. "Sir, I reckon I've had enough of hanging in trees and lurking behind cover and taking easy shots at Yankee officers and gunners. Sorta felt like I wanted the rascals to see who's sending them to hell for their presumption, sir." He paused and shrugged, "Lots of Yankees were between me and Bragg's army so we came to find you all." He took a short breath. "Mighty fine work you all did, sir, up at Anderson Crossing—fiery trail from the valley to the plateau." J.N. smiled. It seemed he was a salesman or preacher in the making, a witty and smooth talker.

The young second lieutenant pondered the three and their story. He thought, "Sharpshooter, farrier, and bugler—Lord knows we could use some fresh troops, and these say they got more of what we need than lots of these dunderheads around here. Hope that sharpshooter won't be any trouble. He's awful uppity."

The second lieutenant, a graduate of Jefferson College in Natchez and heir to a six-thousand-acre delta plantation east of Greenville, told the three newcomers where to put their stock, make a camp, and find a mess to get some food. He told them to find a place to sleep near his squad of troopers, and that he wanted to see them in the morning first thing after they got some vittles.

"Sir, I've got some boys who need tending to. One says he's been with the 24th Tennessee Sharpshooters, and the others want to join up," reported Second Lieutenant James Tyler Muskgrove, late of Green Laurel Plantation, after that Jefferson College, and now in charge of a cavalry troop.

Major Stevenson, as the chief of staff to General Joseph Wheeler, was taking his morning coffee around a campfire outside his tent. "Well, hell Muskgrove, assign 'em to one of your units—you got plenty of vacancies. Give them that needs it the oath, and get your "Top" to sort them out," the still-sleepy major said impatiently.

"Well, yessir, but … but, it's this—one says he's a farrier, another claims to be a bugler, and the older one, as I said, says he is a sharpshooter from the 24th," Muskgrove apologetically recited.

Major Amos Solon Stevenson, late of Carmargo, Lincoln County, Tennessee, had spent a dozen years as an enlisted trooper in the 4th US Cavalry, six months as a walking soldier, and now over a year as an officer with the cavalry of the Army of Tennessee. He got the important details about these new men from his nervous but efficient subordinate.

"OK, OK, Lieutenant, bring them around in about an hour and we'll see what we can do with them," Stevenson responded more attentively.

"Fields is it? Twins from Sequatchie Valley, Lieutenant Muskgrove says?" Major Stevenson began the session leaning forward on a campstool, carefully whittling a long, smooth thick piece of cedar. The shavings were piled several inches high between his worn cavalry boots.

"Yes, sir," Alex, standing nervously in front of the unkempt questioner, responded respectfully, but firmly. "We came a lot of miles with our cousin Corporal J. N. Mayberry hoping you'd take us. We want to help, sir."

"Crittenden's raiders visited y'all's place and did some murdering, did they?"

"Yes, sir, they truly did," Alex's voice broke as did his steadiness. The major noticed Alex's struggle.

"There son, I see, we'll see you get a chance to make things right. You the farrier or bugler?"

"Bugler," Alex said, thankful that the subject of his father and brother's killings was past. He nervously continued, "Well sir, bugler, sort of. Well sir, I'd like to take a crack at it." He patted his calling horn slung over his left shoulder and resting on his right hip. Major Stevenson looked up from his carving and took in the speckled-brown, large bovine horn and smiled up at the boy's pink face. Alex fumbled his horn with his right hand, and with his left drew it to his mouth, blowing loud, clear long notes into the sky.

Braying mules and whining horses created a real racket from the corrals around the camp. Heads all around turned towards the source of the intrusive sound. Several men jumped up from where they sat, or lay confused as to whether it was a call to attention or alarm. Slowly the troopers who were nearest the "bugler" offered chuckles, and then laughter echoed from all directions. The major and second lieutenant were looking at Alex, shocked and dumbfounded. The laughter chorus turned Alex's face bright red, his moist eyes turned down to the toes of his brogans.

"Great day in the mornin'!! What the dickens are you doing boy?" a voice from behind Alex carried clearly over the laughter. The question closed Alex's throat and his eyes made tears. Major Stevenson stood to attention, stick dropped on the shavings, knife closed and into his pocket. Second Lieutenant Muskgrove had stretched as tall as he could and coughed nervously. A short, digni-fied, dark-bearded officer in a big black slouch hat, gold-trimmed medium blue/gray jacket, and lighter gray trousers stuffed in freshly polished cavalry boots walked to Major Stevenson's right side, facing Alex. His countenance was of concern and confusion. His eyes were bright, and directed into Alex's soul.

Second Lieutenant Muskgrove piped, "General Wheeler, sir! These two want to join up. The older one claims that Yankee raiders murdered these boys' father and brother up in the Sequatchie Valley. The corporal there claims he's been on sick leave and that he is a sharpshooter with the 24th Tennessee." Major Stevenson smiled when Joseph Wheeler looked at his senior staff officer.

"Solon, what's the story?" General Joseph Wheeler asked the man who was his strong right arm. The major put his left hand over his moustache, pulling it down firmly across his freshly shaved chin.

"General Wheeler, the younger ones are twins, one is a farrier, the tall one. The other has the makings of a bugler, as you heard, if he can get his timing right," Stevenson chuckled. "The older one seems to be a sharpshooter away from the 24th Tennessee. He was sent home, he says, for that hurt hand to heal." The major's voice took on a serious note, "Civilians, family folk of theirs, were killed by some of our noble boys in blue from up North way." Taking on a lightened demeanor, he added, "All of them want to become part of this merry band."

The chief of the cavalry looked over the three, beginning with J.N., the tallest. Then he took in Alex, and finally Lou. It was an interesting ragtag trio, much like his command—a disheveled and mixed bunch.

Joseph Wheeler had come to terms with his short stature at West Point. He'd learned in New Mexico four years ago that good fighters, especially horse soldiers, come in all sizes. It's about brains and courage, not how big you are. Those persistent, ruthless, hostile, and often successful Apache were all small, but they were formidable adversaries. Their spirits were giant-sized. Even with his learnings about size and men, in every new encounter he was aware of the other man's size. He didn't judge them or himself, but he was aware of his size in relationship to others.

J.N. stood over a half-foot taller and weighed thirty more pounds. Alex was about the general's height but outweighed him by at least twenty pounds. Lou was about his shape and weight, 110 or so, but a few inches taller. When his gaze came to each one in turn, the cousins respectfully looked down, not into, the little general's probing eyes.

The young general said to Lou, "Son, you any good as a farrier?"

Lou was silent for a long moment and then, in a quiet, low voice, said, "Well, General, sir, I've been working with my grandfather and father a long time learning how to tend mules and horses. Daddy always told me, 'Lou, them animals work hard for us and they deserve being taken good care of for the job they do for us. Keep them healthy and well shod, always.'" Lou surprised herself with her lengthy report. She wasn't the talker; Alex and J.N. took care of that. She saw in the general a kindness; she didn't feel at ease, but she didn't feel scared either.

"Well, farrier, your father told you right. Guess we'll have to see if he taught you anything to go with those good words. Won't we Major?" he said to his chief of staff, humor in his expression.

"Yes, General, we surely will," was Major Stevenson's answer.

"Bugler, you think you can learn to play a brass horn?" Wheeler's soft Georgian accent flavored his inquiry.

Alex's face smiled broadly, "Well, sir, if I must, but sir, this horn carries a mighty long way and can sing three-dozen different calls."

Wheeler threw his head back, laughing. "Very well, bugler. Major, see to it they get sworn in and they'll ride with you and my escort. Better keep them close to make sure they do a good job. I'd really like to hear if that bullhorn can call charge and reform. But not now, Son, not now." He chuckled and turned full to the major. "Charlie still chief farrier?"

"Yes, sir, he keeps finding us no matter how far ahead of him and his section we move."

"Well ... ? What's your name again smithy?"

"Lou, Louis Fields—Lou—General Wheeler."

"Bugler?"

"Alexander, sir."

"You, sharpshooter. You're a Fields, too?"

"A cousin, sir—Mayberry—J.N. Mayberry."

"Corporal, I guess you need to stay close to these two green hands?"

"Yes, sir, I'd like that."

"OK, Major, the corporal here is assigned to you. He can watch your sides and back. You're too reckless. The unconventional bugler, major—you see that he gets with some of our more traditional ones for a bit of instruction." Wheeler's face was relaxed and gave off a fine glow.

"Thank you, sir." Lou smiled and relaxed a little for the first time.

"Yes sir, General," Alex joined his sister's appreciation.

"Much obliged General, sir," Lou said as color filled her swarthy cheeks.

J.N. took up the thank yous: "We'll be fine, sir, and I'll watch out for the major good."

Chapter 6

In the Field with General Joe and the Major

"Long" Charlie Maddox was full of himself—and that was quite a full package. At just 5 foot 3 inches, his nickname "Long" was a joke he'd been given when he was twelve. Now he weighed at least two hundred pounds and had a waddle on his fat neck the size of one of Mama Bear's good sausages. His arms were exceptionally long, and hard as hickory wood. His relatively good mood this morning was because the major had assigned him a green hand recruit—a willing and talented "gofer." Charlie was just shy of fifty years old, and was fond of good sour mash whisky, fast horses, tall skinny women for hire, sugar-cured ham, and yeast rolls. "Long" Charlie was outwardly gruff, short-tempered, and foul-mouthed. His near toothless jaw clinched a beat-up cobb pipe all his waking hours. Rumors among the skittish headquarters' farrier section was that he had been a popular and successful jockey twenty-five years ago in Richmond, and that he had courted a big planter's baby daughter—

a sweet strawberry blond. When he got over-saturated with rotgut, he told the story:

Her daddy hated him and ordered him not to see her, and, when Maddox ignored his demands, the girl's father had Maddox horse-whipped and thrown unconscious into the hold of a French freight ship out Norfolk. The busted up jockey somehow made it to New Orleans after several years in France. He said he'd showed those fancy French how to ride a winner. He was in New Orleans when the vol-unteers came through in '46. He joined up and was with Zachary Taylor in Texas when he tangled with the Mexicans across northern Mexico. Charlie had joined up with a Tennessee unit routed through New Orleans. He served with the major, then a corporal in Taylor's infantry, throughout the war. Seems he was assigned to a farrier sec-tion after the fighting stopped, and those two young soldiers, a long way from their homes, sweated through the idle occupation in north-ern Mexico. He and Major Stevenson had been friends since the war, and they had served off and on at different forts in the old army out West since then.

Lou had been working for Farrier Sergeant Charles F. Maddox for three days from before dawn to well after sunset. Maddox had eased up on her only because of darkness. Lou was dog-tired, but she didn't let up. The farriers had been covered up doctoring and shoe-ing beaten up, tired out, and near broke-down stock. They'd been bent over shoeing horse after horse. Every other mount needed cuts tended, and some even needed stitches. Lou knew how to sew up cuts, and she reeked of the foul salve they used on them. It was a blessing for these poor animals that north Alabama's corn and hay crop had been good that summer. Folks brought in wagonload after wagonload of animal and human provisions. The stock was beginning to look like they might just do for the next spell with the Yankees. The men looked like human beings, mostly. The expansive Jones plantation, Caladonia, near Courtland, Alabama, had full food larders, and the troops had shared in some real tasty food cooked up by accomplished black slave cooks. Sweet potatoes were Lou's favorite. Alex ate his weight in warm, buttered corn bread. J.N. was fond of the rich, thick, spring-chilled buttermilk.

Lou's deception had worked. Her look, manner, and toughness had not betrayed her gender. She didn't have to act. She just had to be herself and not be noticeable or talkative. Her moon time had not come yet, and she was a little anxious about it, but in the last two years that monthly event had not been much of a bother. Besides, Mama Bear knew her medicine. The pouch of herbs her grandmother had prepared was hung around her flat stomach, centered above her butt under her drawers.

Alex came bouncing up to the farriers. "Lou, Lou, you heard? We're moving. There have been more stars whirling around General Joe's tent then stars on a clear winter night. Generals by the names of Phillip Roddey—I think he's with us—and a Stephen D. Lee have been in long loud sessions with the general and the major. That Lee is uppity as hell. Word is that he's old money—cotton brokers or doctors—from South Carolina. Granddaddy John L. would call him 'trash aristocracy.' This guy is chief of an independent cavalry bunch over in west Mississippi, I guess. They've been ordered over here to serve with us for whatever's next. Boys say this General Lee never saw a fight he could not go head-on into. Lots of work for the sawbones and gravediggers in his command. Lee tried to bully General Joe, but General Joe stood right up to him, and I mean up to him, and wouldn't bulge. Lordy, Lou, that little gamer is something. Reminds me of my cat, Tiger. Remember Tiger? Little old runt of the litter, but by the time he was two years old, he had put every dog and other cat in the valley on notice. Lordy, no truck from nobody, either one of them. We're going to be OK with him."

"Alex, looks like he's been all over the place in the time we've been here. I've seen him and his big black hat a half dozen times, I bet, checking out the men, corral, and the farrier work," Lou confirmed.

"I heard the major told Lt. Muskgrove, 'Joe Wheeler is the gamest little banty I've ever seen in uniform,'" Alex reported. "And then Major Stevenson said, 'The general ain't afraid of nothing or nobody.' Just like my little Tiger!"

Alex paused, looked at his sister's tired, dirty, and gangly face. "Ain't it something, Lou, we're going to see the elephant—that's what the old hands call going to battle for the first time." Alex stopped work for a moment, looking mystified at her chattering brother. "Mighty strange that saying. Wonder where it came from?" The query got no response.

Lou finished up on a skinny, gaunt bay and walked over to a tree. Alex followed, excitedly telling her his headquarters' news. She reached into her haversack and gave Alex a big greasy biscuit and a strip of dried beef. Alex automatically offered his canteen to her in exchange for the vittles.

"Good, good, brother, that's fine, just fine," Lou said absently, responding to her brother's chatter. She surveyed the dozens of tents and campfires around them. The smell of a wood fire gave her chill bumps, as it reminded her of her mother's fireplace at home in Tennessee.

Frustrated, Alex protested, "Oh come on Lou, this is exciting." He paused and noticed the look in her eyes. "Where'd you just go, Lou?"

Lou said quietly, "Home."

"Oh," Alex paused and looked at what Lou was seeing. They observed the strange sight of a roughly organized cavalry encampment set against the background of a setting sun—day's ending. This time of day, just before dusk, was a melancholy time for Lou and had transported her to another place and time.

"Oh yes, Mockingbird, I see, too," Redbird confirmed.

Lou cleared the vision, but savored the feeling. "Yes, we're going about what we came to do, for sure," she said. Her spirit returned to her body as she sat beside her twin brother under the big locust tree in the moonlight, under the violet sky of a fall night in North Alabama.

"How's your bugling coming along?" Lou said after a few moments, offering a lighter mood to their shared homesickness. "You know all them fancy brass horn calls yet?"

"Not all of them yet," Alex smiled, his spirit restored. "You know there's over a dozen calls: 'To Horse,' 'Assembly,' 'To The Standard,' 'Charge,' 'To The Left,' 'To The Right,' 'About Face,' 'Rally on the Chief,' and some others. Sure has made my lips and tongue hurt something awful. Still think my old horn has a clearer, fuller sound. We've been practicing for hours over in the woods east of camp. The major has me working with a tall, fancy guy from Charleston. Get his name: George Henry Pinkney II. The guys call him 'Pinky Two.' He's been a bugler since the summer of '61. He claims he's from a rich rice-growing family in South Carolina. He is supposed to have run away from home to the war when he was sixteen. He first hitched up with 'Cajun' Pierre Beaugard down south 'fore this. He says the major is a good officer. Only when the major wants something or gives an order, best not to be tardy about getting to it. He ain't got much on patience. He's cheery and full of fun except when on the attack, according to Pinky Two. He says the major served with Zach Taylor at Buena Vista. Didn't Grandfather John L. say he voted for 'Old Rough and Ready' once? Oh, never mind. The major is from over Fayetteville way. Joined up for the Mexican War and stayed in."

Lou nodded.

"He joined up with the company from Lincoln County called the 'Lincoln Legion.' The major was seventeen, said he was nineteen. First with the infantry, he later served in the 2nd Cavalry out in Texas with Colonel Lee—that's the General Robert E. Lee of the Army of Virginia. How 'bout that Lou?"

"Fayetteville—Lincoln County, huh—supposed to be nice country around there. I heard a stock dealer down at Ross's Landing say once that they raise some of the finest mules in middle Tennessee.

Dealer said it was because of the good, pure limestone springs and rich bottomlands, good hay and corn. That makes for some mighty fine stock," Lou asserted. "They've got gentler coves and hollows than us, I've heard. Those ridge sides make for a fine breaking in of a green team. Wears 'em out."

"Lou, hey, how is old Sarge Maddox? He as much a demon as they say?" Alex smiled.

"Well, he blows mighty hard, makes some noise, but there's more thunder than lightnin', looks like. He tells me what to do, I do it, and he grunts. He hasn't corrected me yet or been mean to me, so it's OK with me."

Major Stevenson and Sergeant Maddox were standing alone upside of a glowing campfire. "How's the kid working out, Charlie?" the major asked the overweight, red-faced, wheezing chief farrier who stood beside him blowing his morning coffee tin.

"He's alright, Solon," Maddox answered. Both old army veterans and friends, the formalities of command were lax between them when they spoke out of earshot of others.

"Well, tell me more about that, Charlie," Major Stevenson prompted the taciturn, squatty man who was smeared with soot and grease from headband to shoes.

"Well, Solon, I'll say this about this Fields kid—Fields, right? He has had some good teaching. He's strong, too. Maybe a little slow for me, but he don't miss nothing."

"Charlie, don't you go and be so hard on him. His father and brother were killed by Crittenden's raiders up the Sequatchie two months back. Give him some room and set a good example, which for you will be a stretch. You hear me?"

"Yes, Solon, I do hear you," Charlie said as if he meant it. He might.

Call to Advance

Chapter 7

The General and the Widow

This was his fifth visit to the big house at Caladonia over the last twelve days. He'd kept count. Because of several childhood dislocations, several educational institutions, a mixed heritage—Connecticut Yankee, New Yorker, and young Georgia gentleman—Joseph Wheeler had not had much exposure in the realm of romance. His Connecticut aunts, who raised him from six to sixteen, were warm and good to him, but they were certainly not demonstrative. Their kind spirits molded much of his mannered and reserved character. Their kindness and friendship had shown him women were people—but still different. He liked them from afar. At West Point, the 5-foot 4-inch, 110-pound cadet had not cut an impressive figure at the few mixed socials he had attended. His basic shyness had been a foundation to his means of interaction with people, and his experiences had not made for adventures into Venus' domain. He knew from his own body what sexuality felt like. The early examples of farm animals, conversations overheard at boarding school, slave talk on his father's plantation, and bull sessions in his dark quarters at the Point had informed him about men and women sexually. In truth, he had not been that attracted to any female. Yet there were a few who had inspired his imagination. But there it was: Cupid had found the heart of the young cavalry chieftain. Five visits to a lady in less than two weeks attested to that reality.

Working from before dawn to just past sunset on every job was required of a good commander of nearly three thousand worn out, unruly soldiers—and all the accompanying equipment and stock of an army cavalry command. Drills, instruction, inspections, medical attention, supplies, and getting his troops and their 4,100 mounts, mules, and horses taken care of had been a fourteen-hour-a-day, hands-on job. The job was not complete, but he'd accomplished much. He'd found his second wind, cleaned himself up, and his uniform was as neat and squared away as it had been at the Point.

Mrs. Daniella Ellen Jones Sherrod was a twenty-two-year-old widow. She'd buried her husband, Benjamin Sherrod, three years ago—he was twenty-four, she nineteen—and her month-old daughter, Ella, shortly after that. Her little boy, three-year-old Richard Jones Sherrod, ruled the manor.

"Miss Daniella and General Joe were really a matched team," Major Stevenson had thought so when he'd seen them together for the first time walking in Caladonia's garden a week ago. Watching them a few seconds, he noticed that they talked easily to one another; she did most of the talking. They smiled a lot and were amazingly similar in stature and coloration. She was 5 feet 3 inches tall, he was 5 feet 5 inches. She weighed maybe ninety pounds. Both had fair complexions with dark hair. She had a few freckles and an easy smile that complimented her dark blue eyes. Her hair was a rich brown, and his was prematurely thin and nearly black.

At a big dinner for General Joe and his staff, the Jones' household treated the soldiers to a feast and festival not to be forgotten. Miss Daniella sat at her father's right. The general sat to the left, and beside him sat Major Stevenson. The major's demeanor and uniform were equally proper.

"General," Mrs. Sherrod said, sitting across from the young general and getting his undivided attention. "I've seen you before. I couldn't remember when or where at first. But I knew I had. I remembered today. It was before the war in the winter of '59. Benjamin and I were on our wedding trip to New York City."

"Mrs. Sherrod, you truly have me at a loss. I certainly would remember having met you. Yes ma'am, I surely would," he blushed, smiling with warm eyes that reached out and touched hers.

"Oh, we didn't meet. I said I saw you. It was at a play in New York. You remember. A fire broke out on stage and several of you cadets in the audience, all in your fancy uniforms, leaped up on stage and put the fire out, stamping it out, and you had the thought to grab a sand bucket in the stage wings to smother the flame. You all put it out in short order. We all clapped. You all looked back at us shocked, and you were the one who stood erect and led the others in a deep bow towards us. It was most exciting and then most humorous."

"Well, well think of that. Yes, yes, Mrs. Sherrod, I do recollect. There were four of us just graduated West Pointers. We were all celebrating our first posting. Grand play, till the flames. We did come to the rescue, and then I fear made fools of ourselves. Are you sure I led the bow? I don't remember that," Joseph responded with feigned innocence.

"Yes, yes, my general, it was you. I shan't ever forget that scene," Daniella Ellen Jones Sherrod protested. "Quite gallant too, Joseph," she added, breaking the formality of "Mrs." And "General."

"Oh then, I can not challenge your memory Miss Daniella," Joseph joined in the new familiarity, readily. "I plead guilty, and I was awful full of starch then. Seems so very long ago," his joy turned to something else—wistfullness or longing or something else.

The host took the silence as a time and place to divert the conversation, which to him was becoming uncomfortable.

"General, glad to see you all going back to some action; the sooner the Yankee's get beat, the better. Know you have my full support, sir," Colonel Jones assured him.

The major thought, "Well this prosperous 'big mule' is tired of our company. Guess if I were him, I would be too. Lots of pasture, fodder, and vittles leaving this part of the world with us—inside or carried. And now 'my general' talk from his daughter!" He smiled as he favored a fine piece of baked ham and a big fresh yeast roll.

"Joseph, can you tell us any of your plans?" Miss Daniella said directly to the crisply attired, and now fully smitten, young general.

"Ma'am, it's a bit uncertain. Of course you may ask such." He offered an open face and warm countenance. "We're off to Gunterstown. The command will camp there while I go to confer with General Bragg at Dalton."

The party ended earlier than the general would have wished. It seemed that Jones wanted his guests and contingency to have adequate time to get ready to get away from him and his, especially the young, single, and gallant general.

At the front porch farewell Daniella said, "My General, know my prayers and best wishes attend you. Please come this way again. Caladonia will always welcome you."

"Miss Daniella, may you and yours be safe. My thoughts, wherever I go, will include you, young Richard, and family. Until we meet again." The general bowed slightly and gently shook her small-gloved hand.

He paused after that gesture and added, "Ma'am, be assured Caladonia and all who warm by its hearth are dear to my heart," Joseph said to the little hostess as he smiled into her deep blue eyes.

"General Wheeler, you and your troops are welcome at my place anytime we can be fortunate enough to have you," the scion of north Alabama said with the dignity of a medieval baron. It was an attempt to put a good face on his obvious feelings about this man and his attention to his daughter.

"Anymore cake, ma'am?" J.N. asked the big gray-haired black cook as he and another of General Wheeler's escorts sat in the servants' table at the Jones mansion. The kitchen was in one of the spacious separate buildings twenty feet from the backdoor to the Caladonia Plantation house.

"Yes, course I got more cake. You want a third helping soldier?" Betty, the Jones' cook for thirty years, inquired of J.N. with a laugh.

"Yes ma'am, if I may," J.N. quietly replied.

"Nothing like a third helpin' to make a cook feel good 'bout her cookin'," Betty said with a deep accent and a bass voice. She cut a hearty piece of the white cake for the complimentary young soldier.

"Why you calling that old darky, 'ma'am'?" J.N.'s fellow escort asked, loud enough for Betty to hear.

"Cause she's old enough to be my grandma, and I've been raised right, you damn barbarian," J.N. said under his voice to the smelly South Carolina backwoods private sitting beside him. He then thought he'd as soon whip the smart-ass swamp rat as have his cake.

"Well, it ain't fittin' in to treat niggers like people," the offended remarked.

"Yeah, you heathen, and that's why we're fighting this damn war, ain't it," J.N. unloaded on his unsavory comrade-in-arms. The soldier with badly stained teeth just grunted.

Betty smiled and shook her head as she left the room, saying under her breath, "Amen boy, amen."

Next morning the farrier sections fell in behind the main cavalry column as they rolled east-southeast. The morning sun was in their faces when they skirted Decatur. The sixty-mile trek's destination was Guntersville, Alabama, the major had told Sergeant Maddox as he moved up and down the train getting the movement underway. J.N. was riding at his back and to the right. General Wheeler, staff, and escorts, which included Alex, were ahead two miles behind the scouts. Chill welcomed the ragged group. The sun shone on the tones of tan, brown, and gray—a bright red check here and there—and hats of every description: kepi, slouch, broad wool farmers, even a few straw ones. The weapons included sabers, muskets, rifles, carbines, shotguns, pistols of a dozen makes, and a few side knives. Among their spoils of war were varied instruments of war from many battlefields and many Union and Confederate soldiers. A saving grace was that the dampness kept the dust fairly limited. In the sun of mid-morning the migration appeared a colorful cavalcade, all different, yet one as of a whole. Maybe it was as a crusade, or maybe a circus.

The major doubled back about noon with Alex and a few of the general's escort unit. J.N. was the only non-com; all the others were privates. The party came up to the traveling forge with Lou riding Ben. Sergeant Maddox was beside her on a big chestnut. Bess trailed Lou on a lead line.

"How's the finest farrier section in the whole of this grand Confederate Army this beautiful fall Alabama day?" Major Stevenson greeted the attentive recruit Lou and the nodding Sergeant Maddox. J.N. pulled Sister's reins back as the major slowed pace. Alex, on Tess, was by his side. The others in the escort turned and fell in behind J.N. and Alex.

"Young farrier, you got a weapon?" the major said to Lou.

"No sir, I ain't."

"Corporal Mayberry, give me that navy pistol." J.N. pulled the revolver out of his saddlebag as ordered and gave the pistol to the major. He, in turn, handed it over to Lou.

"Sir, the ammo," J.N. said to the major as he handed him two packages of ammunition he had slung on the saddle horn.

"Yes, corporal. Here Fields. Charlie, when we stop, you give this boy some training on this weapon, you hear."

"Check," Sergeant Maddox said sleepily to the major.

"Thank you Major, just the same, I've fired a gun a few times but sure don't like to," Lou responded mildly.

"Well Private, you're in a strange land, dangers all around. If you ride with Joseph Wheeler's boys, then you shoot, if'n it's called for," Major Stevenson ordered firmly.

"Yes, sir." Lou looked down to her Ben's neck.

"Charlie, looks like we're going to be in Gunterstown for a bit. Guess we'll learn after we get there where we go next," Major Stevenson told Sergeant Maddox. "Carry on, troopers," he added, smiling. He nudged his big old ugly warhorse and said, "Lets go, Carmargo," and he was off in a sprint back toward the front.

Chapter 8

Knoxville and Beyond

Since the success of Confederate General Braxton Bragg in halting Union General William Rosecrans's advance south in late September 1863, little had happened in America's Great Civil War outside of Virginia. Yet a new day was in the making. There was a new Union commander, Ulysses S. Grant, who had been, a year before the war, an unsuccessful farmer and firewood peddler, and then clerk in the family's tannery in Galena, Illinois. "Old Rosey," William Rosecrans, was shifted to St. Louis and oblivion. Privations in Chattanooga had been severe, but Joseph Hooker, sent by Grant with twenty thousand seasoned troops from the northern Army of the Potomac, had broken through from Bridgeport, Alabama, and reopened a supply/communication line. "The cracker line" from Chattanooga connected with Union resources in Nashville and elsewhere north. James Longstreet, greatly outnumbered and outgunned, had attempted to halt Hooker but was repulsed at the Battle of Wauhatchie.

U.S. Grant, the conqueror of Ft. Donelson and Ft. Henry—and new commander of the Union efforts in the mid-South—intended to have an active offensive to push the Confederates south. He was on his way from his headquarters in Memphis to begin a new Union offensive. The winter looked bleak for Confederate fortunes. Grant meant business, even before spring. He had sent Hooker on his breakthrough, and Sherman was on his way to Chattanooga to add reinforcements there.

Grant, a forty-one-year-old native of Point Pleasant, Ohio, east of Cincinnati on the Ohio River, was a diminutive, underachieving West Point student. He graduated near the bottom of his class in 1843. He served in the Mexican War, of which he said later, "I have never altogether forgiven myself for going into that ... I thought so at the time, when I was a youngster, only I had not moral courage enough to resign."

He proved nevertheless a hero. Assigned a quartermaster, he chanced shot and shell to supply his soldiers with ammunition during the bloody attack on Mexico City in September 1847. When an infantry assault was stymied by a heavily defended Mexican walled position, he scraped up a small cannon, had it hauled up a well-placed church's steeple, and fired hell down on the defenders.

Posted in lonely and isolated forts, especially Vancouver, Oregon Territory and Humbolt, California, after the war, he pined for his wife, Julia, and his two little boys in St. Louis. Abusing liquor to dull his loneliness or make it worse, he was urged to resign as a company commander (captain) in 1854. He scratched out a living for Julia and their four children by the hardest, first by farming near his father-in-law outside St. Louis, then by selling firewood, and later real estate. He failed at those efforts and as a bill collector in St. Louis. From

1860 he worked until the outbreak of the war (April 1861) in his father's Galena, Illinois tannery and leather store.

His letters requesting reinstatement in the regular Army went unanswered. Sponsored by his congressman, Elihu B. Washburn, he organized and trained Union volunteers from Galena. He was appointed colonel in the 21st Illinois Infantry in June 1861. Promoted to brigadier general, he quickly proved to be a good commander and an effective, tenacious leader, capturing Ft. Donelson, Tennessee, in February 1862. When sued for terms of surrender by his old West Point classmate, Simon B. Buckner, he answered, "No terms except an unconditional and immediate surrender can be accepted. I propose to move immediately on your works." With that capture of a vital Confederate waterway (the Tennessee River), he gave the Union their first major victory and launched his reclaimed military career and reputation.

In early November, the struggle in eastern Tennessee and north Georgia was heating up. Bragg, struggling with suspicion of his officers and the intentions of the Union Army, anointed James Longstreet, Lee's "War Horse," savior of the situation. In a brilliant plan, impossible to execute, Bragg sent half his force—ten thousand men—with Longstreet and his Army of Northern Virginian boys to Knoxville to attack the Union force there. The idea was that this would draw off the Union buildup in Chattanooga, and with Knoxville pinned down by Longstreet, Grant would be forced to send troops to reinforce Ambrose E. Burnside in Knoxville. The Confederates could then strike a weakened and disoriented Union Army in Chattanooga. This had to happen before Sherman could get deployed to Chattanooga. It didn't.

The major had been back in Dalton for two days. He walked away from Bragg's headquarters and moved into the tree line nearest the clearing. He had gone far enough into the woods for the bustle of headquarters activities to be mostly muted. Pulling out the stopper of his canteen, he took a long drink of old, cold coffee.

He put his canteen on the ground and rummaged into his haversack. He pulled out a one-inch-thick, beaten leather-bound notebook he had bought at a fancy store in Mobile in June of 1861. He sat down on an abandoned rail-field fence. The book had a five-inch by nine-inch cover with a faded gold imprint of an oil lamp. The first half had been written in. The other half awaited notations.

He read the first page:

Journal of Amos Solon Stevenson, born Fayetteville, Lincoln Co., Tenn. Sept.14, 1829. This journal commenced June 5, 1861.

Halfway down the first page was written in pencil:

5/5/1861 - Mobile, Ala., joined the 19th Ala Infantry with rank of 1st sgt.

He flipped a few pages to find the general's place.

Sept. 4, 1861 — We got a colonel today, a Colonel Joseph Wheeler from Georgia. Lord he looks like he ain't 20 years old yet. Must be in early twenties. He is a graduate of West Point, class of '59. He was with the old army's Mounted Rifles in New Mexico, dancing with Apaches for a spell. One of the first sergeants, from Huntsville I think, says they christened him 'Fightin' Joe' out there. We'll see, I guess.

There was a sizeable gap of time in the notebook. The next note read:

Oct. 1, '61 – near Mobile, Alabama. Cold winds off the Gulf, rain, sand and hard work. The colonel has been trying to get us in shape. Called me in to his headquarters tent last week. The rest of the bunch of "officers" are holed up at Battle House in Mobile—nice hotel. The colonel is out here in the pine barrows with the enlisted. Colonel asked me last week about my experience in old army. I tell him. He then said, "Well, Private, you're now a regimental ordinance sergeant. Think you can handle it?"

Blew me over. I said I reckoned I'd try. Didn't take long for me to be suspicious of this promotion. We're a pretty poorly organized military! Colonel Wheeler has had us working our a——off getting into the shape of a fighting infantry regiment. Guess who gets to try to show these Alabama Butternuts how to be soldiers? Here's our day:

Out of the sack at 5:30 am, then:

6–7am: Officers drill

8–9: Regimented drill

9:30–10:30: Officers recitation/lecture on tactics

10:30–11:30: Sergeants and corporals recitation on tactics

11:30–12:30: Company drill

12:30: Noon meal (Poor, even when ample—which ain't often)

1–3pm: Police the camp

4–5:20: Regimental drill

Sunset: Dress parade of command. Posting of guards. (Insects eat us alive during the day especially at dusk.)

The notebooks next entry was:

March 1, 1862 – Corinth, Miss. Ordered north last month to join Beauregard. We're to keep the Miss. River open and protect the Memphis and Charleston RR that runs across north Miss. and Ala. Generals think Savannah on Tenn. River will be point of Yankee's advance south from Fort Henry and Ft. Donelson. Lots of other of our units merging up here. A. S. Johnston commanding general. I knew him out West near 10 years ago. Good officer, maybe our best. He's got a mess to organize and get ready for Grant's push. No rest for the righteous, I guess.

Turning a page, then two, Solon read:

April 20, 1862 near Corinth, Miss – Hell of a battle at a place called Shiloh (after a Meth. Church, I think) April 6-7. We won first day, lost the second. Johnston killed. Beauregard in command. We stopped 'em, though. They bruised but not beaten.

19th Ala. and Colonel Wheeler did fine, lost too many, but fought as hard and as good as anybody on the field. The colonel proved he deserves those three stars on his collar. I'm thankful we were assigned to rear guard with Kentucky boys. Shows how we gained a little respect. General Breckinridge and his orphans from Kentucky, lead unit of reserve, given the job of keeping Grant and Sherman from our backsides as Beauregard and army moved south. We helped.

August 30, 1862 – Tupelo, Miss. We're horse soldiers now! Colonel transferred to cavalry. Asked me to go with him. Thought hard about it. Reckon a change'll be OK. Was a trooper for years, am again. Colonel given three regiments—3,000 or so troopers on paper, we're short that. The stock is decent but we need half again what we've got. New commanding general of this Army of Miss. is William J. "Old Reliable" Hardee. Temporary assignment I hear. Shake up of command. General Hardee made up cavalry—the colonel's training in the old army put to good use, I reckon. We're off to test our metal as horse soldiers in Tenn. and Kentucky in three days. Lots to do getting us ready.

September 29, '62. Completed two days of raids on Union boys north of Nashville. Tore up Buell's railroad and wire lines.

Some of Forrest's boys joined us for a spell for Kentucky adventures. We sure raised some fine hell: Buell's cavalry didn't know which way to look or ride. It was some lark. Twenty-two lost, fifty-one wounded. Captain Towry of D Company, 5th Georgia, killed. Colonel's fourth horse sent to "Elysians Pastures." Name, Augusta, small gray mare. Near Perryville, Kentucky today. We blocked Yankee advance with downed trees. The colonel said felling trees to mess up Union passage is just obvious.

Oct. 13, 1862 – Colonel named chief of cavalry for this army (Miss.). Guess we got the Western war to tend to.

Promoted to captain today (Nov. 1, 62). Colonel was made a brigadier yesterday. Word is he's maybe the youngest at 26. He said when he promoted me, "I figured you've earned some gold tracks if I got a wreath around my stars, Captain."

November 16, 1862. The new brigadier named chief of all the cavalry by General Braxton Bragg. My boy general given command over wild Forrest and hard-driving John Hunt Morgan. The general asked me to be his chief of staff. Well it's a long, long way from my being a seventeen-year-old buck private at Monterrey with old Zach.

There was a gap in notations of nearly a month, then:

Jan. 3, 1863. New Year and we're busy. We have been giving Old Rosey's boys hell along his supply line from Murfreesboro to Kentucky. 20 different hot fights during the last six weeks! Old Bragg sent a "reprimand" for "reckless exposure." My Gen'l don't send the boys anyplace he don't go. Hell for leather!

    Last week we took and burned 450 Union supply wagons. Captured 2,437 prisoners. "Old Rosey" is in trouble.

January 18, 1863 – North of Nashville near Ashland City. We got a new name, "Horse Marines." Some Georgia boys calling us that. Around Christmas we got word they calling us "Wheeler's Lumberjack Cavalry." If we had a lot more boys they could call us anything they want. As is, we're surviving. We'd been busy burning bridges around Ashland City on Cumberland R. We're watching river for traffic. Fired on steamer "Charter" with boat in tow. Boats came ashore and surrendered. Next morning at same spot two gunboats raked the shore with shot hoping to get us. They missed. Colonel Wade's detachment had been successful farther up the river. He and his boys captured an unescorted transport up at Ashland landing. Next day "Trio," transport also captured. "Hastings," a hospital ship full of blue boys hurt from Murfreesboro was next and transport "Parthenia." Hospital boat sent on to safety. What a sad ship. "Slidell," a gunboat then came up blasting the banks. Our little field pieces out-shot them terrible gunboats' firepower. We got her too. Five vessels in a row—a gunboat and four transports taken in two days! Horse Marines, indeed.

Feb. 15, '63. Forrest blew up at the general and offered him his sword this week. A stupid, hotheaded, senseless action by General Forrest. He took exception with General Wharton as he read the report of Fort Donelson attack. Bragg had ordered General Wheeler to attack Ft. Donelson. Forrest had been given the task. It was cold, snowing, with two inches on the ground. Union forces too strong. Forrest withdrew and cussed Bragg, Wheeler, and the elements. General Wheeler defending Wharton said, "the report does ample justice to your (Forrest) men." Forrest would have none of it. All I can say is we're cold and the weather is misery and Bragg's headquarters ordered a senseless offensive against a strong fort. The attack was a "forlorn hope." Everyone knows

Forrest hates Bragg, threatened to give him a whipping. Bragg has no grievance against General Wheeler. The general gives General Wheeler a job and we do it. No trouble, we do our job. All can be said is that there is bad blood between Bragg and Forrest and General Wheeler is Bragg's chief of cavalry and Forrest is his subordinate—General Joe is caught in the middle. Politics everywhere in this here army.

The major paused from reading about what seemed the far past; he looked north and a little west toward Chattanooga, thought a few minutes, and began to write of the last few days' happenings. He thumbed ahead to the next clean page:

November 25, 1863 near Dalton, Georgia – It wasn't a disaster but it surely was a mistake. Time, time is the abiding enemy in living and in war. What Bragg planned, or was it Longstreet, or both? Just couldn't work. We had a mere three weeks to get to Knoxville and flush Burnsides out of his stronghold. He had plenty of shot and shell with good artillery soldiers. Idea was, with Burnsides threatened and maybe whipped and Knoxville and northeast Tennessee in danger, the Yankees have to take men from in front of Bragg at Chattanooga. Great idea, terrible in reality! Stalemate in Knoxville. Burnsides hunkered down and made good use of artillery. We couldn't budge them. Bragg called us back from Knoxville to Missionary Ridge November 23.

Yesterday, Nov.26, near Ringgold, Georgia — Thomas and his bunch just plain walked over us as the Yankees marched over Missionary Bridge yesterday. The general, staff, and escorts got to the battle at the beginning of the party. We were able to pull together some cavalry, not near enough, a puny group, and tried to do some good. Retreated with Cleburn's division and we turned on those arrogant SOB's. Hooker's bunch couldn't get past us. Lord, what a fight. Cleburn and Wheeler were tasting fire. A vicious ordeal. The general wounded by shrapnel in foot. Sent by ambulance east around Union positions. I'm moved back to Dalton with rear guard.

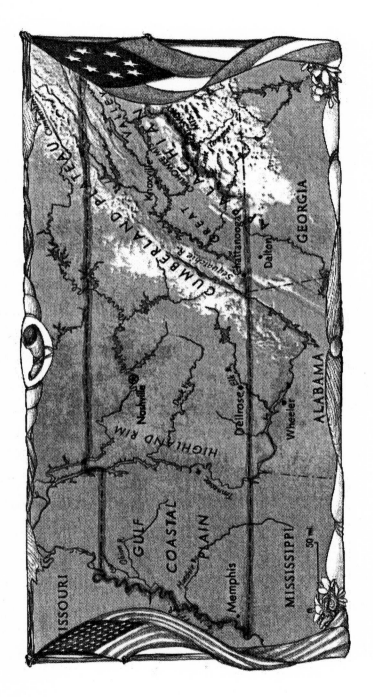

The Heartland

Chapter 9

Spring Place and the War Women

Lou accompanied the general and his staff on November 23–26 during the hasty return from Knoxville to Bragg's army near Chattanooga. The general had wanted Lou and a pack mule with some farrier equipment in case the mounts and remounts needed attention. Bragg needed the general to urgently report to him just south of Chattanooga. So off they went lickety-split, the general, staff, and escort with farrier rushing south from Kingston to North Georgia.

By dark the staff and escort group (which consisted of sixteen soldiers plus Lou on Bess) were some distance down in southeast Tennessee on the way to north Georgia. Crossing the mountain passes was slow. The general kept them in the saddle some four hours after sundown. He halted his caravan near a secluded creek. Two privates built a campfire and cooked up some coffee and corn bread. The general kept his own special corn bread mix in a handsome, well-finished canvas pouch Miss Daniella had made for him after she'd asked what she could send with him to ease his work. With fresh water, a skillet, and a bit of fatback, he enjoyed hoecakes whenever "dining" was difficult.

"Private, see to the mounts," the general said to Lou as the camp took shape.

"Yes, sir," she replied. Dismounting Bess, she bent over and touched her toes, freeing up her cramping. Her bottom and low back hurt. Tending the chores, she mused about the exchange when Major Stevenson had ordered her to rest back at Kingston. They'd been hot at it, and the mounts needing attention had overrun the farrier section. The other farriers and even Sergeant Maddox had worked sixteen hours straight. The major had ordered Lou to rest and told Sergeant Maddox to lighten up on the "kid" and stop letting Lou do Maddox's work.

The major had said to Lou, with a weak sternness and twinkle in his eye, "Youngun, there's always plenty of work, so don't kill yourself trying to finish. We ain't going to ever be finished. Pace yourself, boy!"

What was it about those words? They were no different than the ones J.N., Alex, or her father would say to her. But the feeling, her feeling, in reaction was most curious. She was not able to figure out her feelings of anger and appreciation. The major's attention preoccupied her mind as she went about tending the mounts and remounts. The major bothered her.

Lou approached the general as he sat on the exposed root of a big, snarled chestnut oak. "Excuse me, general," she quietly said, some eight feet in front of him. A good fire crackled, and a blackened coffeepot sat on burning hickory branches.

"Yes, son?" the twenty-eight-year-old general asked. The general was about the same size as sixteen-year-old Lou—and maybe even a little smaller. Lou's smeared, crusty, and sweat-dried face had the appearance of a barn owl—white around the eyes with smudged brown everywhere else.

"Your mount, sir—well, sir, she's got a ugly place on her left front leg, about mid-way between the knee and hoof."

"Bad, son?" the general asked, concerned.

"Well, not yet, general. Must have pulled through some strong and rough brambles or skinned it somehow. It needs tending, though, before it sours," Lou said. Then she quickly belated, "Sir, might be best not to ride him the rest of the way. We've got two remounts, the bay and black."

"I'll take your guidance, doc," the general said pleasantly. Then seriously, "Do what you can, farrier. You can patch her up?"

"Yes, sir. I think so. I brought some of Mama Bear's good medicine and salve. That ought to do the trick."

"Well, seems we got a bear-cub horse doctor here tending our fine war horses," Wheeler said without meanness.

General Wheeler had left his cavalry under the watch of General William T. Martin, one of his two brigade commanders. He and his escort got to Bragg's headquarters mid-afternoon the next day, November 24. It was a mess in the region.

Grant had thrust Thomas at the Confederates on Missionary Ridge, east of Chattanooga, which was Bragg's vital holding force for Chattanooga. Later, Sherman joined Thomas. Then Hooker pushed two divisions through the mist up Lookout Mountain. The battles of Lookout Mountain and Missionary Ridge on November 23-25 were the beginning of Grant's successful brawl with a succession of Confederate commanders of the Army of Tennessee.

What had been Bragg's nail-down of the Union force in Chattanooga became a Union breakout all along the Union front and the southern edges of Chattanooga. The Union offensive put Bragg into a stumbling defensive posture. The Union forces were like a stunned fighter who had been hugging and protecting his head with his fists. Then suddenly when it looked like he was ready to drop he had gotten heart, bowed his back, and punched away fiercely at his stunned opponent. The blows were left, right, and then George Thomas's eleven brigades finished the attack up Bragg's center. Left shot, right shot, and then a pounding of the mid-section. The Confederates, stunned and whipped, retreated to save their hides. Grant and the Union forces were on the move. All that Bragg could do was backstep south into north Georgia. Patrick Cleburne and Wheeler's soldiers and scraped-up cavalry were charged with slowing and, if possible, stopping the Union advance south after Bragg's army.

General Wheeler desperately pulled together a small, makeshift cavalry force from the few hundred of his command he left with Bragg. Wheeler and the majority of Confederate horse soldiers had gone with Longstreet two weeks before. Now the boys he needed for an effective fight were one hundred and fifty miles north!

At Ringgold, in Georgia, the Confederate retreat led by General Patrick Cleburne, an Irish-born Southern division commander, turned. They were ordered to halt the Union pursuit. Wheeler and his cavalry hugged Cleburne's flanks, battling as mounted and dismounted cavalry. Grant sent Hooker with two divisions to drive over Cleburne and Wheeler. Hooker failed and then sent two brigades to roll back Wheeler's forces on the Confederate's southern flank. In a difficult and fierce fight, the Union movement to the south was halted by Wheeler's troops. General Wheeler was wounded in the foot. Grant temporarily abandoned the Union pursuit of Bragg's army.

A forty-plus, well-dressed woman riding sidesaddle pulled rein of a big white stallion beside an ambulance that had stopped in front of the mansion. "Soldier," she confidently addressed the medical orderly sitting on the driver's seat. Lou sat quietly beside the driver. His shoulders were crunched down, and it made him look like a frog. "Who is in that conveyance?" she asked assertively, waving her riding crop like a scepter.

The six escort riders looked like some were going to laugh, and the others looked likely to pull their guns on the uppity woman. The driver just stared at her. A disembodied, weak voice from inside the canvas covered wagon said, "Corporal, who's there?"

"Sir, it's a lady, sir," the uncomfortable orderly answered, turning his head back towards the patient behind the canvas.

"My complements, madam. I am a bit indisposed. Would you kindly come to the back of the wagon so that I may speak to you directly?" General Wheeler requested.

She moved the thoroughbred to the rear of the wagon.

"Madame, I'm Joseph Wheeler of the Army of Tennessee cavalry," the General said to the attractive blank-faced woman dressed in expensive riding fashion.

"Yes, well general, might I be of an assistance? Sir, you may gladly avail yourself of the shelter and hospitality of Spring Place. I'm Amelia Vann. Spring Place is my farm and welcomes all who defend it," the mistress of the region said.

General Wheeler, his left foot bound in a dirty red and brown wrap, leaned up on his elbows. "Ma'am, you are most gracious. That is not required. We'll move on to Dalton to find headquarters. Medical services will be there."

"Nonsense general. They'll kill you with their ministrations. Quacks. You tell your driver to drive up that way and come up to the front door of my place," the regal lady on horseback ordered. Then she turned her spirited mount and said to Lou, "Boy, follow your general and help get him inside."

The next day Charlie came by the plantation and saw the ambulance from the road. He pulled in behind it in the drive. There, around a fire on the gravel driveway, sat the three troopers eating ham and biscuits. Lou had a fancy china cup held by both hands. It gave the smell of cocoa. Charlie's mouth watered.

Just as he was about to get some information from Lou there was a commotion at the house's front door, and his lust for grub was suddenly dampened.

"You gentleman take this villain!" the dark, well-dressed woman with a scarlet turban said as she stormed out of the house. Beside her was the biggest black man Lou had ever seen. He was holding an unconscious rebel with a green stripe on his sleeve—the medical orderly.

"Damn villain drank the bonded whiskey meant to clean the General's wound," she said, looking at the offender with pure loathing.

"Any of you know any doctoring?" she angrily asked.

The youngest of the four troopers piped up, "Ma'am, this here boy knows doctoring. He's patching up wounds all the time." He was pointing to Lou.

"Boy get up, follow me," Miss Vann ordered a shocked Lou.

Lou was so taken aback by this assertive woman's directive that she struggled up, brushed herself quickly, adjusted her dirty black slouch hat, and followed the red-turbaned, bossy woman toward the big house's porch. Charlie was left with his mouth open. He forgot about the ham.

Miss Amelia Alice Vann, forty-three, spinster, was mistress of 1,700 acres, Spring Place, twenty-one slaves, a flourmill, a blacksmith shop, a store, and a tannery. She was the only child, the heiress, of "Rich" Joe Vann, a mixed-breed (white/Cherokee) who had become quite "white" after the "Trail of Tears." Her grandfather had been James Vann, a scoundrel, madman, and thorn in the side of John Ross, the chief of the Cherokee. He had been an ambitious and successful planter and trader, before killing himself many years ago.

This woman had held together her inheritance for over twenty years against ne'er-do-well suitors, suspicious and corrupt state officials, and the trials of a civil war in both her front and back yards.

"Ma'am, he's bad, real bad," Hannah, Amelia Vann's middle-aged and dignified personal servant said to her mistress as Miss Vann glided into the curtained, darkened room.

"Yes, Hannah, thank you. Boy, what do you need?" Miss Vann said to Lou.

"Ma'am?" Lou squeaked.

"Boy, pay attention. Your general here has a bad wound. You and I must see what we can do to relieve his suffering. If he's lucky, we may save that foot. I surely am not going to let one of your surgeons at him. They saw wounds off!" Miss Vann informed Lou.

Miss Vann turned to Hannah and said, "Get us some lye soap, clean soft cotton pieces, and some good strong string. Check for the string in the sewing room." Miss Vann next turned to Lou. "Well, let's see what we've got here, boy."

"Ma'am, please don't trouble yourself. Wrap it up, if you'd be so kind, and I'll be on my way to Dalton," the general whispered, lifting himself with difficulty onto his left elbow, hazily finding that the people around him were planning his treatment.

"Nonsense, sir, you'll get lockjaw or lose that foot. I surely am not going to trust your health to the barbers posing as healers. Sir, I am the granddaughter of Joseph Vann, daughter of James Vann. Cherokee blood flows in my veins and we are a mighty civilized people. We know more about medicine than the butchers who stole our country!" Miss Vann stopped herself, realizing she was wasting time preaching and justifying her actions.

"Sir, rest. Boy, in that cabinet, hand me that decanter and glass in there."

"Yes, Ma'am." Lou surveyed the direction Miss Vann had indicated and accomplished the chore.

The willful hostess administered to her wounded guest a half-glass of ten-year-old sour mash whiskey.

"Boy, find Hannah upstairs and tell her to get a sharp pair of scissors from my sewing basket and a sharp knife from the kitchen," Miss Vann directed Lou.

Before Lou could react, the general stirred and said, "Ma'am, here, my pocket knife." He fumbled into his worn blue trousers and drew out a shining, burnished, silver-plated five-inch knife and waved it.

Miss Vann handed the warm knife to Lou, "Well son, cut that bandage off and let's see what we have to deal with."

"Yes Ma'am," Lou said and got busy doing as told.

Between Amelia Vann's will, dried herbs, lye soap, Lou Field's tender ministrations, and Mama Bear's Cherokee medicine, Joseph Wheeler's life was saved. So was his foot.

The general gave Lou his knife, which she tried to return before they moved out. His father had given it to him when he had left for West Point in '54. It was silver and had an inscription: "Honor." The general told Lou, "Consider it a gift. You surely gifted me with your Indian conjuring." He smiled and saluted her.

She blushed and looked at her worn out brogans. "Much obliged, sir."

Chapter 10

A Soldier's Pilgrimage

Major Amos Solon Stevenson sat in the large yard of Spring Place under a huge spreading sycamore tree twenty feet from the troopers' fire. He held a hot cup of real coffee between his gloved hands. After waiting five days longer than it should have taken for the general to show up, the major had rode out to find General Wheeler. He and half of the general's escorts had doubled back, hoping to find sign or notice of the general, ambulance, Lou, and escorts. He'd arrived at Spring Place two hours ago and found the wayward detachment and sick general. Sergeant Maddox was here too. This was the beginning of the second week of the general's convalescence. Miss Vann and the farrier youth were caring for the general's wounded foot. Damnedest story he'd ever heard from this mighty peculiar woman. She declared that she was the descendent of a Cherokee, and the Field's kid tells her—once the kid got over her fear of the crisp old maid—that Lou had a grandmother who was a Cherokee healer. Hell, the kid even had some Indian medicine his grandma'am had sent along for any cuts or wounds. The boy cleaned the wound, lanced the festered wound with a pocketknife, administered some Indian medicine, and the general was on the mend.

The major shook his head, "God almighty." From what the troopers told him, the general was in as awful bad way before those Indians got hold of him and his sour wound. Now the general was getting anxious to get back to his troops and away from Miss Vann.

The morning was a little chilly but bright, sunny, and clear. As the major blew on his cup of real coffee—courtesy of Miss Vann's tiny black slave cook—he thought of the softness of the occasion. Weeks—no, months—of whirling around hills, splashing through creeks and rivers, slipping and sliding on mountainsides in all sorts of weather, cold and hungry and more scared than any self-respecting horse soldier admitted, and now here he sat in this quiet beautiful place with the loyal sun warming his fatigued body and wasting soul. Life was "interesting" at least.

The major stretched his neck and twisted his head. He relaxed and went away from the present and into his past, soon losing all sense of his surroundings. Taking a deep breath and stretching his arms wide, he noted a bird two branches from the lowest limb on the old oak. It was singing as if it was the first day of creation. A clear sweet song weighed gently on the seasoned warrior's soul. The major had often felt the darkness of his soul. He knew the depth and breadth of a rage from hell. In a hot fight it came forth and occupied his soul and body. He called it the "wolf." Lots of blood and other men's souls were on that wolf's soul—on Stevenson's soul.

"Corporal, that's a mockingbird, ain't it?" he spoke quietly so as not to scare the bird across the yard, addressing himself to the three horse soldiers stretched around the trunk and roots of a larger live oak.

"Yes sir, a mockingbird."

The major's soul smiled. He felt blessed—and maybe even forgiven. "Odd," he thought, "very odd." Nature for him had always been something to overcome, not appreciate. But on this occasion, and at this place, he had noticed.

"Major, sir," Lou quietly spoke, standing eight feet to the front of the napping, brown and gray, buff figure with a battered kepi pulled over his eyes. An old brown book lay under his left hand on his lap.

"Yes," a groggy voice answered from the sleeping officer.

"Sir, the general asked me to tell you he wanted to see you in about an hour," Lou said.

Coming awake, Major Stevenson pulled himself alert, put his notebook in his haversack, and picked up the overturned coffee cup made of blue and milky white china. He handed Miss Vann's fine china cup to Lou. Lou stepped forward and took it.

"Hey, Bear Cub, it's you. Here, go get me some more of that store-bought coffee, would you? Get yourself some too. I need to talk with you."

"Yes, sir." Lou was off to the errand.

Sipping his coffee, the major spoke. "Private, what possessed you to practice medicine on the general. Hell, boy. A man ain't a horse."

Lou looked slapped, "Well, sir, well …"

"Well, well—well what?" Major Stevenson's attitude softened, and his eyes sent out a twinkle.

"My grandmother, sir, well folks from all over the valley come for her healing. Plenty of cuts: axe, knife, saw, scythe—even gun shots. Usually by the time they come, their hurt is in a bad way. Mama Bear has medicine she gets from plants, trees, and even certain mosses. She grinds it, adds lard, and makes a poultice, and her treatment works most of the time. Her poultices are really good on sour wounds."

"And you just go and decide to doctor the chief of this here cavalry with your Indian medicine?" the major said with a smile.

Lou's feelings—mind and heart—were all confused. It seemed that the major was grilling her as if she'd done wrong, yet his spirit was warm and kind. Mighty confusing.

Lou struggled for a response. "Sir, some of my people are Cherokee women. Cherokee women are different, different from most white women I've known in the valley, at church, and at the store."

"Different? Cherokee women are different? We're all different one way or the other, so what does that have to do with you doctoring on a senior general officer of this here army?" the major asked with slight irritation, but more like a friendly sparring with words.

Lou looked right and left, then down. "Miss Vann, sir, she's like Cherokee women: she's strong, mighty strong. She acted like her way was the only way. She told me to doctor General Joe, and I did, sir," was the only answer Lou could offer.

"OK, boy, OK," the major said to Lou, as if to say, "I see, I understand some." He smiled again.

The major sat alone again under the sycamore tree on a fine north Georgia fall morning.

He pulled his notebook, again, from his haversack. Turning to where he'd remembered being in the journal, he thumbed through several pages to find the pages he'd written about the Sequatchie Valley raids in the fall of last year.

He stopped at a May notation.

May 1, 1863 – General now major general. He's the youngest major general ever commissioned in American history, so says General Whalton.

May 5 – The new major general made me a major. Said no captain can be an MG's chief of staff, now can they, Solon? More I'm with this man the more respect and regard I have for him. He fights like a hell-yun and has the lightest of hearts. I couldn't serve in this storm with a better man.

June 29, 1863 – Southeast of Shelbyville, Tenn. Lost thirty-seven men in Shelbyville two days ago. Forrest was the fault. General Joe, me, and 51 troopers with a few foot soldiers of the regiment were to hold Shelbyville bridge over Duck River. Forrest, who was, "he said," a few miles out of town needed it to get his command across. We gave and took the dickens from the Yankees who wanted that bridge. It got down to three choices: we could get killed, surrender, or make a jump for it into the river. Had to be twenty feet down and the water was deep and running fast. We jumped. The general was the last in the river. He had to hold on to Augusta's pommel as he kicked and swam and as we bobbed and whirled. I somehow stayed on Carmago. The Yankees were shooting at us from the bank. I take it that 50 to 51 of us went into the Duck River in a jump. 13 made it.

That passage caused the major to pause. He listened for the bird's song. He needed to hear that song, he felt, to get his soul some relief from the hurt. He did not hear anything but the troopers across the way talking. He'd started trying to find his Sequatchie Valley notes but had became engrossed in the Shelbyville scrape. He turned a few more pages and finally found the valley notations:

Sept. 29, 1863 – near Jasper, Tenn. Along Anderson Pike. Yesterday we took 900-1,000 of Rosecrans's supply wagons on their way from Nashville to Chattanooga. What a blaze. We rounded up some of the Yankees. Had to dispose of most of the wagon teams. A hard business, putting those creatures down. We kept a couple hundred of the best.   *Rough skirmish with*

Union troopers at Fayetteville's fine Elk River Bridge. We stopped them. They high tailed it back. Bridge safe. Safe for both sides. We made it across north Alabama to Chattanooga. Chased hard, but successful on our raid of Old Rosey.

He closed his notebook and looked to the tree line to the west. The blue sky was clear and rested on the greenish-brown distant ridge.

He thought, as he soaked in some of life's beauty, "The Field boys said their father and brother was murdered about then up that way by Yankee raiders. Stole their mules, too." He wondered if any of those mules they had saved and brought along to north Alabama had belonged to the kids' family.

The mockingbird flew across, above his head—he'd found his mate. Husband and wife flew to a nest. Both sang as if celebrating supper and home.

Elk River Bridge

Chapter 11

December 1863 —
August 1864

The winter had been hard, and the spring was not any easier—and much busier. The summer was more of the same, lots more. General Joseph E. Johnson's assumption of command in late December 1863 had brought change. Joseph Wheeler was retained as chief of the now Army of Tennessee (changed in name from the Army of Mississippi under General Bragg). A reorganization of responsibilities, territory, and strategy had been put in place. Johnston, a master academic military leader, assumed that Grant and Sherman would be intent on the destruction of the Confederate Army and its will to fight. Territory, he assumed, would not be as vital as the grinding down of the rebel military. So give them territory, and not the chance destruction of the second most important army except Lee's. He planned accordingly: no full "big" offenses for his command. It would be jab, feint, wait; jab, pester, move, and wait. Give ground to get Union casualties.

Maneuver and rabbit punch. Don't get into a full-blown "great battle." No gambles, just patient, technical hide and seek. The fifty-seven-year-old Johnston, a native of Virginia and an 1829 graduate of West Point, had thirty-two years of impressive service in the U.S. Army before Fort Sumner. At the Civil War's opening he had been a brigadier general and chief quartermaster in the old army.

Johnston knew his numbers; 63,408 soldiers, including some 8,000 cavalry under Wheeler, with 189 pieces of artillery could not out-brawl William T. Sherman's muscle-bound Yankee Army.

Sherman was a forty-four-year-old Ohio native, and as a nine-year-old orphan had been raised by a power politician, Thomas Ewing. He was an 1840 graduate of the US Military Academy. He had given up the military in the 1850s to make a fortune in California. He had not accomplished that goal. At the war's beginning he was superintendent of the Louisiana Military Academy, which later became Louisiana State University. "Cump" Sherman had turned down a Confederate commission. Occasionally a bit insane, Grant valued his abilities. He was a hell of a fighter.

Sherman's 97,797-strong force was divided into three prongs under George Thomas, James B. McPherson, and John M. Schofield. Three to two, it was Sherman over Johnston.

"Yes, Major, whatever it takes. It must be done," General Wheeler said to his chief of staff, Major Stevenson. Wheeler's foot was healed now, and his spirit was driven. The actions of 1863 had worn, beaten, depleted, and nearly demoralized his cavalry of the Army of Tennessee. They had near-constant action. There was a new "Pharaoh in Eqypt," and General Wheeler was going about responding to his edicts: refit, retrain, restore, and re-inspire the outnumbered Confederate Army. Wheeler took to his part of making that happen with a sprinter's energy. As he had with the 19th Alabama Infantry, he worked tirelessly to get his boys in shape. For usually fourteen hours a day, six days a week, the little general in his oversized black hat was all over the Confederate cavalry encampment near Dalton, Georgia. Major Stevenson was with him half the time. The major was the only one who worked longer than the general. He brought the general his coffee in the darkness of before sunrise and finished his duties after the general had gone to a few hours rest near midnight.

The major sat by his commander beside a campfire at about 10 p.m. "Yes, General, we've—you've—accomplished a near transformation these last seven weeks. I've never seen or done as much training since my time with General Taylor down in Mexico after the fighting was over and we were waiting to come home. Your work here with these ruffians is showing. They ain't ever going to be good book soldiers, but, by the Eternal, they are gonna be better fighters. They were pretty good before, now they're gonna be better." He blew on his tin of coffee. "We still haven't got enough of anything, especially troopers and guns, but we sure to hell are more ready with the little we've got than maybe we've ever been."

The general, warming his hands beside the flickering hickory and cedar fire, said, "Solon, we're going to face real hell this spring. The Yankee troopers don't fall off their mounts when we show up anymore. Damn if they haven't learned to be cavalrymen. We'll have more than we can say grace over soon enough. Heard my old classmate at the Point, Judson Kilpatrick, has taken over some of Sherman's cavalry. There will be the devil to pay, Major. They don't call him 'Kill Cavalry' because he's timid. Tough and crazy as hell. We're in for it, Solon."

"General, when haven't we been?" the major said quietly.

Major Stevenson sat against a large exposed limestone boulder ten feet from a small campfire. It was early August 1864. This August was hot as blue blazes, and the cavalry's activities had involved nearly daily actions against Sherman's pushes to get into Atlanta—and to kill John Bell Hood's army along the way. The major thought, "What a change from Old Joe Johnston's cautious slap and run, hit and hide, never engage head on." It had worked for nearly six months, but Richmond had wanted offense, brawling, the great underdog victory over the bully—a regular David and Goliath story. Jeff Davis wanted the victory in July of 1864 in north Georgia, with J. Bell Hood as the young shepherd. Johnston was out, and Hood was in as commander of the beleaguered Army of Tennessee.

Major Stevenson grunted to himself, "Didn't know hell could be any deeper or hotter than what it was in this spring. We've had bad, tough, hard fighting in this the summer of our Lord, 1864."

He pulled off his worn-out, old, dull-brown kepi with the crossed-swords insignia. He laid it beside him on the green grass.

Pulling his left hand slowly from the top of his head forward to his throat covered with week-old stubble, he sighed heavily. It was as if the friction of this movement would draw out the poison. Shaking his head as if to clear his mind, he rummaged in his haversack. In his notebook he read a passage of some three months ago:

May 26, 1864, near Cassville, Georgia. Day before yesterday we had a rip-roaring fight. Lost near fifty-nine men, but ran off Yankee troopers and took Union supply train. Over 80 filled wagons taken and we captured about 110 prisoners. Worn out. Carmago has had stone bruise. The young farrier, Lou Fields, has been doctoring him. I used a big red mule for a week or so while Lou tended Carmago. Fields said he worked with the mule some and it was a jumper and had good speed that stretched out 'bout as far as he'd ever seen. Mules sure have a different gait and feel. By the Almighty, that Fields kid was right. He did the work and was ready for more. I've got a regular "War Mule"! Fields calls him "Cousin." I'm having Lou keep him with the farrier section as a remount. I may use Cousin some and rest Carmago. He sure has earned some time off.

Lou Fields, our apprentice farrier from up Sequatchie way, has become a real trooper and pure pleasure. Kid doesn't miss anything and those brown eyes got a brightness about them that shows something special. I tease him too much. Not sure why. When he's around I pick at him something awful cause of the way he reacts—open, kind, and gracious. He just smiles and blushes. He's a good kid. It feels like his youth and brightness draw me away from this killing and dying we're about. That

surely is taking its toll. Losses, great losses. I feel so very, very bur-
dened of soul ...

Word came from General Johnston yesterday. He congratu-
lates the general and us for our efforts at Cassville. Much obliged,
I'm sure. I'll tell the graves.

He looked up to the bright sunny patch, and sadness covered
him like a big heavy quilt. He nearly couldn't breathe. Then he
sucked air into his lungs and blew it out slowly. Wetting the short
pencil he'd squirreled out of his tunic pocket, he wrote:

August 5, 1864, southwest of Dalton, toward Macon — 5 gener-
als and near 3,300 Yankees taken in raids of McCook division
at Newnan. We also captured a big chunk of Sherman's cavalry
and General George Stoneman and 700 of his troopers at
Macon. Near a hundred supply wagons and six artillery batter-
ies, 21 guns acquired. Bet "Red" Sherman is fit to be tied.
Rough, mean work—79 dead, 63 missing, 116 wounded.
Whole cavalry command down to a little over 5,000; 4,200
effective. Last few weeks have been as hectic as we've endured.
They keep coming with more of everything and we keep having
less and less to fight with. Dog tired.

Lou had set up the farrier station. Sergeant Maddox was asleep
under the wagon. Thinking to clean up, she grabbed her kit and went

towards a creek she'd noticed when they'd driven into the tree line. The troopers were spread out to the west in groups of twenty or so, doing a search of the area for running Yankees. Some of Stoneman's boys had taken flight, and the Tennessee boys smelled equipment and Union rations. The pursuit was on. Lou had heard some faint gunshot reports from time to time, maybe a half-mile off, as she built the campfire. Not really concerned, she had nevertheless put her pistol in her belt. She had checked, and it was loaded. She'd done the target practice as ordered many times and had gotten adequate in the skill, but she didn't like it.

Just as she approached the sound of running water, she heard the canter of hooves behind her. Quickly turning towards the source of activity, she caught sight of Alex about thirty yards behind her.

"Hey, trooper," she cheerfully greeted the bugler. His calling horn bounced on his thigh as his mount briskly moved closer to her.

"Farrier Boy! I'm fine and dandy and how are you this fine day? Lordy, lordy, we whipped 'em every way and a couple of new ones!" Alex was full of residual excitement from the disaster Wheeler's cavalry had brought down on Sherman's horse soldiers. "We got Stoneman, Lou! And supplies, yes some fine vittles." He sat on his horse a few feet from Lou. Reaching behind himself, pulling up his saddlebag flap, he jerked out a greasy, formerly white cotton bag. "Ham, Lou. It ain't salt pork. Reckon old Long Charlie would quit his complaining if he got hold of a big helping of this?" Holding the ten pound bag out towards Lou, he laughed and answered his own question: "S'pect so!"

As he leaned forward, swinging his trophy, Lou caught a flash. Startled, she focused on the sparkle. Alex was too much into his

prideful celebration of a big supper to notice the activity behind him
and his mount. As the spectre took form in Lou's mind, she froze for
a second then grabbed her navy Colt revolver. In what seemed an
instant of movement—a methodical flow—she cocked the big gun,
took six steps away and to the side of her confused brother, aimed,
and fired. The charging rider's chest exploded in scarlet, his head
stretching toward the sky, then falling back, his saber tumbling from
his limp hand. The attacker seemed to bounce as he hit the ground
and was hidden in the foot-tall grass. She aimed again, sighting the
second rider coming up just behind the fallen one. His carbine was
bouncing as he tried to aim at her and Alex. The pistol roared again.

Alex's shock quickly passed as he turned in his saddle to see what
was the reason and result of Lou's actions. "God almighty, you got
both of them. They ain't moving!" The first Yankee's horse had
turned away from Alex and Lou and was standing perplexed fifty feet
from the two. The second one stopped two feet away and looked
back. The big, slick black stallion and fine roan mare looked over the
scene. It appeared as if they understood what had happened.

Lou held the smoking pistol and looked at Alex, the grass-
obscured Union trooper, his horse, and then to the right and left. She
was as white-faced as Alex had ever seen her. There was fire in her
eyes, and Alex was struck by the heat and starkness of her look. She
put the pistol in her belt and looked up to her still-mounted brother, tears in her hard eyes. "Brother, we've done it." She paused, took
a deep breath, and then said, "But I forgot to offer prayer before I
shot 'em!" She went to Alex and grabbed his mount's placid face. She
hugged the warm horse's head as if her life depended on holding on,
and she cried into its sweat-soaked mane.

Chapter 12

An Ending and the Uncertainty of the Future

"Hell, Fields, that Yankee pork was just what the 'doctor' ordered, Doc," the sergeant laughed as he complimented and teased his assistant the next morning after Lou's gun play. He had come to appreciate this kid's quiet strength and tireless hands, arms, and back. It didn't seem that this abuse fazed this accomplished farrier and healer. Unrelenting in his attempts to irritate Lou, he had learned not to expect a response of anger or sullenness—but still, he tried.

Lou said distractedly, "Yes, Sergeant."

Maddox had failed again to get any energy back, or to elicit any tone of resentment or aggravation. That game was always the same: Maddox tried to rile Lou, and she always resisted being out of sorts.

Then Lou realized she was suddenly hot, very hot. The August sun had moved to shine right on her and the sergeant. It was hot, Georgia August hot. Two layers, wool trousers and cotton jeans, were most uncomfortable in the ninety-plus temperature of an August day

113

in Georgia. She unbuttoned her coat, pulled it off, and unbuttoned her vest and shirt collar. Tugging at her homespun, heavy cotton shirt, she fanned the shirtfront, trying to get some air down the unbuttoned collar. No relief was achieved. Getting up, she went over in front of Sergeant Maddox and squatted down to pick up his eating gear.

"Damnation, that ham fill you out? You've gotten thick, boy! Devil almighty, you gaining weight? A person would think it would be contrary. Hard gaining weight on half rations. That ham sure filled you out." The sergeant chuckled, trying again to shake Lou's placid behavior.

"Well, Sarg … well … I guess I'm just still growing," Lou said haltingly as she felt a wave of panic. She thought, "My secret must not be found out!" She quickly stood up, pulled her vest together, and turned her back to Maddox. She walked away slowly; she wanted to run, but she restrained that impulse.

The sergeant went on to a new topic. "God almighty! It's sure hot. Been in this infernal clime all my life but damn if the down South summers don't sap me." With that complaint, he moved out of the sun into the shade of a big, bell-shaped chestnut tree.

"Yes Sergeant," she said over her shoulder as she buttoned up her vest and moved away from the stirring sergeant. She needed desperately to be away from the sergeant and everybody else. Her panic and dread bounced inside her soul like a rubber ball Alex had played with for months when they were five. "Sergeant, think I'll find a creek and wash up a bit," Lou told the fat, smelly man who was settling in. The robust, short man pulled his hat down over his face, his arms folded above his big belly. She walked away as he mumbled something she didn't hear.

Lou had traded some wormy fatback with one of the general's escorts a few days before for some soap. She needed to take the waters, to cleanse her spirit for her action yesterday. She saw this as the opportunity she needed. Scared of exposure, her thoughts went to sorting out what she must do—wash her clothes and scrub herself, take the waters and offer a prayer. The lye soap was wrapped in a cotton rag. She took it from her haversack and unwrapped it. She sniffed it. The smell invoked the presence of her grandmother Mama Bear's iron wash pot over a hickory fire just down from her back porch. Mama always boiled bedclothes early Monday morning, cold or hot weather.

With her mind bringing Mama Bear into its consciousness, she felt a chill even in the August heat. She felt the hard, translucent, and rough-cut bar of soap. Putting it to her nose again, she drew in the strong, chemical, clean odor, as if to be with her grandmother beside the black iron wash pot at home. Her spirit yearned for Mama Bear's presence and blessing—and Grand and Mother. She blocked her yearning for Johnny and Daddy. The dead were not to be bothered.

Directly in front of her, about twenty feet away, standing out alone in front of the tree line illumined by the high sun's strong light, was a cedar tree. The tree was over twenty feet tall and was snarled, thick, and full-needled. A huge moss-covered limestone boulder, three feet tall and five feet long, lay to the tree's left. A bit startled as she took in the scene, her spirit smiled. Her heaviness lifted.

Standing six feet from the tree and rock, she spoke to them, imagining that her grandmother and mother's spirits filled them. "It is done, Bear Woman, Lone Cedar. Mockingbird has fulfilled the blood law, the obligation honored." She went to her vest, put her hand through its opening and into her shirt. She carefully pulled out a soft, small, tan deerskin bag. She breathed in deeply, taking in the sun's warmth and the deep green tree's vigorous fragrance. Taking a pinch of her grandfather's shredded burley tobacco, she walked forward and tossed it up and toward the cedar tree, then onto the limestone outcropping.

"Mama, Grandmother—Great Fire, Life Spirit—the balance is restored."

Dog tired, he'd not had any real sleep in three days. Two-hour naps somewhere in the haze of that space of time didn't count for much. The major rubbed his low back and thought, "Damn, Solon, you're getting to be an old man! What is it ... thirty-four? Well, well, it's thirty-five." His dark brown—nearly black—hair had become a bit thinner on the top of his head, and in the places above his ears there was some gray. His chin stubble also had some increasing gray. The staff meeting with the general and commanders had been brief, and he'd thought to get away from war for a little while. Taking his haversack and saddlebags, he walked deeper into the woods away from people.

As he was about to get away, a voice called from his back, "Major!" It was Lieutenant Muskgrove. "Sir, sorry I missed the meeting. Some trouble with captured supplies. Some of the Texas and

Alabama boys didn't see eye to eye about the division of goods. Took a little strong persuasion, but I got it worked out for now. Sir, those Texans are the meanest bunch of outlaws I've ever come across." Muskgrove offered more than the major wanted to know.

"Lieutenant, we move out at five in the morning. You see to getting headquarters broken down and ready by four-thirty. Now get some rest out of this heat, and I'll see you at dinner," Major Stevenson instructed the aide. Turning away to let Muskgrove go about his business, he thought, "Boy has lost some of his starch. He might make a decent officer if he can just lighten up and calm down a bit."

The creek, near a mile from camp, was some twenty-five feet across, mostly shallow, and full-running. Lou walked along it a little ways and found a big overhanging willow with some exposed roots out in the creek. She thought the creek looked deep at that place. Testing it with a broken long branch as she leaned down over the willow roots, it seemed like the place was four or five feet deep. It would do for her purposes. The roots and willow provided some screen, and the hole was deep enough to get a good bath. She looked around and listened for a bit. Nothing. No sounds or activity were detected. Nice. She listened again—nothing but woods' sounds.

After she'd taken off her brogans, socks, and trousers, she sat in her drawers and shirt, washing her stained feet. Checking again, she eased into the creek by way of the willow roots. The rocks were sharp on her bare feet, but she shifted her weight and found a soft-bottom space. Her dirty wash was in one hand and the strong lye soap in the other. It had a harsh, greasy acid smell, and her clothes smelled mighty sour. Wetting the clothes, she laid them on the root. Taking a piece at a time, she stood waist-high in the creek and started scrubbing her wash. Her soul was in a better place than it had occupied in months, but she was still little confused when she thought about it. She'd killed, and there was a shallow grief—but a deep peace of mind. The place and the quiet rays of sun coming through the trees were surely a comfort. With her obligation accomplished, her mind at rest, and her soul soft, she went about her task with a peaceful spirit. After lathering, scrubbing, rinsing, and repeating the process, she worked through her washing and laid each completed piece of clothing on some of the branches of the willow. There was a slight breeze coming through the trees, and a patch of sunshine warmed the place where she laid her washed clothing.

With her outer clothes washed and hung to dry, she proceeded to lather up the drawers she was still wearing, and then her hair. Alex had kept it cut pretty short during their enlistment. She closed her eyes tightly after lathering her drawers and head. Then she went under the water, slowly moving her head around to rinse. She ran her fingers through her shining black hair. She enjoyed the feeling under water for as long as her lungs would allow, and then she slowly reemerged. She felt as if the world was fresh, if only for just a few seconds. Letting the sun warm her wet drawers and the creek water drain off her hair, she stood motionless for a few moments. No sound, no movements could she detect, except for some birds singing in the woods along the creek. Assured of her solitude, she went under

Taking the Waters

the water to her shoulders and unbuttoned her shirt. Lathering up her hands, she went on to scrub under her arms. She stood up out of the water a bit. J.N. had told her, not long after they'd joined, about lice getting on the body hair. She had checked from time to time during her very infrequent bathing and had found the things a few times—and felt them once on her head and once in her down-below hair. She doubled her scrubbing when she thought about those creatures on her body, clinging to her hair. Satisfied that she had accomplished as much as possible, she went on to soap her chest and midsection. She'd not really seen her breasts for what seemed like quite a spell, and she was a bit shocked to see how they'd grown. They were now the size of one of Mother's good china cups. They felt weighty, and they would lift as she soaped under them. Her nipples, dark brown, offered feelings when she soaped them that she found surprising and pleasant. Preoccupied with her feelings and washing, she gloried in the experience. It was a spell of peace in a relentless hell.

Major Stevenson was drawn to the splashing sound. As he cleared a thicket of scrub brush and middling cedars, and brushed bramble away from his knee, he looked at the sound and saw. The brown eyes looked like those of a doe he had killed when he was sixteen and over which he had grieved for a long time.

Lou grabbed her breasts instinctively as she stood to scramble out of the creek. The major saw everything and with a rush retreated into the cedar thicket in a panic.

Chapter 13

The Sentence

Lou seeped a cold sweat from the crown of her head to the soles of her feet. There were droplets rolling down her face. She felt cold in the August heat. General Joseph Wheeler was sure that there were tears mixed with the perspiration. Over the year that Lou had been with the cavalry, the general had taken to him—to her. The doctoring Lou provided at Spring Place might have saved his foot if not his life. The general was truly confused, sad, and a bit humored by the situation. A strapping teenage girl had fooled a whole cavalry of unruly, ruthless, restless horse soldiers; fooled them, Sergeant Maddox, Major Stevenson, and him. What a hoot! He was astonished and amazed, but he knew what had to be done.

Farrier First Sergeant George Maddox and Major Amos Solon Stevenson stood on each side of Private Mary Louise "Lou" Fields, farrier, Cavalry of the Army of Tennessee. General Joseph Wheeler, chief of cavalry, sat before a makeshift desk in the musty hall of a big old poplar-logged barn near Lovejoy, Georgia, on the hot, humid, and steamy morning of August 6, 1864. General Wheeler sat on a

121

rickety porch chair, his elbows on the table, his ungloved hands crossed before him on the empty table.

To the general's right, in a kitchen chair leaning on its back legs against the log hall wall, sat Brother Paul Israel Robertson, volunteer Baptist chaplain with the Army of Tennessee. He happened just that day to be on only his second visit to Wheeler's cavalry in eight months. Brother Robertson was not much older than the general—maybe thirty; he was clean shaven and had a head fringed with stringy, greasy hair that hung down to his shoulders. As with Shakespeare's Cassius, he had a hard, lean, and hungry look. Slight of build, 5 feet 8 inches, 130 pounds, he rested his head on his narrow chest, his thin long arms wrapped around his dirty and tattered black frock coat. A tarnished Maltese cross insignia was present on his coat lapel. He was without caveat and wore a faded butternut homespun shirt buttoned at his throat. He was listening intently, his eyes closed, his breathing expressive. None of the four others in the hall were unaware of his presence.

"Let me see if I got this right, Major," General Wheeler addressed Major Stevenson. "Yesterday you accidentally discovered while skulking around in a cedar thicket up that creek over yonder, oh yes, you were just getting away from camp to walk out your stiff limbs to find a good cedar stick for whittling or whatever, that this boy is a girl?" Joe Wheeler's voice and face were solemn, but his eyes betrayed his sternness. The major took comfort in his awareness of that contradiction. But this was no joking matter. There may be good internal feelings, but rules were rules—no women soldiers. The major, daring to not make light of this situation, remained alert and empty-faced, his eyes looking over the general's head to the bright sunshine at the opening of the barn hall.

"Sir, well, General Wheeler sir, the trouble is," he realized he was stalling by trying to find his jumbled thoughts and match them to the necessary words. "Yes. General, Private Lou Fields is a female," the major said finally, quietly and simply.

Brother Robertson jumped up, his chair bouncing against the wall. "General, beg your pardon, sir, but this won't do, won't do at all. You're here to say, Major, that neither you nor anyone in this command noticed that this, this strumpet was not a male! Lord knows what sins she worked on your troopers. On you! It's a scandal, a sinful scandal. She's nothing better than a whore, general, a harlot of temptation, agent of Satan!" The fire of the righteous man of God unleashed a damning stare at Lou, whose eyes stared at the front of the general's desk. Solon drew in a long necessary breath and caught the preacher's eyes and soul.

The chaplain drew up his most terrible sin-whipping voice. "And you, Major, you lurking around to see her sinful nakedness. Why sir, that could only mean that you are a whoremonger!"

The wolf's eyes fired gold red, and in two heartbeats, three steps the possessed major had the frail preacher a foot off the ground, pinning with his arm the reddened, stretched "holy Joe's" throat against the rough-dressed, gray brown poplar log wall.

"Major! Solon, at ease! Major?" General Wheeler had hopped up around the table, his hands on the major's rock-hard shoulders. He tugged at the major's frozen back.

Sergeant Maddox had come to the general's aide. "Major, this son a bitch ain't worth the strain." He was trying to get a hold on the man and his rage. It was a formidable task.

Lou just stood at her place, taking it all in. She was trembling, her eyes wide open, her heart in her throat, and her hands in white-toned fists. She felt badly sick with an anger new to her. She then realized she was in the presence of evil. Evil in the form of an agent of the holy that had condemned her and the major.

An hour later, two escorts aided the shaky chaplain's departure from Wheeler's headquarters. Lieutenant Muskgrove had told them to not harm the man, but to get him as far away as they could, toward the Union lines, without risk to themselves.

The major and first sergeant were beside the water trough fifty feet back of the barn headquarters. The major knelt on the smooth quarter-inch gravel around the watering place. He was pouring water from his cap over his head. Shaking the water off he said, "I would've killed him Charles. I sure would have rung his damnable pious neck."

"I know, Solon. If you hadn't, I would have," the first sergeant allowed. Then he chuckled, "What do you reckon—firing squad or medal—would have been our reward?" Charlie broke out in a belly laugh, his red face becoming redder.

"Yeah, wonder which," the major said and broke into a smile. The wolf was caged with that gesture.

The general paced in front of his desk in the barn hall. His soiled, scuffed boots knocked up barn dust and decayed chicken droppings. J.N., Alex, and Lou stood fifteen feet from the desk.

"Boys, I could have you court-martialed for putting us through this hoax. Might just do that, too." He quickly went to his chair behind the desk, saying to himself, "Yes, I might just ought to do that very thing."

The general turned back to face the three recruits. "Sharpshooter, what do you have to say? By the great Jehovah, man, you're too old to be playing such a dangerous game."

"General, sir. You don't understand, sir. I tried, sir, I truly did. Her grandfather tried. There just was no way she would not come and get in this war. No way, sir, that I know of short of crippling her. No sir, no." J.N.'s steam was released, and his engine ran down.

"And you, bugler, what about you. This 'sister' got some power over you, too?"

"No sir. Well. Sir, that is—she was going to come, sir, and she is the most determined person in our whole family. Heck, sir, I haven't ever known anybody as stubborn." Alex paused and looked at the front of the general's desk. Then he said, "She came, sir, and I came."

Wheeler shot up from his chair, dust rising from the ground. He whirled and walked away from the desk, his back to the convicted. His head was shaking slowly, his hands finding purchase across his low back. He muttered, "Damnation!" He was one part exasperated and one part impressed by this kid and family.

It had been decided by noon. Orders had come for the cavalry to move out the next morning to make mischief with the Union's stretched supply line through the Sequatchie Valley, Cumberland Plateau, and on to Nashville. General Hood wanted a major disruption of communication and supplies. Sherman had to respond by pulling off troops on the offensive to take Atlanta. Hood needed to diminish as much as possible the great number differences in north Georgia.

The major sat in his shirt at the front of his tent, shell jacket spread to air on a branch of the middle-sized elm. In front of him First Sergeant Maddox and Lieutenant Muskgrove braced the three condemned.

"OK, this is what is going to happen. J.N., you are to stay close to these two, your creative and daring cousins. All three of you are to stay close to me. First Sergeant, you've lost a farrier!" The major took a long pause. "We'll be in your home country within the next week or so. You three are going home."

"No, sir. No," Lou found her voice and it carried authority beyond her gender and age.

"Alex and J.N. here didn't do anything wrong. No one ever asked them if I was a boy or girl. They kept quiet because, well sir ..."

"Because, because, young lady!" the major barked at Lou.

"Because, sir, I had a duty, we all had one." She went quiet, her anger and nerve modified by grief. Then she looked the major in the eyes, a custom she struggled to adapt to, but she needed to join his spirit, to connect.

"It was because of the killing last year of your daddy and brother. Girl, is that what you're telling me?"

Lou's eye contact broke and she looked down. "Yes sir, the murders, sir. Murders."

The major's displeasure, sternness, and resolve were broken by Lou's words and eyes—and her diverting gaze. They had to go, but he didn't like it.

The next morning at an hour before sun-up, Major Stevenson, astride Cousin, came up to the campfire as J.N. put a small rotten sycamore log on the small fire.

"You three. Listen up!" he ordered as he patted Cousin's neck. "When we get within twenty miles of y'all's place, you, Mayberry, take these two home. Swap for some civilian clothes all of you before we leave here. Girl you keep that hat off. Find a kerchief or bandana. No hat. You need to look something like what you are. There's Union patrols and partisan reported all over that area. You all are three farmers coming home from town. Understand?" No answer. "Understand!"

"Yes sir," J.N. responded with a bit of energy.

The twins mumbled, "Yes sir."

Chapter 14

Home Again,
August 1864

The sun was bright and high in the sky. The air was warm. A faint breeze moved the green-brown leaves of the big yellow poplar. Bess stood munching the lush bahalia grass ten feet behind Lou. The hillside graves had patchy growths of wild grasses. The new headstones read:

Wm Norman Fields
August 3, 1822 - Sept. 3, 1863
and
John Ross Fields
June 14, 1843 - Sept. 3, 1863

A space separated the graves—a place for Lou's mother.

Lou had removed her hat. She held it to her side. She patted it slowly against her the side of her thigh. With her left hand she rubbed her tearing eyes.

"I'm back," she said quietly and went silent for several long moments, then, "It is done." With that she looked up past the old tree to the ridge's crest and the shadowed tree line. Swiping her face with her big bandana, she blew her nose. She turned and went to Bess, reached her hands around the big scruffy mule's neck, hugged it hard, and sobbed heavily into her musty, animal-smelling gray black coat.

Grandfather John L. was busting ten-inch-wide, foot-long hickory sections with his razor-sharp double-edged ax. The crack of the wood resonated crisp and clean. Lou came around the house toward the big woodpile. In mid-swing, her sixty-five-year-old grandfather saw her.

"Praise the Lord, and serve the wine," he hollered as he popped his ax into the chopping block and was with Lou in five long steps. He grabbed her shoulders in his hands, caressing and squeezing her. Tears rolled down his red cheeks and over his chin.

"Lone Cedar! Sarah!" he called as if trying to be heard in the next hollow.

"They're back. Sarah, they're back," he exclaimed with a smile that crunched up his eyes. The back door of the house slammed open and closed as Mama Bear came bounding down the back steps.

"Yes, yes," she said with assurance and joy.

"Where's Alex, J.N.? They tending the stock?" John L. asked as he visually searched toward the house and the corner where Lou had appeared. Lou's eyes went down to her grandfather's shuffled, worn brogans.

"What, Lou? What? They hurt, girl?" John L.'s joy evaporated and he was filled with foreboding. "Dead!?"

"No, no, they're fine, Granddaddy, fine," she assured her grandfather. "They are with General Joe in Athens. We came up nearly a week ago from Dalton to make a mess of Sherman's supply line," Lou reported. "They'll be here in a few days."

"Lord in heaven, they ain't with you? You all got within fifty miles of home and they didn't come? I swear." Totally flustered, he swung his axe like a hickory switch, the axe head embedding three inches into his busting block.

Mama Sarah took charge. "That's enough John Longstreet. They're alive. Lou's here." She looked deep into Lou's brown eyes and Lou kept her eyes locked on the woman who was her life's touchstone. "She's here and we're going to keep her if I have to tie her to a barn stall with a log chain." She smiled at her granddaughter and turned.

"Well, lets get this girl some food, John L. Quit your questions," Mama Bear ordered her excited husband as she pulled her out of her grandfather's grip and started toward the house, her arm in Lou's.

At supper she told the family the whole story. There was no conversation on the subject. Mama Bear went and gave her granddaughter a hug when Lou moved to leave the table. No words were exchanged.

"OK, A. Call the boys to reassemble," the major said to Alex as he stood high in his stirrups surveying the trail ahead.

The sky was filled with smoke from the two-dozen Union supply wagons attacked at daybreak. Alex made the bugle call. The troopers regrouped and moved out.

Later that day, six hours after the small raid, the major sat in a thin woods filled with cedars near McMinnville. He'd made camp there to rest and tend mounts and troopers. Rock outcroppings disturbed the sparsely grassed ground. Taking a long pull from his canteen, he put his near-empty container of stale water down. Pulling his notebook from his haversack, he turned to the next unwritten page and wrote:

Sept. 1, 1864, near McMinnville, Tenn. Last week we captured a Yankee command of three companies near McMinnville. Surprising them, they made haste to depart our presence. Left ten wagons, an ambulance, and three teams. The general has been urged by some of his officers to take Nashville. Gen'l Joe wanted to come up and around Knoxville to give Sherman's backside a kickin', but we're too few and they are so many. The general was right early on. Them Yankee horse soldiers have been tough opponents over the last two years. Give us both equal mounts and weapons and it is no contest, but when it's two to one and they've got everything they need and we haven't got much more than our bull headedness, well it's ...

Sent Lou home two weeks ago when we came by northwest of Chattanooga. Alex talked the general into staying. General Joe asked what I thought he should do and I said he'd learned a lot

for us to lose all that education. He laughed and said, "Very
well." Lou wasn't too upset as the family might need her and
J.N. at home with all the excitement in the valley and along the
Cumberland from Chattanooga to Nashville, Alex said.

He paused, seeing again, briefly, that day at the creek and his dis-
covery of Lou's secret. The vision of her disturbed him in a way he'd
not been disturbed before. The senoritas in Monterrey were friendly,
warm, beautiful, and generous. He'd known, in the Biblical sense, his
share of women since he was twenty. He'd like to have shared more
time and life with two or three, but he'd learned he was not the settling kind. The next horizon, trail, or duty post always seemed to be
more important than trying the civilian life and being in one place
with the same person or people. He realized then that he needed new
activity—physical and mental—to live like he wanted.

Seeing Lou, turning over the last year and her place in it, caused
him pause. He couldn't name it, but there was something new and
different in his thoughts and feelings. It was a threatening thing, and
it was troubling.

Putting off the image and the feelings accompanying it, he
wrote:

The cavalry of the AOT is a mighty pale version of itself these
days. We've been stinging the Yankees, trying to give them some
pain, but not having much success, skirmishes from
McMinnville to south of Nashville, Franklin, Columbia,
Pulaski, and near Fayetteville, but this has been a foolhardy,
mostly trifling adventure. Too many lost, half the command, too

little accomplished. Wish I could have seen some folks in Lincoln Co., but I've been gone near 20 years now!

The next day General Wheeler and his cavalry forded the Tennessee and held up in Tuscumbia, Alabama. John Bell Hood recalled his less than 2,000 (down from 4,500) horse soldiers to the Atlanta area. Hood gave up Atlanta on September 2nd, and moved west to come up and around to pounce hard on Sherman's line of communications from Nashville to Chattanooga and to Atlanta. The plan was to cut Sherman off in Atlanta, draw him out, and give battle somewhere in the mountains of north Georgia. Wheeler and Hood joined up October 8th, fresh from Tuscumbia with new recruits brought out of middle Tennessee. Along the way, near Decatur, the major's journal notation read:

Oct.4, 1864, Courtland, Ala. Partook of the Jones' hospitality for the afternoon. The general and Mrs. Sherrod went for a long walk in the garden. He saddled up with a lightness I had not seen for a very long spell.

Chapter 15

The Pea Patch

C.S.A. Ex-Colonel Amos Solon Stevenson's journal:

May 15, 1863 – Augusta, Georgia (Savannah River)

It is done. Some Union troopers woke us up a couple days ago, but not for breakfast. If I don't laugh about this mess, I might cry and, well, I don't cry, haven't since I was fifteen and mama died.

We are northbound—to prison. Gen'l has had time with family this morning on shipboard. There is word from one of our guards, a young strapping boy from Batavia, Ohio, that it's Fort Delaware for us. Davis and some of the Richmond crowd are set for Fort Monroe up near DC. Guess the Washington boys want to keep an eye on them. It's been a soldier's life since '46 for me, now prison. Well. Being out of saddle for a spell might be good for this aging soul and body. Time to sort things out. No one real-

ly to care where I am or what happens. Could get down if I don't watch it. No use in that. Don't think they'll kill me. Might go to Arizona Territory afterwards, if there is one. Heard there was some raw country out there and the boys in blue will be trying to keep the Navajo and Apache in line. Might get work scouting. Better not do that. More killing sure don't seem the thing I want to do or be around ever again. Could try to scrape up work on some of them big spreads or Wells-Fargo. They'll need someone who knows horses.

I just don't know what. Better to take it as it comes. I reckon. I haven't got no mount so I can't ride off—no retreat to regroup now!

In the summer of 1863 there were 12,500 new arrivals at Fort Delaware, Pea Patch Island, in the middle of Delaware Bay. The legend was that a boat in the early years of the state ran aground on the soft, swampy shore and peas grew from the wreck's cargo. The fort dated from 1814 and was a defensive response to the British invasion of Washington and threats to Baltimore and Philadelphia. An experimental floating steam pile driver made possible the construction of the giant pentagonal fort just before the Civil War. One hundred and twenty-nine political prisoners in 1862 were the first of the prisoners who transformed this grand old defensive fortification into a military prison. More than 30,000 unfortunates passed through the gates of this island fortress during the war years. Over 2,400 died there, and the majority were buried at Finn's Point, New Jersey, just across the bay from the fort.

A prestigious dream for America's military and the defense of a vital water route to three of its greatest cities became, in 1865, the prison for over fifty Confederate expatriates. Isolated on an island miles from New Jersey or Delaware, reachable only by boat, its depth of infamy did not reach that of Andersonville, but neither is it of any pride for a nation or its people.

The bed was hard, rough boards with soiled ticking stuffed only with horsehair, he hoped. The cell was damp, lice-infested, with malaria-carrying mosquitoes and little or no circulation of air through the high two-by-two-foot barred window.

Retired from the Confederate Army, thanks to Union forces in the Georgia thickets not far from Atlanta, Colonel Stevenson had been in prison for three weeks. Before he was captured he had put his notebook in an old Bible he'd found somewhere, and had been able to save it. A short pencil was hidden in his boot. The sun of late June cast enough light for him to read his notations. He turned to the page that began:

March 12, 1865, near Fayetteville, N. Carolina. Such a hard, hard time. We are able to pester Sherman's march but he has everything we don't: men and equipment. Another dance with "Kill Cavalry" and his troopers two days ago. Our morning attack caught him in his nightshirt. Our wounded include Generals Humes, Hannon, and Hagan. Generals Ashby and

Allen had mounts shot from under them. Carmargo, number three, got me through. That little black is a gamer.

The general made me colonel. Don't feel right but little it matters. We cannot continue for much longer. In Wellington's army against Napoleon's legions, there was at one battle a unit of "forlorn hope." Feels like that's true of the A. of Tenn. Calvary. We're sacrificial, that's for sure. I sure don't want to try to count up the lives I've taken and bodies I've maimed.

He turned two pages and read:

April 27, 1865, near Durham Station, N. Carolina. Gen'l. Joseph E. Johnston surrendered the Army of Tennessee. I cried like a baby when General Wheeler said farewell to his troopers. I made a copy of it from his order's book:

"You have fought your battles; your task is done. During a four years' struggle for liberty, you have exhibited courage, fortitude and devotion: you are the sole victors of more than two hundred severely contested fields; you have participated in more than a thousand successful conflicts of arms. You are heroes, veterans, patriots. The bones of your comrades mark battlefields upon the soil of Kentucky, Tennessee, Virginia, North Carolina, South Carolina, Georgia, Alabama, and Mississippi. You have done all that human exertion could accomplish.

"In bidding you adieu, I desire to tender my thanks for your gallantry in battle, your fortitude under suffering, and your devotion at all times to the holy cause you have done so much to maintain. I desire also to express my gratitude for the kind feel-

ing you have seen fit to extend toward myself and to invoke upon you the blessings of our heavenly Father, to whom we must always look in the hour of distress.

"Pilgrims in the cause of freedom, comrades in arms, I bid you farewell."

The Gen'l. is going to join up with Jeff Davis as he moves south in front of the Yankees. I ain't got nowhere to go so I'm going with him. Near 600 of us are sticking.

And then he went to this notation.

June 1, 1865, Ft. Delaware, Del. Some of Miss Barton's people came through Sunday afternoon. Gave out small parcels of writing paper, pencils, soap, and hard candy. Preachers also came. A Universalist came to my cell. Two guards flanked him. He gave me four pamphlets and said "My God is one of love not vengeance. Brother, our God is not partial. Read these and learn of our Father's love and salvation." His words struck me hard after he left. I remembered a preacher came through Lincoln County when I was twelve or so. Preached on the courthouse steps. He didn't scream. Talked just loud enough for the twenty or so folk to hear. I thought that was a strange way for a preacher to preach. Don't remember what he said. Didn't care then.

Lincoln was dead. Old Andy Johnson of Tennessee, who'd embarrassed the man who had selected him to be his vice-presidential candidate on the "Union Party" ticket in 1864, was in Mr. Lincoln's White House office now. Appointed military governor of Tennessee in March 1862 with the rank of brigadier general, Johnson had dealt roughly with Nashville rebels, made a fortress of Strickland's majestic state capitol building, and widened the Union hold on his home state.

At their inauguration in March 1864, Johnson was feverish, recovering from typhoid fever, and had taken one to many shots of whiskey to brace him up in an overheated, standing-room-only, US Senate chamber. His skill as an accomplished stump speaker was overcome and corrupted by the whiskey, his illness, the heat, the crowd, and the occasion.

An orphan boy, whose wife taught him to read and write competently when he was eighteen, Johnson had come a long way from abject poverty, isolation, and the opposition of his neighbors. He'd stayed loyal to the Union after Sumter. His public life had been as an archtypical populist, striving to improve the status and life of Tennessee's working folk. He deeply hated the Southern oligarchy that had duped so many Southerners.

One of his earliest efforts in congress in the 1840s was to introduce a Homestead Act so that those who would improve land on America's frontiers could have their own place. Lincoln signed the Homestead Act in 1862 after nearly two decades of effort by Johnson.

The Washington power brokers and national papers protested to Lincoln about the shameful behavior of his unworthy vice-president.

His response was simple: "Andy ain't no drunk." Several days later John Wilkes Booth killed Johnson's defender, and Johnson became president.

The burden of rebuilding "... the mystic chords of memory, stretching from every battlefield and patriot grave to every living heart and hearthstone all over this broad land, will yet swell the chorus of the Union, when again touched, as surely they will be, by the better angels of our nature."

—Abraham Lincoln

Lincoln knew that this must be done without vengeance, and this task suddenly fell on the broad shoulders of a tailor turned Tennessee politician.

In the months since becoming president, Johnson had slowly and intentionally followed his mentor's charge. His initial toughness towards the defeated had softened, and he'd allowed the wayward Southern states to return to the union with what the radical Republicans thought a drastically too lenient process. The common soldier had to take an oath of loyalty. Many of the higher ups in the rebel government—Jefferson Davis and several of his cabinet—and many Confederate military leaders were still in prison in Fort Monroe and Fort Delaware. Joseph Wheeler was in the middle of the Delaware River in Fort Delaware Union Military Prison.

Joseph Wheeler, twenty-nine years old, former major general, former chief of cavalry, the Army of Tennessee, Confederate States of America, extinct, awoke from a fitful sleep. He'd been having a nightmare in which he saw himself and a few of his troopers riding in a land of death—bloated, butchered corpses everywhere; burned houses; dead, fly-infested horses; and trampled-down crops under a full moon against a slate-blue Alabama sky. The feeling was uncertainty, grief, and loss. His face and shoulder ached. His prison cell in the bowels of Fort Delaware was ten feet square and contained a cot, a table, and a chair. A washstand sat in the corner of the stone room. A rickety four-drawer clothes chest sat against one of the damp walls, and a coat rack stood beside it. His terribly worn, two-year-old uniform coat, vest, and slouch hat hung there. His worldly goods were thus diminished. Everything he owned was in his cell. All had been spent for a dream—which became phantom, then nightmare.

After his capture on May 13, 1865, near Atlanta, Georgia, he was held prisoner of war by his Union captors. Taken to Augusta, he had been visited aboard the prison boat by his father and two sisters. Shipped from there down the river, the prisoners of war were placed on another prison boat, the Tuscarora, and escorted by a US Navy man-of-war north. These orphans of the Southern Confederacy included President Jefferson Davis, Vice-President Alexander H. Stephens, former USA/CSA senator and national leader Clement C. Clay of Alabama (and his wife), former Governor Francis R. Lubbock of Texas, Postmaster General/Secretary of Treasury John H. Reagan of Tennessee/Texas, the president's small staff, Colonel Stevenson, Captain Muskgrove, and the general.

The general was in his shirtsleeves in his deathly hot and humid prison cell. Going from his cot to the chest of drawers, he withdrew a small packet of letters and his writing supplies. He first opened a two-week-old letter from Mrs. C. C. Clay:

My good general, I have, as you requested, written Mrs. Daniella Jones Sherrod of Courtland, Alabama, on your behalf. I told her of your nobility and valor. I'm still disturbed beyond remedy about that incident on the Tuscarora. The insult by that villain Tennessee Yankee was deplorable. You were defenseless. His assertion of your breaking of the rule about leaning on the boat railing was totally a scandal. Your endurance of his vile tongue was truly chivalrous. Your telling him that if you'd known the rule you would not have infringed on it thrilled me. That was as estimable an act as I've ever witnessed. You have my deep admiration.

I pray hourly for the release of our people in Fort Delaware and Mr. Davis and Mr. Stephens in Fort Monroe. I fear terribly for my dear husband's health.

Putting the letter down, he gently touched his hurting shoulder and then his whelped neck. Looking vacantly at the dripping wall, he thought of that wounding. Wounded three times in the war, sixteen staff members killed, six horses slain, and thousands of fellow warriors giving the ultimate—their lives—it all saddened his heart and inflicted his soul.

Turning to another letter, he read:

Courtland, Alabama
June 10, 1865.

My General,

Mrs. Clay's letter came with this morning's post. I'm truly stricken by the unprovoked attack and your injury by that coward. This act against their grand lecturing about the moral rightness of their civilization surely does confirm their hypocrisy ...

I share Mrs. Clay's appreciation and admiration of you ...

Know the memories of your attendance of me, Father, and my son are treasured ...

Please know the hospitality of this family is always available to you, my dear friend.

With the warmest of regards and admiration,

Daniella Sherrod

Two weeks later, Joseph Wheeler and A. Solon Stevenson, along with two-dozen other former Confederates at Fort Delaware, were released from US military imprisonment.

Chapter 16

Two Pilgrims: One Southbound, One West

Sterling Smith, Joseph Wheeler's New York brother-in-law, was tending some business in Baltimore this warm day in late June 1865. He had come to Fort Delaware when the general was paroled and released from military imprisonment to get him on his way to Georgia. Giving the general ten twenty-dollar gold pieces without ceremony or comment, he had excused himself. The former general joined the former Colonel Stevenson at a saloon near the depot.

At a table in the back of the saloon, the two former Rebels had a parting meal. Joseph Wheeler, twenty-nine years old, looked gaunt and soul-weary. Solon Stevenson looked the same. Joseph forced half of his coins on Solon. They shared ham and sharp cheese sandwiches, sweet pickles, and drinks. Joseph had a lager beer and Solon a frosted, foaming glass of root beer. Solon had sworn off spirits last month in Fort Delaware US Military Prison.

Wheeler opened the conversation, philosophically. "Solon, I haven't done anything but be a soldier since I was seventeen. You neither. You bent the truth in '46 when you went with Taylor to Mexico, as I remember."

"Yes, sir, Old Zach's boys. I talked a recruiting officer over in Pulaski into believing I was nineteen. I was barely seventeen, but he saw I was near grown and let me in. Got transferred to the Lincoln Legion at Monterrey and, well, been in uniform ever since." Solon paused a moment and took in his young general's worn, gaunt, troubled face. "General, you ought to have become that merchant your daddy wanted you to be." Wheeler's brow frowned.

Solon continued, "Oh, sir, the boys gossip something awful. Ain't no secrets. Yeah, you a wealthy merchant, say in Charleston or Savannah, making thousands off of this nightmare. You know lots of those sons of bitches did." His face was reddening, and he was letting out some of the grief and anger of a man who has been deceived in the worst way possible by something he deeply believed in—a righteous cause.

"Fools, fools … all of us, all the dead … fools …" Solon confessed to the saloon table. His voice trailed off, and he looked out towards the big glass window at the other end of the saloon, its window like a mirror reflecting bright sunshine. He returned to the moment and gulped a deep drink of his now warm root beer. His face was the color of some of the bloody creeks he'd ridden through.

"Solon, I understand what you feel," Joseph began, "but you're too harsh." He paused a minute, letting the silence settle, and then continued, "Bitterness will mean the others won both on the field and in our hearts. We fought 'em to hell and back. They beat us, sure, but what a fight we put up. They aren't going to beat my spir-it. No, Colonel, never."

The twenty-nine-year-old, nearly emaciated little fighter took on the visage of a Celtic sage with his bright focused blue eyes, his beard longer and now with traces of gray, and his nearly bald head. This beaten but undefeated twenty-nine-year-old messenger ministered to the thirty-six-year-old man's spirit. Solon's eyes became moist, and then tears came. He smiled through them. "I'll take that as my last order, sir." He blew out a gust of air towards the smoky saloon. "Yes sir, I surely will, much obliged ... Joseph." Wheeler smiled and pursed his lips, then downed his warm beer.

"I am leaving for Chattanooga on the 4:16 p.m. train," Wheeler told Stevenson. "First I'm going to Augusta to visit with father, and then I'm going by Caladonia to see Mrs. Sherrod. Right now I can't imagine what will happen. All I need to do is get some good food, get home, see what's what, and call on Mrs. Sherrod. Sterling has told me about a plan he has for me in New Orleans. We'll see."

Stevenson offered with a chuckle, "Not sure the old army will take back a sergeant the Rebel Army raised to colonel. Last few years experience might not sit well with any Union recruiter." Sobering after receiving Joe's smile, he said, "I'm for Cincinnati. Seems like I need to check out something there." The ham was good, the cheese divine, the mustard zesty, and the different beers satisfying. Melancholy and uncertainty was thus acknowledged and shared by the two who had been together to hell and back for nearly four years. Now what?

The Memphis-Charleston depot in Courtland, Alabama, was a small, shabby, war-damaged building. The general's heart didn't see the ugly reality; he only felt the meaning of this stop. Mrs. Daniella Jones Sherrod lived only a few miles northeast. Wheeler's civilian suit was a new experience that he still felt uncertain about. Uniforms had been his wardrobe for over ten years. The hat was more familiar. It was similar to his army slouch hat, his last and favorite military headgear.

Checking his suitcase and big trunk labeled "J. Wheeler, New Orleans" with the baggage master, he went about finding the livery. He needed a mount to ride out the half-dozen miles to Caladonia. His father in Augusta had outfitted the former career soldier for his new life as a civilian. The items were partly from his father's wardrobe and neighbors' households, and partly from what goods the Augusta haberdasher had in its limited inventory. This equipment for a new life was simple and unpretentious—as was the present owner. Standing on the depot porch taking in the crisp October morning, he surveyed the north Alabama landscape on this mid-South fall morning. It was the ending of harvest time. Soon the acreage would be laid by for the dreary winter's passage. The land looked as if it would never revive: brown, shaggy, dreary—he knew spring would change all, but his spirit fully understood this shadowy time.

After adjusting his dark gray frock and tugging down the matching vest, he patted his vest pockets. In one rested his father's silver pocket watch attached to a plain fob.

The national trial was over. The verdict was definitive. The adversaries were spent.

Robert Jones's success had been inspired by ambition and provided by opportunity. The second-generation master of his domain had successfully gotten into developing cotton raising in north Alabama during the expansion of cotton production in the 1840s-50s. He had been able to become a rich and powerful man owning 22,000 acres, several businesses, and over a hundred slaves. The well-drained, good-watered red land was rich and productive, and Robert Jones made his fortune from it, his slaves, and his cunning. Daniella, his daughter, and her children were heirs to his wealth. Colonel Jones had weathered the storm of civil conflict, economic upheaval, anarchy, and social revolution that was the "War Between the States," the "War of Rebellion"—America's Civil War. Some folks gossiped that he worked with both gray and blue. He still had wealth after the war. Most didn't.

Daniella Ellen Jones Sherrod, widow of Benjamin F. Sherrod (who died in 1861), had turned twenty-four in August. She was her father's joy and hostess, tending the mistress duties of the fine mansion, Caladonia. Now with the end of slavery, both she and Colonel Jones were challenged with all the implications of former slave owners. The freedman had no life-skills except what they had learned in the slave system. A new system of capital and labor, employer and worker, was in its early development phase. Within twenty years the sharecropper arrangement would be the production arrangement for most of Southern agriculture. It became a new, troubled experience in peasant-and-landlord relations. New challenges require creativity and toughness. The Joneses of north Alabama had those qualities.

"Daniella, I'm so very pleased to learn of the health and security of you and yours. The times are most disrupted," Joseph Wheeler said as he sat in the Jones plantation mansion's parlor.

Mrs. Sherrod, dressed in an attractive day dress of pale lavender and brown, responded, "My General, we have been fortunate, and I deeply appreciate your concern. The receipt of your letters has been such a delight. It is most touching that you, with all your trials, have thought of me."

"Mrs. Sherrod, Daniella, the thoughts of you and our friendship was as a light in the darkness. Yes the time in Delaware was difficult, but I'm here now. It will take time for the past to be past. But I am ready for what comes, save one thing," Joseph responded.

"Joseph, please let me be of assistance. It is a difficult time but we have been fortunate, thankfully. If it is within my means, I would be honored to provide whatever you might need to be successful in New Orleans or wherever you choose."

His clothing seemed odd and uncomfortable. He was aware of the difference in the feel of his civilian boots, boiled shirt, and differently cut suit. His cavalry boots, military tunic, and sturdy uniform trousers had been his shield, his armor, for over a decade. Now he was unarmed in a place of civilization, not conflict. He was no longer a warrior who knew his place and job. His new assignment was not a scouting chore, planning tactics, a raid, or movement around the flank of a menacing opponent. The chore ahead of him was of a different nature, an unfamiliar task.

Joseph Wheeler, late of the Confederate States of America's military, had, under the CSA flag, been in hundreds of armed skirmishes. He had lead troops and commanded in 127 full-scale battles. Eighteen faithful horses had died in battle during the last four years of warfare. Thirty-six staff officers riding by his side had been killed in battle, and he had survived three wounds. Courage was not absent from the character of Joseph Wheeler. His personal valor had been proven countless times. But alone with this young woman, and fulfilling the task that brought him here to this place in this time, was harder than anything he'd undertaken as a seventeen-year-old cadet or horse soldier.

"Miss Daniella, I'm not an elegant fellow. My prospects are now known. As I told you in June, the position in New Orleans has great potential. Honestly, success has not been a pattern considering our efforts for the Confederacy. But I feel assured of one thing ... no, two things. I love you deeply, and the delight of my life would be to have you as my wife." He paused, realizing that the fear had lifted, and that he had done what he came to do. Waiting and feeling embarrassed, he smiled and took Daniella's hand as she looked into his dark blue eyes. Drawing the plain gold ring from his vest pocket, he said,

"I sure hope it will fit, it was my mother's." He turned her hand over and placed the ring in it. He looked into the deep brown eyes of his beloved and sought a sign, a recognition that his passion was shared. It was.

"Joseph Wheeler, I'm most pleased." She paused and took up a marital manner. "Yes, sir. I'll marry you, my general." She radiated joy as she put the ring on her finger and smiled at her fiancé.

A dreariness, not related to the gloomy winter season, was evident over Caladonia Plantation on February 7, 1866. Inclement weather was the background for the wedding. Daniella and Joe's wedding came that day, a month after a funeral. The bride's wedding gown was trimmed in black. Richard Jones Sherrod, Daniella's little boy, five years and ten months, had been buried on January 7, 1866. Two wounded souls were pledged in matrimony: a young vanquished horse soldier and a young grieving mother. A widow, Daniella had also endured the deaths of her two children, little Ella Sherrod in 1861, and now her little boy.

In the fall of 1865 in Cincinnati, sitting across from the Universalist church on a park bench on a bright late December afternoon that was warm for the season, Solon Stevenson took out a brand new journal, turned a few written-on pages, and wrote:

December 6, 1865, Cincinnati, O.

Been going to church and helping out since August. Classes with Reverend Everett L. Rexford going good. It's about 10 a.m. on Sunday, December 6. Tried to push this down, but it feels like it must be done. Damned, if I ain't called! Must answer.

He straightened up his sack coat and squared away his hat. He walked across the street, after a fancy carriage passed, to the modest stone church with a simple sign that read:

First Universalist Society
God is Not Partial
10 a.m. Sundays

He had to tell Brother Rexford.

Chapter 17

A Veteran's Journey

The Louisville-Nashville railroad depot was busy when Solon's train from Cincinnati pulled into Nashville at 2:33 p.m., April 22, 1869. The former "hell for leather" warrior appeared different from what he had three years ago. His Fort Delaware pallor was gone, and his weight was back to 160. His hair was thinner and grayer. His oversized black three-piece suit, white cravat, boiled shirt, and wide-brimmed black hat made him look like what he was: a preacher. Any comparison with an officer of the Confederate cavalry would be difficult. His appearance was that of a well-scrubbed agent of God, not a bringer of death and destruction. A transformation had occurred in Amos Solon Stevenson. Still light hearted, the destructive fire in his soul was converted to a passion for ideas, sermons, celebrations, and sharing the tonic that restored his being—God's love.

Walking through the bustling lobby, he smelled cooking food. Finding the source of the temptation, he entered the depot's well-appointed café. The lean years of the war and hunger of Fort Delaware had left him constantly with an appetite, yet his weight was the same as when he joined the Confederate Army in Mobile in the summer of 1861. He had the look of a 6-foot 2-inch, sturdy, slim, proportioned, and purposeful man in his forties. He was forty-one.

He found a two-seated empty booth midway down the wall opposite the ornate mirrored bar and took a seat. An alert waiter took his order, and he was soon partaking of a thick roast beef sandwich with tart German mustard. The coffee tasted as fine as any he'd ever had.

Finishing his meal, he found his way to an empty bench in the large lobby. As he took his place a tall, thin, dark girl/woman passed him and took a seat a little way down the bench. She clutched a ragged, dirty bundle that Solon at first thought was her clothing, but when she held it away from her breast, he saw the face of a tiny pale baby.

The mother saw him looking at her and her child; she blushed, diverting her dark eyes down and then anxiously turned away to nurse the child with her back towards Solon and the busy lobby. The look moved Solon, disturbed his thoughts, judgments, and attitudes about pity. The look was not of some beaten spirit. There was fire in the eyes and the strength of her defiance. As those realizations assaulted his assumptions, he saw again Lou's eyes that time in the creek in Georgia five years ago. This memory and the feelings invoked were alive. He thought he could again smell the heat of that August morning, the dust, the cedar freshness, the honeysuckle and musk of the woods.

He felt absolutely alone—lonesome—without a place. In the middle of the crowded Union Station in Nashville, Tennessee, he was shaken by the shudder of aloneness. His awareness returned to the smoky, busy lobby in a few seconds. To reorient himself and settle back into reality, he looked around at the variety of people moving through the lobby: the immigrants still in their native dress; country-dressed farm folk; dudes in outlandish styles and colors; women, righteous and otherwise; neat, scrubbed ordinary families; and rich folks moving hurriedly through the common people, not looking at them. They were going to their private train cars, he speculated, servants and porters hauling mountains of luggage behind them. Solon also saw half a dozen young Union soldiers in bright new clean blue and yellow uniforms—cavalry. There were also three soldiers clad in blue tunics with red trimming—artillery.

Turning to the girl and baby, he didn't hesitate as he fished a silver dollar from his vest pocket and leaned towards where the two sat. "For the little one, ma'am," he said as he handed the coin to the dark-eyed young mother. She didn't move. Not frightened, her eyes messaged surprise and tenderness. Solon gently put the coin in a fold of the child's wrap. He then stood, took his small carpetbag, went toward the café, and found his former booth. Pausing before he took the seat, he went to the bar and ordered a cold, frosted root beer. A part of him, a small part, wished it were a schooner of good Cincinnati Heidepohl beer. He'd taken the temperance pledge in prison, but had bent the vow a few times in Cincinnati. Tennessee might make fine whiskey, but their beer was only so-so compared to the beers of Cincinnati, Ohio.

Drinking beer discretely from time to time these last four years, he greatly appreciated the health belch it produced. He didn't plan on ever drinking the hard stuff again.

Settling into the booth, he went to his bag and took out a black notebook with a cover of good leather. It was about half used. His full brown one from the war was packed in his valise in the baggage room. The flood of loneliness provoked by the encounter with the unknown young mother inspired him to find his place, any place, and the journal would testify to the reality of his being for the last four years. He opened the cover and read:

Amos Solon Stevenson

Book Two – Commenced August 10, 1865 – Cincinnati, Ohio

August 10, 1865 – Cincinnati, Ohio. Arrived four days ago from Baltimore. Found the church, 1st Universalist, without any trouble. It was just north of the old Mechanics Institute building on Walnut Street between 3rd and 4th streets. The Reverend, Everett L. Rexford, was kind to me, a little amazed, but kind. We talked for two hours until he had to leave for a visit to some of his sick folk. He was startled to hear my story—the war, prison, and reasons for coming to him. He didn't seem surprised when I told him of my being given a copy of George Rogers' The Pro and Con of Universalism. I learned from this Cincinnati-printed book of Rogers' missionary travels south in Tennessee and Alabama. Brother Rexford said over 5,000 copies of the 1840 book had been sold all over the Midwest, South, and back East. John Gurley of the Universalist newspaper, Star of the West, had printed Rogers's book in seven editions over the past twenty-five years. I resolved to go to these offices and learn about the paper and books they print by ministers and teachers.

Pausing at the commotion in the lobby, he saw folks rushing towards the boarding platform. He guessed the 3:45 Cincinnati North train would be pretty full. Returning to his journal, he turned a few pages and read:

January 14, 1866 – Mt. Carmel, O. Driving lumber company delivery wagon on the route from riverfront lumberyard to Salem, Fruit Hill, Forestville, Withamsville, Tabasco, Mt. Carmel, New Town, and back to Cincinnati. Deliver to thirteen places: carpenters, feed stores, general stores, cabinet shops, and small lumberyards. Make trip twice a week, full loads on freight wagon pulled by two mule teams of Tennessee Reds. Big ones, two matched pair. Wheel horse is "Champion" and lead is "Hustler." Fine animals. I take care of them at company stock barn. Sleep in upstairs loft/room. Company's daddy was from Pulaski, Tenn. Mr. Angus had brother with AOT; Cheatham's Tenn. division killed at Murfreesboro. He pays me good money and the free room helps me to save money. Reverend is giving me Bible and theology classes nights. I'm not sure he's ever had an older student or a slower one! I'm cleaning church as payment on Saturdays and shoveling snow in winter.

He paused a minute, looking at himself in the large mirror behind the counter, and reflected on the changes in his life. For nearly twenty years he'd been in uniform, on horseback, chasing Indians in the deserts of west Texas and Yankees in the hollows, pastures, and mountain passes of the Tennessee Valley. He thought, "By grace, by grace."

He found another notation a few pages later in his journal:

September 10, 1866 – Vevay, Indiana (Switzerland County), 50 miles down river on the Ohio from Cincinnati. Preached today for first time away from Cincinnati church. Have preached for Reverend Rexford's folks four times. Listeners seemed to appreciate my efforts. Brother Rexford was concerned when I preached at 1st Church that I was too "light hearted." Looks like to me that the knowledge of God's love and the faithfulness of Jesus' gospel ... the restoring of all of us to salvation is something to be happy about. Let the "hell and damnation" Bible-bangers give out hell, I'm going to give out love and hope!

After turning a score of pages or more, the journal recorded:

November 19, 1868 – Cincinnati, O., lumberyard stock barn. Been doing supply preaching at New Town, Amelia, and down to Louisville when Mr. Angus lets me have a Monday off from time to time. The Montgomery Church hired me for six months first of year. They found a Buchtel graduate in summer for permanent settlement. Am feeling more comfortable as a preacher. Folks seem to appreciate my twenty-thirty minute sermons— most preachers last for twice, three times that long. Wears folks out! General Grant to be president. Seymour of New York, the Democrat, didn't do badly given that so many whites in the

South couldn't vote. From what I can read of the voting, the new
freedman voters made the difference. Lord, I pray nearly every
night when I remember my blindness about slavery and the
African race. We Southerners' sins of omission and commission
are mighty heavy. Grace descend! The coloreds at the Angus
Lumberyard are just like the whites I know—some trifling and
some good people. I believe James (a thirty-seven-year-old Negro
born in Batavia) could do anything or be anything if he were
white. I swear he knows the Bible as well as Reverend. He told
me he went to public school from time he was six to sixteen.

Taking pencil to his journal, he wrote:

April 22, 1869 – Union Station, Nashville, Tennessee.
The Miami association ordained me at New Town,
Christmas, Dec. 25, 1868—thankful and scared. I'm testing
Jesus' teaching about a "prophet in his own land." It's been over
a quarter of a century since George Rogers did his last fieldwork
around here and south. I've wondered a hundred times if he was
the preacher I saw on the Fayetteville square forty years ago.
Reverend Rexford told me there was a Universalist church in
Fayetteville in the late 40s. Must have been Brother Rogers that
day in '43. What circles there are! I'm going to try and do what
he did, where he did. Lord knows if I can be half of what he was.
Those beaten-down people in my part of the world surely need
the hope of the Universal Gospel—Hope in Salvation—Life in
Grace. Prophet or fool? I dare say I'll find out.

Chapter 18
Fall 1865

Lincoln County, Tennessee

S old," the high sheriff rapped the gavel on the crude pine-plank
desk on the south side of the square in Fayetteville, Tennessee.
Alex, Lou, and Grand John L. stood near the back of the
dozen or so bidders on this cool, overcast April morning. The three
days of rain had broken, but the sticky mud of farm lot, field, roads,
and streets was evident on everything that moved, man or beast. John
L.'s mud-heavy work boots made sucking sounds as he moved forward toward the county clerk sitting on the new bandstand at an old
campaign desk.

"Name?" asked the bespectacled little man, who looked exactly
like a small rural county government scribe should. Appearing at first
impression like a clerk or schoolmaster, a covered stump where his
right hand should be identified him as a veteran and survivor of the
war. He placed the damaged appendage on his papers to hold them
in place as he prepared to write with his left hand.

"M. L. Fields and A. A. Fields. $250 in gold," John Longstreet
Fields, a sixty-nine-year-old new face to the county, told the record

163

keeper. The clerk wrote those names down on a half-page piece of paper. "Mr. Fields is it? Take this letter of sale to Mr. Gleghorn over at the Lincoln State Bank and pay for this farm. Bring the receipt to me in the courthouse after dinner and we'll work up and record the deed."

"Yes, sir, we'll do just that," Grand John L. said, smiling.

Lou had returned home in late August, 1864. Alex and J.N. were to stay two days and then return south to join up with the major and general in north Georgia. The cousins found Grand John L., Mama Bear, and Nancy Bird well but besieged by Unionists and partisans. Alex and Lou's mother, Nancy Bird, was well but still distant. Her husband and son's deaths a little over a year ago were still daily presences in her living. She let the grief have its way, and she was slowly claiming a life that was different from her last twenty years. The three caretakers of the two Fields' places were watched over by Mary Jane and Joe T. across the valley—John L. and Mama Bear's daughter and son-in-law, J.N.'s parents.

Union partisans had been bold and ruthless up and down Sequatchie Valley over the last few months. With Grant's buildup of Yankee forces in the Chattanooga region, and the absence of Confederate military presence in the area, raiders, self-styled as Union raiders, had hit several real and suspected Confederate sympathizers' places; they stole stock and food and threatened folks with worse if they felt like it. Over the last year, five barns in the county had been torched, and several residents had been horsewhipped. The sheriff hid out in his Dunlap jail.

Joe T. had been honored by a corrective beating at the pleasure of seven rough, maddened, and cruel self-ordained saviors of the Union. His bruises and cuts had pretty much healed, but his zest, energy, and purposefulness was weak.

J.N.'s rage, when he learned of his father's ordeal, was measured. He kept to himself for a few days after they returned home. His mind was in turmoil, and his spirit was burdened.

The second day at supper with his family he said to the other seven, "I ain't going back to the Army. I'd planned to go and finish this thing. But the war is here and some of our so-called neighbors are the enemy. It's here I need to make a stand. Let 'em come again. They'll drag some of their brave dead scalawags outta this hollow feet first."

His demeanor and message was stern, focused, and left little doubt of whether or not he would do what he said he would do. Alex and Lou took note of his calculated rage.

The next morning at breakfast, as the family ate with quiet appreciation of one another's closeness and togetherness, Alex said, "You all, I'm going back. I ain't no shot so I couldn't help J.N. here and the major and general need me."

J.N. and Lou looked at him, surprised at first, and then concerned, especially Lou. They were a pair, a team. Alex received the feelings of his sister and cousin through their eyes. He looked away from them, stared at the plate of biscuits in the middle of the table, and said, "I've got to. You all, I'd be in the way here and, well, tarnation, I need to do what I can …"

His reasoning trailed off, but his determination was fixed. There was some arguing, mostly J.N. and Grand, but he kept his position. Lou didn't join in the pleading. She understood. Alex had taken to the major as a big brother. His place was with him.

The next morning the family stood in the front yard as Alex prepared to leave. Lou was checking Top, Alex's current riding mule. Tears rolled down Lou's frozen, wounded face as she went about her inspection. J.N. fumed, but he kept his tongue.

His mother, Nancy Bird, shared Lou's emotions but said only to Alex, "Come home, Red Hawk. Come home."

Alex hugged his forlorn mother, and when he released her, his grandfather stood holding the stirrup.

"I can't agree with you Alex, but I know you must do what you see is called for," said John L. as he bear hugged Alex; he whispered, "We'll be here, we'll be here, little brother."

Mama Bear stepped forward as her husband turned away from their grandson. She took his hand and placed a small, dark leather bag in his hand. "I made you strong, good medicine for your journey. Bring it back and we'll renew it together."

She pulled up the hand with the bag, kissed the back of it, then drew him into her strong embrace. She patted his back lightly before releasing him. She stepped back and Alex gazed around at his folks then up behind them at the valley ridge.

Alex pulled up into the saddle and touched his hat, turned his mount, gave it a gentle heel, and trotted off across the yard and down to the road.

"See ya when I see ya," he called with false cheer as he headed off.

Early in March '65, while the family was eight miles away at Sunday church, the Mayberrys', senior Fields', and Nancy Bird and Lou's houses were set afire. During the winter there had been some raids throughout the valley, but, by fate or by luck, Lou and her family were not disturbed. It now seemed like it had only been a matter of time.

By some grace, the family was gone when raiders came for their stock. There were no killings, but the next worst thing visited the family—the violence of fire. Frustrated at the disappointment of an unsuccessful mission, the Yankee partisans had gone house to house and fired the families' homes. Joe T. had insisted that they take the last of their stock with them to meeting. Most of what they had was lost in the hateful burnings, but something had been saved: foundation stock, a mature jack stud, three young mares, and work stock— a team of four-year-old, big matched mules.

That night after the family had put out the remainder of the dying fires, extinguishing their past, Lou counseled them about a future. The atmosphere was filled with gloom and poisoned by destruction.

"Grand, Uncle Joe T., we gotta leave. It won't work here any more. The war is lost. It's just a matter of time—and not much time. Major Stevenson told me that Jeff Davis will order the last company of infantry to make a bayonet charge even if they're cornered on the tip of Florida!" Her bitterness was directed towards the stubborn Mississippian in Richmond. "It's lost, and this valley is going to be unfit for us to live in. We could make a stand, and Alex would come home to graves as well as burned houses. We're going to leave!" Her determination grew and replaced the confusion of the day's cruel gift. "We moved with General Wheeler through some great farm land over in middle Tennessee on the Elk River. We got enough wagon parts to repair those old frames in the barns. We've got one, and there's the rickety old freight wagon in Grand's barn. We fix them up and take whatever we can salvage."

Mixed reactions showed in the others' faces. Lou expected Grand to be the spokesman for the six. He wasn't. It was Mama Bear.

"I've got forty-six twenty-dollar gold pieces in my special place in the barn. Been building that white man's fortune for near forty years," she smiled. Then with sternness she said, "This is a land of death—we didn't make it that, but it has become that. Mockingbird is right. We can go. We'll make a new place and a new home." Her face changed from authoritative to reflective. "My people have had their homes made into places of death by others for generations. We start again, we start again." Resolve and a touch of abiding grief were in her tone, not anger. "We go in three days."

They did.

Burned Out

Chapter 19

1870 Reunion

The icicles were six inches long on the edge of the back porch roof. The great light had just crested over the tree line east towards Dellrose. Lou pulled her heavy coat tight at the worn collar with one hand. In her other hand the steaming coffee mug offered a cloud of steam that was trapped in front of her face by her broad hat brim. She liked this time of day best—light renewed, sunrise. She greeted it most days right on this spot on her house's small back porch. To her left was sunrise, and to her right was the barn she and her family had rebuilt four springs ago. She could hear the stock shifting in the barn stalls and lot pens. The old Dominicker rooster had sung his harsh morning reveille just a few minutes before. Lou and he were in an ongoing contest to see who would be the first to recognize the beginning of the daylight.

Alex came through the back door with his coffee. "Sister. Dang, it's brisk, wouldn't you say?" was his greeting to his twin sister.

"Yes, Alex, but it's the third of December, don't you know."

At twenty-two years old the twins were the shape and size of adults. Lou was now 5 feet 9 inches tall and weighed 118 pounds, and Alex was 5 feet 7 inches and 189 pounds.

Alex had left the major, who had raised to colonel and Wheeler's shadow cavalry, in April after the colonel had near kicked him out. "It's over boy, git home, they need you," he'd said.

Alex had showed up late spring of '65, worn out and sickly. By fall the family had restored his physical health, and Lou's dreams had restored his spirit. He was her counsel, alter ego, and jester. He was a good worker in spirit and a good talker all the time.

"The long and short of the Fields," Grandfather John L. teased them. He, Grandmother Mama Bear, Mother Nancy Bird, Uncle Joe T., and Aunt Mary Jane were stirring in the kitchen. The women were working on breakfast, and the men on the stove and fireplace. In spring and summer the house was awake and functioning quite a bit before the rooster's morning song, but in winter the waking time was later.

The Fields and Mayberry families had come to Dellrose to begin again in late 1865. Mama Bear's thirty or more years of herb sales and doctoring folks over in the Sequatchie had provided them enough hard money to buy their new place at a sheriff's sale. They started a new life in a place less poisoned by the war. With Grand John L. as straw boss and Lou as working boss, the new farm had taken shape. The first crops of corn and tobacco had been poor, but the women's garden was abundant. The second season's row crops were better, and the garden was faithful. Good corn crops followed yearly. The mules and horses were healthy, and their numbers had increased from five to nine. Two milk cows provided enough milk for them. Five pigs had provided enough meat to share with neighbors. The chicken pen was home to nine hens and the rooster. Guinea fowl found the leavings from stock feed to be ample provisions. They provided eggs that were richer than the chicken's eggs. A barn had been rebuilt, Lou's forge set up, smoke house improved, cistern under the back porch repaired, and some of the rock field walls had been put in fairly good shape, but there was still more to do on the border of the other fields. Lou and Alex would be working on that this Friday morning after milking and feeding the animals. Tomorrow the family would go the fifteen miles to Fayetteville to get some supplies.

Mama Bear, Nancy Bird, and Aunt Mary stayed at home that Saturday. They liked town well enough, but the day was cold and dreary. Mama Bear had said, "Too much work to go to town on a day like this. Nancy, Mary, and I'll piddle around here. We'll find something to do. Supper is my pork loin, Mary's potatoes and greens, and Nancy's pecan pie. You all be back before milking to eat, or I'll give it all to the pigs."

Saturday in rural Tennessee was a busy trade day in its some ninety county-seat towns. Weather didn't hamper that occasion. The country folk came to town to get needed supplies, from groceries to clothing to farm items. Dellrose had most of what the farm needed, but Fayetteville was the center of the county's life, transportation, politics, and big social events such as revivals, dances, electioneering, land sales, stock auctions, travel-through peddlers, even the occasion-

al minstrel show. The Chicatauga, a recent nationwide traveling cultural event in late summer and fall, with featured speakers and varied
entertainment and educational programs, was hugely popular in the
heartland, and citizen's gatherings around the courthouse square just
to visit and catch up with the family news and general gossip was an
ongoing event.

Lou and Alex rode big, red matched mules—"East" and "West."
Uncle Joe T. drove the wagon team pulled by the big black mule
team—"Jack" and "Bill"—brought out of the Sequatchie. Grand
John L. sat regally in the big chair in the back of the farm wagon. He
faced the rear. He told folks that he wanted to remember where he
had been and make sure no villains were about to overtake them. In
the winter he was always wrapped in a big, gray wool blanket that
Alex had procured from the Army. Mama Bear had put a patch over
the hole with the bloodstains. He called it his "Chief's" blanket. He
brought some herbs from Mama Bear. He would see Mr. Damron at
Carter's Drug Store about them. The tall, quiet druggist was Mama
Bear's biggest customer. Joe T. pulled the team in beside Davis'
Hardware atop Jailhouse Hill on the west side of the square. Alex and
Lou hitched their mounts in front of the store. The county judge,
Leland Mansfield, greeted them as he strode towards the courthouse.
His father-in-law, Claude Moore, was the new principal at Dellrose
School.

Lou dismounted, being careful with her petticoats. She could or
would not ride sidesaddle like some of the ladies from Mulberry
Avenue, but she did somewhat conform by wearing voluminous
dresses of current women's fashion, albeit without a corset. She had
two going-to-town, Sunday outfits—one light brown with dark pur-

ple and yellow trim, and a middle-toned gray one with scarlet and light-blue trim. Her felt hat was hanging on the hat peg back in the kitchen at home. Today she had on a fashionable black bonnet with scarlet accents that complimented her gray and scarlet ensemble. Kathleen at the millinery shop beside Sherrill-Stone's had told her it was being worn in New Orleans this season. Her heavy shawl was black.

As she stepped up on the wooden sidewalk from the dirt street and was straightening herself, a voice cheerily said, "Miss Fields, isn't it? From down Dellrose way?" The voice came from a well-dressed, well-fed man in his middle fifties.

"Yes, sir, Mary Louise Fields. Eagan Place towards Bryson," she responded a bit uneasily.

"My pleasure, ma'am. I'm John Morgan Bright, attorney-at-law and your new congressman," the self-satisfied, well-suited man boasted.

Lou gave him a cold stare.

"Not mine, sir. I can't vote in this land of the free," Lou shot back, instantly disliking the slick talker and obvious blow-hard.

"Now, now, Miss Fields, it is a man's job to take care of business and government. Our gentle Southern ladies shouldn't have to soil their characters or virtues with such unseemly activities as politics— or business for that matter. No ma'am, women don't have the necessary faculties for such. Their virtues are domestically inclined and rightly so."

"Mr. Bright, you come down to my place Monday, say about 5 a.m., with gloves and work clothes and I'll show you what's men's work and what's women's work. Now if you'll excuse me, I've got some unsavory business over at Mr. Gleghorn's bank!" She breezed by the startled politician towards the bank over by Ashby's Hardware on the north side of the square.

"Sister, you got more things to do?" Alex asked Lou an hour later as they walked on the south side of the square past Mr. Moore's grocery.

I've got to go by *The Observer* and do some window shopping, Brother," Lou answered.

Each one's breath made steam as they passed the poolroom. Mr. Stewart at the *Lincoln County News* tipped his hat and inquired after their families' health. He reminded Lou of his ad rates for her spring mule sales. Then they moved on across the southeast corner of the square.

"Alex, let's go to the hotel and get some dinner. I told Uncle and Grand we'll be over there about now, and for them to meet us there."

"Lordy, that's a walk—what, five town blocks at least. We got to double back from Mr. Wallace's paper," Alex reminded Lou. She liked to walk. He liked to ride.

"Suit yourself, Brother. I'm walking," Lou said and kept her pace.

"Oh, I'll walk with you, stubborn, stubborn Mary Louise, but slow down some. Hey, I thought you were going to whip that Bright fellow back there in front of Mr. Davis' store," Alex chided his twin.

"Oh, he is just another one of that pompous courthouse gang. They think they know everything. General Brown got elected governor, and now the 'brigadiers' are top dogs with Parson Brownlow now gone to Washington. I know who this Bright fellow is. He rode with that fire-eating Governor 'I-sham' Harris during the war, sitting back with the brass in the rear. Damn Harris and that crowd. They got us in that mess that got Daddy and Johnny killed. Grand was right when we left to go to General Joe's. Trash aristocracy ain't worth the sweat it'll take to horse whip 'em," Lou said without losing her breath.

Alex was keeping up but was winded by the time they went by Carter's.

"Forty cents! Forty cents for someone else's food. I'll never get used to paying for some stranger's made-up food," Grand John L. groused; he spoke his words with the same zeal he displayed in his eating. Uncle Joe T. grunted his agreement.

The Pope Hotel was a few blocks up the hill from Fayetteville's Nashville-Chattanooga railroad depot. The family had been to the Pope twice before. A new hotel was being built out on Mulberry—the Largen—but the Pope was now the place for travelers and "town" food. It was nearly two o'clock by the time Alex and Lou had started crossing the square. Uncle Joe T. and Grand John L. were going to Moore's for ten pounds of coffee and forty pounds of sugar, and then they planned to meet the twins at the wagon. Lou and Alex had stopped by *The Observer* office on the way to pay for their subscription for the weekly. As they came around the northeast corner of the square to cross the courthouse yard, Alex said, "Looks like something is going on over at the bandstand. Reckon what's happening? Election is over, so must be something else. Preacher, I'd bet."

"Probably right," Lou agreed, distracted by the fine dark green silk dress in Sir's Department Store window. She'd remember that dress and talk with Mr. Joe Sir about its cost come spring. She'd heard some tacky comments on "the Jew," but it seemed that he treated everybody the same—rich, poor, or whatever. That made him all right in her eyes. Heck, Jesus was a Jew in her Bible. Right now they needed to start for home, and she still wanted to go down to the mule barn to see what Mr. Rambo was allowing. She had heard at the Dellrose Post Office that Mr. Rambo had gotten in some fancy Spanish jacks recently. The dress shopping would have to wait. Money for stock came first.

As they neared the courthouse bandstand, Lou recognized a voice. It represented a distant memory, but she knew the voice—cheerful, strong, and familiar.

"Gather round folks, let me have a few minutes of your time. It could change your life," the speaker announced.

"Lord, Lou, it's the major—I mean Colonel Stevenson!" Alex explained just as Lou brought his face to her consciousness. When she saw the speaker, her memory was confirmed.

The Fields twins stood well back of the crowd of some two-dozen, maybe thirty, listeners.

The preacher began, "Folks, I left this town in '46 for the war in Mexico—served with the Lincoln Legion. All my folks are gone now or moved to Texas. I'll tell you that Dr. Sloan's horse medicine pulled me through a fever when I was ten." He smiled. Dr. Sloan was a medical doctor of sorts, not a veterinarian. He was so dignified a character that the kids had joked about him when he was a youngster. There were a few chuckles as Solon continued. "I've seen a lot of this world in the last twenty years, most on the back of a cavalry mount. Fightin' Joe Wheeler and the boys of the Army of Tennessee fought, bled, and died from yonder to yonder. We spent a lively afternoon over at the Stone Bridge in September '63. Yes, real lively." He swept his hand from his far right to his far left. "Those days are gone, thank the good Lord."

He paused and took in the faces—some affirming his presence and words, others leery but interested. Preaching was a form of entertainment for many. For others there was a hunger for something, something real but unfocused. Those who were needful conveyed a soul deficiency with their eyes and lost looks.

Lou and Alex, on the far edge of the group, were in the shadows of a big oak that shaded the courthouse. Alex's interest was seeing the ex-soldier again and seeing what he'd become. Lou's attention was for that—and maybe something else.

"Yes. 'Good Lord,'" Solon's voice went from a light conversational tone to that of a confident speaker. Not a huckster, his eyes offered a purpose and sincerity Lou had seen before in him. "Yes, I said *good* Lord. I'm not here to say any man is wrong in how he understands God or how one finds God's grace. I am here to say that where many folks look for that redeeming power is in the wrong places!" Solon message had begun. "My faith tells me that God's love is real and all encompassing. His strong arms and big heart take in all—all—the family of man. Yes, all folks, not some! I'm over forty years old but I am a child of God. Blessed Jesus' gospel and sacrifice saved the whole of mankind, not just some. God is not partial. Let me say that again. God is not partial! Saved and condemned? Good and bad, saint and sinner? All such are blessed by God's salvation through Jesus Christ! Jesus, the son of God, taught it and gave his life for it. But God did not give his only begotten son so that we would be divided or condemned, but that we would be saved by his grace and through the blood of his son, Jesus Christ, and with him usher in the kingdom of God. Heaven is a big place—room for all—so big it runs over and washes over even Tennessee, even Fayetteville!" He pointed up to the sky, blue and bright. "It ain't up there. Jesus said it: 'the kingdom of God is among you.' That's you, me—us. We got to tend to it, build it up, through living the Son's gospel—the golden rule.

"Open your eyes. Open your hearts. Are you trying to follow a god who keeps playing tricks, setting traps so he can condemn you, take joy in your misery? That's an awful little and mean god. The one I bear witness to is lots bigger. The great and one God is about love, not trick justice and sham righteousness."

Lou was touched, smitten by the message and the man. She often went down to the Methodist church at Dellrose—but not every Sunday. The farm and stock didn't allow a regular day of rest for her and hers. When she sat in the congregation, she listened and believed that she was a Christian. She took part in the Lord's Supper every quarter when presiding Elder Hawkins from Columbia offered it. Her heart was at ease with Methodist Christianity, but her head had reservations. Solon's words found that place of unease, opened it, and had Lou's full attention. An ache of the soul was manifest, and the former horse soldier's words seemed as a welcomed shower on a dry field. Here was a message and man that she need reckon with.

Lou stayed back. Alex had quickly made his way to the preacher after the meeting was over. Sure enough, Alex and the ex-soldier, now missionary, came walking, crunching down the brown grass to where Lou stood.

"Major, Colonel, sir. I mean, what, I guess, 'Parson'?" Lou said, her face flushed, but she carried herself with the confidence of a young successful farmer and individual. Her eyes, however, were quickly averted to the silver watch chain across his black waistcoat.

"Our farrier, well if this isn't something. Girl, boy, now woman. Bugler and farrier all grown up and here. Alex tells me you all moved from the Sequatchie and are raising mules and farming west of here," he said to Lou, his eyes sparkling and his face open and obviously pleased.

"Yes, sir, we sure are," Alex answered, as Lou stood wordless and stark still. Lou could not make eye contact with the one man in the world who had seen her in the natural state. She was not embarrassed, but had that strange feeling she had experienced once before with this man. She suddenly in her heart recognized the feeling: attraction! A few bold, would-be suitors had come calling up Eagan Hill on Sunday afternoons, but Lou had ignored them. Grand John

L. had talked them off the place in short order after they received Lou's cold shoulder.

She thought, "Lou, you're stark raving crazy. The major—this preacher?—is old enough to be your father." But Lou owned that her feelings about him were anything but fatherly.

"Parson?" The word somehow sounded odd. "Anyway, Parson, you've got to come home with us. Mama Bear and Mother's cooking sure is favored by the Methodists. I'll bet you all ... what is it ... *Universals*, will find it right tasty, too," Alex gushed.

"Universal-ist," Solon gently corrected his excited former bugler with a smile. "I couldn't impose, A. Besides, I got to be on the stage to Pulaski to catch the L & N 6:15 passenger train. I'm due in Montgomery on Monday night. Mighty kind of you, but, well, I really need to keep my schedule. I've got folks expecting me in Montgomery. Several faithful are trying to revive their dormant church."

Lou found her courage. "Parson Stevenson. Sir, you'll be back this way?" Her brown eyes connected with his blue ones. She was out of hiding—letting her spirit be open to him. Her heart demanded it.

"Why yes, Miss Fields. It is 'Miss' Fields?" Solon asked of the once quiet and talented boy farrier, now a young and not unattractive woman.

"Yes, it's 'Miss' Fields," Alex informed Solon. He giggled and made eyes at Lou.

She ignored her silly brother and said, "Well then, you plan on stopping up this way long enough for a good farm meal when you next come through. It'll be a bit better than the vittles we 'didn't' have in the Army." She offered a small smile at her attempt at humor, and her brown eyes shined warmth. The smile and beautiful brown eyes took in the warrior-turned-preacher.

Solon visited Lou's eyes and said, "Why yes, yes Miss Fields … and Alex. I'd like that. Might be a few months, February or March, before I come this way again. It all depends on how my Alabama travels go."

"That will be fine." Lou was now more comfortable with the situation and her confidence directed her words. "Write us in care of the postmaster in Dellrose, Tennessee, when you'll be back and can share in our hospitality."

"Miss Fields, I will do that. Yes, ma'am. I surely will."

Chapter 20

Words from Home and the Road

Lou opened the brown paper-wrapped package about the size of a Bible. She noted the faded, dark blue, cloth-backed, and cheaply produced book's title in silver gilt letters, *The Pro and Con of Universalism*, by George Rogers, Cincinnati, Ohio. A caption on the first page of the book read: "… an examination of the condition of man, the character of God, and the hope of Universal grace. What can be the foundation of faith but love of, gratitude to, and trust in a God who loves mankind?"

Between the next two pages was a folded piece of notepaper. It read:

My Dear Miss Fields,

I would count it a personal kindness to me if you would read and consider the ideas in this book. Mr. Rogers traveled to many of the same places I'm now committed to go. Over thirty years ago he brought the gospel of universal salvation to dozens of hamlets, crossroads, and towns from Cincinnati to Mobile. Like Johnny Appleseed, he planted a good fruit for the benefit of those hungry for sweetness in life. I've found his words and ideas most reflective of my own. My education is very limited. I am not a scholar. I have tried over the years since the war to prepare myself to dedicate my life to God's grace and the sharing of God's love, mankind's hope, with the people in and around the Tennessee Valley. With the general and boys, I had enough experience of war and death. I intend for the rest of my life to offer something good and needed. Mr. Rogers voices the ideas that inspire me. I feel commissioned to be about this work. Your prayers and good thoughts will be most appreciated.

Your Servant,
S. Stevenson
General Delivery
Montgomery, Alabama

Two weeks later a letter from Lou arrived in the Montgomery post office. Ten days later Solon retrieved it on his way through Alabama's state capital. He was on his way from Brewton, Alabama, to Meridian, Mississippi. He'd heard of some scattered Universalists over in fast-growing Meridian. It had become a railroading crossroads. Two weeks ago had found him in meetings at Camp Springs in east Alabama near Opelika, with the Burrus folks there. The economic and social upheaval in southeast Alabama, the whole central South, was markedly discouraging. The people responded well to his message. Because of the bad times, folks seeking hope was an idea Solon had come to understand. Setting his work aside, he began reading his letter.

Mr. Stevenson,

I trust this finds you in good health and that your work goes well. We are well and warm. Winter here is cold and wet. We had a sprinkling of snow two days ago.

I received Mr. Rogers's book that you sent and am reading it, maybe better said—I am wrestling with it. I look forward to being able to talk with you about it. Some of it is troubling. It is so very different from what I've heard from preachers in the Sequatchie Valley and here in the Elk Valley. I say troubling because Mr. Rogers's and your belief describe God as a lot more loving and merciful than others.

Grand John L. says for you to watch out for those hard-shell Baptists down that way. He says they really like a mean God and you'd better not go talking about a good God, they won't allow it. Alex asked me to send you his greetings. He is so very fond of you and impressed by your work. He's reading Mr. Rogers's book with relish. He pesters me with wanting to talk about it and we've spent quite a few evenings in talks about it. Mama Bear says it sounds a lot like an Indian God to her. Mother hasn't said much but when the conversation is changed she tells us to go back to that "preacher's book" talk. Uncle Joe T. listens but doesn't comment, and Aunt Mary keeps her quiet, too. I don't think they object to the ideas. They seem worried about J.N. He's been in New Orleans for nearly four years. He got a job with General Wheeler at his carriage company there the summer of '66. Our general and J.N. became fast friends. Miss Daniella has been kind to him too. J.N. is sorta lost because of the general's removal to north Alabama nearly two years ago.

During the war, with J.N. as a corporal and "Fightin' Joe" a general, they didn't seem near the same age. As civilians, they do. J.N. is twenty-nine and the general is thirty-four. The general and little family—Miss Daniella, Lucy—4, Annie—2, and baby Ella, born in the summer—left New Orleans in early winter of '68 for Courtland. Miss Daniella's high and mighty father had been wanting them back with him at Caladonia since they left in February, 1866. He offered the general a farm set up and half the profits. Miss Daniella has a claim on her dead husband's land, and Mr. Jones is scheming to get it for her from his family. There's no end to that man's wheeling and dealing, according to what the general has told J.N. Our general, J.N. says, just chuckles and says Miss Daniella is what he wanted, and her father was an added feature of the situation. Says Colonel Richard Jones has had his way for nearly forty years, and a mere horse soldier is not going to change his plans or check his offense. J.N. is due here in spring. He and the general have made some arrangement about the wagon and carriage business. Grand and I are to talk with Mr. Gleghorn at the bank about a building in Fayetteville and suppliers in Cincinnati. Oh, you might know some of the firms there he should contact. He says there are the best hardware and equipment companies in Cincinnati for what his business will need.

Our prospects for crops I hope will be good come spring. Uncle Joe, Alex, Grand, and I are talking about more corn, maybe forty acres. Tobacco prices are looking good too, so we're going to put in five acres, twice what we had this past crop. Stock breeding and late spring foaling ought to give us four mules. That'll make our stock number two work teams for our place and farming, three yearlings ready to break to plow in summer, and four foals that'll be ready for breaking and training in twelve to fourteen months. We've made a good start with the place, more buildings to fix and build, more acres for corn and tobacco, and growing stock for training and sale. Our two cows provide all the milk we need. Mama Bear and Mother got ten pigs and more due come spring. Plenty of meat to eat and share.

Well I guess that's about all the news from the Fields' place, my clan, and the wintry Elk Valley.

Know my prayers and best wishes accompany you in your travels and work. Any idea when you can claim that meal we promised you? Mama Bear wants to fix fresh port tenderloin and she's worried that we'll have a hog worthy of her skillet and your plate.

Best wishes,

Mary Louise Fields

Solon took his glasses off and rubbed his eyes with his knuckles and his hands. He then looked through his nearsightedness out the depot window into the fuzzy morning's overcast sky. He acknowledged his good feelings with a "Well, well" under his breath. There was no one near him on the depot bench. His train wasn't due for two hours.

Solon sat in the booth near the rear of the café down the street from the Montgomery station. The chicken and dumplings were more dumplings than chicken—and too greasy—but the coffee was passable, and the fresh pecan pie was good. He held and sipped his heavily creamed coffee in one hand and scratched out his letter with the other, his mind and heart miles from the overheated eatery.

The large awkward script read:

Miss Fields,

I trust you and yours share good health. I do. Thank you for the letter. I picked it up here in Montgomery this morning. I've just returned from Brewton, Ala. and am on my way to Meridian, Miss. The time in Camp Springs, my destination when I left Tenn., went well. The Brewton experience was difficult. My train leaves in a short while and I wanted to write you and get this posted before I leave.

That is interesting about the general and his removal from New Orleans. "Squire" Jones, his father-in-law, wanting his little girl and grandchildren to come back to Miss Daniella's home is not surprising. The general got along with Bragg so he can handle the land baron, I expect.

We've exchanged letters since Fort Delaware. The last time was from N.O. awhile back. Then he said his "expanding" family was well situated in New Orleans and that the spring high water and summer fever season had not proved difficult for him and his. The general seems to have adapted to the business world well enough. It's a long way from New Orleans finery and high tone to the fields and hills we ranged in the AOT. The only thing the carriage business and a field cavalry have in common is horses—don't you think?

New Orleans has a bunch of CSA brass. The general says he met up with John Bell Hood one day in his carriage. Our general says Hood is real sickly and that his disabilities plague him, he has aged terribly and that he is a shadow of himself. "Cajun" Beauregard is in high cotton back home in Louisiana and doing fine. New Orleans is his hometown. He's president of the New Orleans, Jackson, and Great Northern RR and goes to Europe for the RR. Raising money, I guess. Our general reports that Beauregard is helping a group called the "Reform Party" that's trying to integrate freed slaves into Southern politics. Maybe he's a better man than he was a general. He really was good at impossible operations and offenses. I'm not hopeful that his political efforts will be much better. It is a pity about General Bragg. He was civil but bitter, the general said. He thinks our old CO carries his lack of success with the AOT as a burden even today, over six years later.

James Longstreet, our comrade in the Knoxville adventure, has become a Republican. "Old Pete" is making a success and is active in politics. Looks like he doesn't venerate Massa Lee like some. He's in a fight about Gettysburg and who should have done what. I expect Longstreet is right, a shift to new ground might have worked, but that's a fruitless business. Why can't we honor our dead, forgive others and ourselves in the past and move on to some new living unclouded by old troubles?

J.N. ought to be able to make a go at business. I'll send you names of companies in Cincinnati for him in the next letter.

Tennessee, from what I read and hear, is better off than Alabama and lots of the South. Word from Cincinnati is that Kentucky and Tennessee are prime targets for Northern dollars and new businesses. RR's expanding all over up there. Investments and such ought to spread and affect lots of people. New Orleans and upper South are recovering but those in the middle—south Alabama, all of Mississippi, south Georgia, and north Florida—are really suffering. Alabama is a mess—divisions and hate—poor, rich, colored, white, towns, and country. Poor always at the wrong end of everything—white or colored. Shame.

Tennessee's new governor, General J. C. Brown, has some sense. He's a neighbor of yours from over Pulaski, isn't he? Did you know he worked like the dickens to keep Tenn. out of the war? Then when it left the Union, he was a mighty fine field officer for us.

I know "The Parson" Brownlow and his crowd were a trial for you in Tenn., but he's safe in the Senate now, up with those

Washington yahoos. I'm wishing J.N. good fortune if he tries his hand at his own business. Folks need wagons and carriages, and, with all his silliness, he's a good fellow. Make a great salesman. Never shirked his duty that I knew and sure served me good. He defended us—he, the general, and I—several times when the dance got dicey.

Brewton is a busy lumber and railroad community. The main movers, the Campbells, are from a prominent New England family who came over thirty years ago and have built up quite a fortune in business. The current patriarch, James Peabody Campbell, made it quite clear when I arrived that he preferred a Yankee Universalist preacher rather than me. "Mr." Campbell said, as we finished the first meeting, "Well said, sir, well said." I was delighted with his remark. Vanity goeth before the fall, you know.

I hope to be back your way in six weeks, maybe by the first of spring, March 20. Tomorrow I take the Mobile-Ohio RR to Quitman, Miss. I'll rent a mount to explore the wilderness south of there. I'm searching for Universalists south of there in Jones County. Bro. Burrus says that that part of Jeff Davis's Mississippi is as different in geography and culture as can be, like east Tennessee and north Alabama hill country. Davis's delta and the Piney Woods see and experience the world mightily differently. Bro. Burrus told me of some folks down in "Free" Jones County I need to meet with, Herringtons and Mauldins especially. After that I hope to spend a couple weeks in Mobile and then back to Birmingham on my way home to you.

My best regards and warm wishes,
Solon

He reread his letter before addressing and posting it. The closing required reconsidering. Those last words, "on my way home to you," expressed feelings that had not been available to him for his face-to-face reckoning. There they stood—free, real, and right. And he had signed, "Solon." With that he had exposed his heart, but it felt safe and good. "Well, well," he softly said to himself. He mailed the letter as written.

Lou laid aside the first three pages of Solon's letter. Before she began the last page, she conjured up a picture of the general with three young children underfoot and that little wife. New Orleans, too, intrigued her—a strange and different place from Chattanooga or Nashville with all sorts of people and sights. Might be worth a visit someday. Solon's newsy letter had been a delight to read. His views and humor invoked good feelings.

She began the last page: "… couple weeks in Mobile and then back to Birmingham on my way home to you. My best regards and warmest wishes. Solon."

Her thoughts and feelings were suddenly in a jumble, a jumble like the ones she'd felt in the cavalry, at the creek in north Georgia, and at the Lincoln County courthouse over two months ago when she had truly looked at him, and Solon smiled at her.

That night she had a hard time getting to sleep. More than an hour after going to bed she got up and, in the markedly cooled kitchen, lit the lamp, sat at the table, drank some buttermilk, and reread Solon's letter. She then smiled and giggled as she put the folded letter in her housecoat. She got up to return to bed and left half a glass of buttermilk on the table.

Dellrose, Tennessee
Feb. 20, 1871

Solon,

Your letter came several days ago. I've delayed writing hoping to sort out my thoughts and feelings. Come home soon.

Lou

Chapter 21

New Arrangements

Lou allowed Solon to drive the carriage that Saturday morning. April had been the gentle heir of a stormy March. Sunshine and gentle warm breezes had dried the mud. The warmth was preparing the land for the renewing of spring. Solon had been staying at Icee Harwell's boarding house up the road from the Sherrill-Stone store for three weeks. He had ridden his big old gray, rented from Everett Clark's livery, up Eagan Hill every other day. He came visiting, helping with milking—a renewed skill—helping Lou tend the stock, and telling the family stories of Cincinnati and his missionary trips in the mid-South. He even told of his travels in west Florida and Appalachicola—a right busy port town and fishing center he allowed. Alex was fascinated by the story about a doctor there who was working on the prevention and treatment of yellow fever, "Yellow Jack." This Dr. John Gorrie thought this reoccurring coastal pestilence was caused by "bad air," and he'd invented a machine to condition—cool—the air. Solon said he'd had some success with treating, but had not succeeded in preventing the mean sickness.

The family had taken Solon in. Alex thought he was the greatest man—after Grand, his father, and the general—that he'd ever known. Nancy Bird accepted him because she saw character and his regard for her daughter. Joe T. and Mary Jane received him warmly because of his patronage of their J.N. Even Mama Bear begrudgingly warmed to him, but not until after he'd raved about her cooking and flirted with her unashamedly. Grand John L. liked to argue, and Solon was a respectful but capable foil. Those practitioners were few and far between for Grand John L. Lou had felt awkward and uncertain when Solon first sat down with her after arriving at her place on stormy Friday.

"Lou," he began, "I'm forty-two, nearly old enough to be your father. I have chosen or been chosen for a calling that hardly pays my expenses. I own one suit, a pair of boots, and my beat-up old hat. My worldly possessions can be put in two large saddlebags. Dr. Burrus is holding eighteen books of mine and $127. That is my real estate. When I get back to Dellrose, I've got to wire him to get the books sent here. I've got little to offer you but a loving heart, warmest respect, and devotion."

At this, their first real conversation since his arrival, he reached over the loveseat's small space which separated them, took her big, hardened farmer's hand, and said, "Mary Louise Fields, I'm her to court you. I want us to marry. I don't want, will not accept, an answer now. Please hear me out." He paused and looked down at his brushed old boots.

She kept her silence and looked at the worn, lined profile of his face and the gray hair that had nearly replaced the dark brown. His moustache's color was mostly gray, a real difference from seven years ago at Caladonia Plantation where she first laid eyes on him. He put his other hand to his upper lip and pulled down on his lip, mouth, and moustache. It reminded her of how she'd pulled on the milk cows' teats before sun-up.

"Here's what I'd like to happen. I need a rest. I've taken a room in Dellrose and paid for a month. My books will be here next week. I'd like to do some reading, sleeping, and just nothing for a spell. 'Course, I want to call on you and if you'll allow, help you, work with you. You've known me as a horse soldier and someone in charge. This is your outfit, not my cavalry," he smiled. "I'd like to get the feel of it and be with you. Ain't saying I'll make a fittin' hand, but I'll work hard at it. Reckon your granddaddy's got some old clothes and brogans I can borrow?"

He'd been talking to the parlor, only occasionally turning to catch Lou's eyes. Seemed he was dreading her response. With her right hand she took his chin, turned his head so as to face him square, and said, "We'll ask. 'Spect he does." She smiled shyly and looked at their joined hands. His hazel eyes met hers. She pulled that hand away and placed it on the side of his face, leaned forward and kissed him with tenderness, and with her eyes open.

Supper was Mama Bear's fresh tenderloin with Aunt Mary's corn bread, and Nancy Bird's fried potatoes and hot blackberry pie. Solon had two helpings and talked lots. Lou listened intently and smiled a lot.

Now, three weeks after his arrival, Lou and her beau were going to Fayetteville for a Saturday outing.

"Wonderful land, this part of the world," Solon offered. "These gentle hills feel old and kind—if land can give off feelings."

"Mama Bear says it can," Lou responded, gazing at the scenery about them. "I believe that, too," she added.

"Those fields, hills, and mix of trees and cultivated land show God's bounty, I think," Solon invoked. "The limestone outcroppings of the scrub thickets with those scrappy cedars show me there is some grace even from poor ground. Well, well, sorry Lou. That sounds like a sermon illustration. I just thought of it, but you know, it ain't bad—might use it on the circuit. It suits lots of places." He chuckled and smiled into Lou's peaceful brown eyes.

He continued after a while, turning the bays off the gravel and dirt road to along side the thoroughfare just before crossing Swan Creek at Cyruston.

"Lou, I've spent twenty years as a soldier, killing for some really unseemly causes. Saw lots of loss and hurt—more death than I could take in without God's love. Two good things came to me in spite of that wasted life—prison and getting a penny pamphlet about an odd religion, and meeting a boy/girl farrier one night down on the south side of the Tennessee." He didn't smile, didn't look at her. Shaking the reins, he said, "Walk on, horse," and the buggy moved forward, back onto the drying, muddy right-of-way.

Lou kept her eyes on the side of his face, and she swore a tear emerged from his eye. Couldn't be the wind that evoked the wet eyes; it was a calm, pleasant day.

"Miss Fields. Good weather down your way, too? When you going to have me down to take a look at your stock?" Mr. Jones asked as Solon pulled the wagon up to the saddle shop. It's whitewashed front gleamed in the eastern sun. The courthouse square, shops, stores, and assorted businesses were busy. Solon was lucky that the space was given up by a work wagon.

George Washington "G. W." Jones was a sixty-five-year-old native of northern Virginia. He had come to Fayetteville with his parents when he was a boy right about the time Lincoln County was founded. He got some schooling and apprenticed with a saddler. Beginning when he was twenty-six, he entered local politics and was elected a member of the county court—justice of the peace—in 1832. He studied law and became a member of the bar in 1839. He'd served in the U.S. Congress from 1843-1859. He worked hard as a Democrat Unionist to avert the civil war. When war looked sure, he was chosen to attend the Peace Convention of 1861 in Washington, DC. Illness had prevented his attendance. After serving a term, 1862-64, in the Confederate House of Representatives, he didn't seek reelection. When the Brownlow regime was overcome by Governor DeWitt Clinton Senter, he represented Lincoln County and his old district at the Tennessee State Constitutional Convention in 1870. Opposed to the poll tax as a requirement to vote in the new constitution he worked for its defeat in the convention. He lost. When the poll tax was approved he told the convention in the most stern of terms what he thought of the elitism and democracy's distortion represented by the tax. Refusing his pay and to sign the finished covenant he left Nashville and came home to Fayetteville disgusted. In public service since he was twenty-four he'd never lost a political race. He had been "Jones of Old Lincoln" since 1835. He was a political elder now dabbling in banking. He still owned part interest in a tannery near Town Spring and puttered around the saddlery on the square to talk stock and politics. Lou thought of him as a friend. Grand John L. found him the most worthy arguing challenge in the county. Mr. Jones stayed with Lou's grandfather in the varied topics they explored and always made him laugh when they got too hot into debate.

Grand John L. and G. W. Jones, in truth, did agree on many things, but arguing was more entertaining. One thing they did agree on was Andy Johnson, late US congressman, governor, US senator and president of the United States. G.W. was a close friend of the east Tennessee Unionist despite the turmoil of the war. The "commoner and tailor" of Greenville had failed in a bid for his old US Senate seat in 1868, but he'd written G.W. about trying for the newly at-large congressional seat in 1872. Grand John L. said he might just vote for the first time since he'd voted for Jones's candidate, Stephen Douglas, for president in 1860. He deserved vindication over the bullies who had tried to run him out of the White House. He said, "Aye, God, they didn't make Andy run!"

Mr. Jones had been referred to Lou and Alex by Mr. Gleghorn at the bank as a good man and someone who could help the Fields establish themselves with stock dealers. He'd visited, partaken of Mama Bear's table fare, and gave the family a tutorial on county politics and business affairs.

"Mornin' Mr. Jones. Spring might come back to us, don't you think?" Lou greeted the tall, lean man, whose gray hair and full beard made him look like a biblical figure. He might have walked the halls of Washington, but he looked like a working man in his leather work apron and turned-up sleeves.

"Most assuredly, little lady," the saddler-politician responded. He always called Lou "little lady," ignoring the fact that she was not little and surely didn't put on the airs of a Mulberry Avenue "lady."

"Mr. Jones, I'd like you to meet the Reverend Amos Solon Stevenson." She paused, then said, smiling and blushing, "We're getting married come June." Solon's neck snapped to look at her as he secured a hitch weight to the lead horse.

"Lou, Lou, we are?" Solon nearly shouted. Then he took his hat off and sailed it across the sidewalk into the saddle shop's open door. Then he rushed to Lou, picked her up, and whirled her around like heaving a shock of corn. Lou's head bobbed above his as the square rotated. She hadn't been handled that way since she was four and her daddy had taken her "for rides in the air."

"You are husband and wife," the Honorable G. W. Jones, lay Methodist supply preacher, announced to Solon and Lou. About twenty witnessed the wedding in the front of Lou's place. The ceremony was at 10 a.m., Saturday, June 7, 1871. J.N. had been home since early May. He and Alex stood with Solon. Grand John L. was with Lou. Mama Bear and Nancy Bird had parlor chairs behind the wedding party on the lush green grass. The big black walnut tree provided leafy shade for the warming morning. A bright sun in a clear pale blue sky anointed the occasion.

Solon had a new suit from D.C. Sherill's, a black frock coat, vest, and trousers in a fine gabardine wool, fine new boots, a John B. Stetson hat—black and broad-rimmed—and a boiled white shirt with white cravat. The general had sent a $200 draft with instructions on the money's use: "… groom outfit, best quality from hat to boots. With what's left use in your work," the general had written. Alex had given him a haircut and made sure he had some Bay Rum aftershave applied for the special day.

Lou's white dress had brocade panels in the skirt, and in front, on the bodice, there were circles from the throat to the belt at her waist. Her cuffs were made of matching brocade. The dress was tailor-made by Miss Virginia Harwell, seamstress over at Hamilton Mill, and had been her grandfather's special gift. He'd said he wanted his women folk to worry about cooking, not sewing, and had insisted on getting Miss Jennie to make the dress. Miss Harwell had become their first friendly neighbor down the road before moving to Harms in the spring. She was the best seamstress in the county. Her husband, Rolly, had been killed at Murfreesboro, fighting with Cheatham's Tennesseans. She made the wedding dress from a pattern they'd found in Godey's Magazine. Lou didn't wear a veil. Over her shoulders she wore a lace shawl that her mother and grandmother had worked on for three months. Her hair was pulled back in a style she'd seen and liked in an advertisement in *The Observer* for women's combs. Alex had given her a new mother-of-pearl comb ordered from New Orleans. She wore it at the back of her bun. Lou's plainness had been transformed. She looked like a handsome mature woman of twenty-three. Her movement showed shyness, but she held Mr. Jones's eyes, listening to his words. When the officiant had told them to hold hands, Grand John L. took her small bunch of spring wild-flowers that Mama Bear had picked, arranged, and tied with a dark purple ribbon. Her brown eyes connected confidently with Solon's hazel ones.

At Mr. Jones's announcement of Lou and Solon's new status— married—J.N. whispered to Lou, "You may now kiss the groom, bride." Lou laughed. Solon joined the good humor and then gently kissed her.

At the end of the ceremony, when the wedding couple was being greeted by family and friends, Nancy Bird, Solon's new mother-in-law, held his eyes as she shook his hands. She leaned forward and said quietly in his ear, "You take care of my Mockingbird, sir."

Solon reconnected with her eyes. "Yes ma'am, I will."

They went on a four-day honeymoon to Huntsville, staying at the Madison House a block from the Big Springs. A week after their wedding day they were working in the tobacco bed, thinning the foot-high plants. Brown sticky soil was clinging to their shoes. They laughed and laughed.

Thirty miles south of Dellrose, the general paced the back porch holding the Wheeler's newest baby, their fourth child and first son, Joseph Wheeler, Jr. A tiny thing, the newest little Joe had started crying a bit past midnight. Miss Daniella had said, half awake, "Joe, would you see to him?" He'd been a helpful father with all their children, and the newest one got his attention, a clean diaper, and a lullaby, "Buffalo Gals." When the former general, now businessman/planter and lawyer, finished walking his fretful boy, Joe, he focused on the trial he had to argue at 9 a.m. over in Huntsville.

A "wool hat" old Unionist farmer from New Market had been arrested for selling untaxed whiskey from a work wagon at Ditto's Landing just before Christmas. Guilty without much doubt, the defense hoped to convince the jury that the hard times of the Panic of '76 were extenuating circumstances, thus getting the old codger off with less than a year. The thirty-four-year-old lawyer was successful. His client got six months and was fined $50. He paid his defense attorney with five gallons of his wares.

Lou & Solon's Wedding

Chapter 22

Bountiful Late Harvest

The pattern was soon established without much fuss. Solon was kind—if not terribly demonstrative—to Lou. That was fine with her. There was warmth and consideration when they retired to the big four-poster cherry bed Uncle Joe T. had made and given them as a wedding present seven years ago. There were no children, but not from want of trying. Lou and Solon's rhythms were comfortable, with him evoking her laughter and her common sense grounding his energy.

On the circuit from late September to about Easter, Solon tended as best he could the Universalist groups he found in little country churches, farmhouse parlors, a few town churches, county seat rental halls, and brush arbors from Columbus, Georgia, to Mobile, Alabama, and from Jackson, Mississippi to Decatur, Alabama. He usually had several dozen public meetings during his six months itinerancy for the revival of the faithful and attraction of new flock. Lou had secured worn railroad schedules from the Louisville-Nashville, Mobile and Montgomery, Alabama Central, Alabama and Chattanooga, and Western RR of Alabama. She knew as much about railroads of the area as any passenger train dispatcher in the South. She was always given Solon's "preacher book," a big leather-bound ledger, at the first meal they shared when he came home the week after Easter. She took delight in reading in his hand the recordings of his sermons and their scriptural source, the places he'd preached, the number of listeners, the weather on the occasion, and the names of those getting married, baptized, christened, or buried. He was nearly halfway through filing his second volume since their wedding.

"Mama Bear, you got any of your yellow salve? My back, here, hurts like the dickens." Lou put each hand behind her and rubbed the kidney area as she came into the kitchen for morning coffee.

"You making water all right, Lou?" Mama Bear began her uninvited consultation. With Lou's affirmation of the regular workings of that bodily function, Mama Bear said, "It's all that climbing and toting you been doing. You don't recognize when you're tired out!" her grandmother chided her.

"I do, Mama. I just don't stop. Too much work to do with Alex in Nashville on Mr. Jones's business," Lou answered patiently. "Brother needed that trip," Lou added.

"Your moon times regular, girl?" Mama Bear asked. The grandmother had not taken notice of Lou's fuller cheeks and tighter clothes. After the first few years of Lou's marriage, Mama Bear had let concern for great-grandchildren decrease and barely be a part of her thoughts. Lou's subtle change of appearance had not registered with Mama Bear until just then. At seventy-one, her vision was not what it had been. Dr. Stone said the cataracts were normal and, short of very dangerous surgery in Nashville, there was not much to be done. Lou looked at her solemnly, "Well, no. I'm overdue for this time and missed the last moon."

"Well, girl, take it easy for a few days. The way you've been working this winter on finishing that new shed, it's no wonder," Mama Bear said with her back to Lou as she took her flour from the kitchen cabinet for biscuits. She smiled at the tin front of the cabinet, her face away from Lou. Mama Bear hoped. No children in seven years had been disappointing, but she'd tried to hide those feelings. Maybe she'd have a baby to fuss over in not too long a period of time.

While Lou's hands and back were busy with the life and work of a farmer and stockbreeder, her thoughts were focused on a variety of ideas. From her time as a six-year-old when Grand had taught her to read, she had cultivated that skill and avocation. Sherrill's had a small news and book corner, and she spent part of her shopping time every few weeks exploring its publications. Solon had told her about *The Revolution*, a magazine run by Susan B. Anthony and Elizabeth Cady Stanton, that advocated her social passion—women's suffrage. Her Cherokee heritage of strong women and a matriarchal social structure, her skills as farrier and stock handler, her love of the land and its tending, her experience as a soldier, and her talents and convictions about business matters were a strong foundation and informing structure for her beliefs and hopes for women. Solon was not threatened by that. It served to endear him to her mightily. She didn't see being married to anyone who didn't let her believe and act as she felt.

He had noticed early on the importance and contribution of women in the church. He'd met Olympia Brown, the first denominational ordained Protestant minister, in 1863. Miss Brown's (she kept her maiden name) husband, John Henry Willis, and Solon had taken to one another when Solon had traveled to Chicago in 1874 on church business. He told Lou that Miss Brown was a pixie with the heart of a lion. He thought she was as good a preacher as he'd ever heard, save Edwin H. Chaplin, an influential and eloquent Universalist minister in New York. A good half of Lou's precious leisure time, usually late at night in the glow of a kerosene lamp, was devoted to reading about the women's movement and writing letters to the field soldiers in that effort from Maine to the Wyoming Territory. Miss Anthony and Mrs. Stanton's organization, American Women's Suffrage Association, got an annual donation—only $5 at first in 1870, now $15 in 1877. She'd tried to enlist G.W. in the cause, but he couldn't bring himself to that challenge. He said he was too old.

She'd written Horace Greeley on behalf of women's rights. The Democratic/Liberal Republican candidate in 1872—and active Universalist layman—had a long-standing record of support for social reform. His *New York Tribune* had carried his words for thirty years from New York to even Fayetteville, Tennessee. Mr. Wallace at *The Observer* often reprinted his articles, arguing with some, agreeing with others. Especially well received by Mr. Wallace, Grand John L., Solon, Alex, and Lou was Greeley's advocacy of reconciliation "across the bloody schism" of the Civil War for North and South. Greeley assured her in a return letter of his support of women's suffrage but lamented its small chance of popular support. It was an irony not lost on Lou that the opposing 1872 Republican Platform of the ill-favored but victorious GOP President U. S. Grant had mentioned more equal participation by women in the nation's life.

Her hopes were long-suffering, but she took heart about a new political movement coming out of the mid and near West: the Greenback party. From what she could learn, it sprang from the agrarian and small town folk of the prairie states and Texas. Lou found the ideas of this progressive agrarian movement, with their principles concerning limiting the power of the controlling elite business interests and halting the exploitation of all working people—from the women in Massachusetts shoe factories to farmers everywhere—to be very appealing. Lou felt that power was about three things: personality, money, and numbers. Money can be trumped by personality and numbers—if there is organization and cooperation. Lou was not wealthy or poor, but she knew in her bones that everyone's condition affects everyone's happiness and well being. The farm provided enough but required much effort and sense.

She was for more freedom and fairness. For her it was just right. Solon agreed. For him it was the way God's kingdom should be manifested. For Lou these ideas and efforts were a matter of politics, and for her husband it was one of faith.

A month later Lou sent a telegram to Solon, general delivery, Montgomery: "Solon. We're going to have a baby."

Lou had gone to Dr. Stone to get his opinion about her health after Mama Bear had finally told her what was what after she threw up her third breakfast in a week.

Dr. Stone came into the hallway outside Solon and Lou's bedroom.

"Brother Stevenson, you're the father of two boys. Twins, sir. Tiny things, but they seem to be working like babies are suppose to," the middle-aged, Vanderbilt-trained general practitioner announced with a smile and the shaking of Solon's wet-palmed hand. In the bedroom, Nancy Bird and Mama Bear, each holding a baby, went about cleaning up the messy miracles. Solon watched them with tears rolling down his cheeks and took a good look at the miracles they were burnishing. He then sat with Lou, holding her hand, patting it gently. Through his teary eyes he held her tired brown ones. "Mary Louise—Mockingbird—you hatched 'em just fine. We got a good-looking matched pair." He laughed quietly through his tears.

Lou was soon asleep. Solon kept vigil until dawn.

"What we gonna name our team here, Lou?" Solon sat in the old cherry rocker holding one of the twins. Lou held the other to her breast, and he was heartily enjoying his first breakfast. Mama Bear had put an end to discussion of the names for the baby during Lou's pregnancy.

"Don't do that, Little Sister! Bring bad on them. Ain't a human being till we hold 'em. We wait till its real. No bad spirit in this house while I'm here. Lordy, such talk. No, no Mockingbird, you mustn't, now you listen to me." The old woman had gotten as excited as Lou had seen in years.

"Yes, mama, we won't," Lou had assured her.

"You got the first born, husband. What you want to name him? We got lots of good strong names in my family: John, Norman, Alexander, Joseph, Thomas, Amos." Through her tiredness she radiated joy and love. Solon smiled back into Lou's warm, brown eyes with unrestrained appreciation and love.

"They're all good, Lou, real good. But let's set this one a new heritage." He paused thoughtfully. "I favor James."

Lou waited a moment, turning the name over in her mind. "Well, we haven't had one. He ... they ... both of 'em are something special after all this time. Thought you were just a dried-up old man there after awhile. And now two boy-children!" She blushed with her joke but stuck to it and played it out. She looked seriously at Solon for a couple of seconds before laughing out loud, bouncing the baby. "Oh Lord, that hurts," she quickly recognized. Solon smiled back sheepishly, and then threw back his head in a full joyful tribute.

"Serves you right, mocking your virile husband, woman." The baby in his lap, wrapped in Mama Bear's special quilt made and saved since the wedding for this use, looked startled, and Solon stopped his frolic and tended the wrap and his boy. He returned to the business at hand.

"James, Lou, for Jesus' brother—not that the other one there is the Savior—but because James' Letter says, 'Be ye doers of the word, and not hearers only ... faith if it hath not works, is dead, being alone." I like that. Dead faith without doing something for others and God. What you think?"

"I like it fine, real fine, Solon," she said and did. "How about James Taylor Stevenson? Taylor for the governor! Why not, since we're plowing new ground!"

"And for old Zach! Yes, Lou, that's a good name."

"What about this little, sweet, puny one?" Lou said with tenderness.

"Puny you say. Well let's see. I've thought about names ever since we knew we had a baby on the way. Now two, well, James was what I'd come up with. This 'uns James." He gently jostled the pink, black-haired bundle he held protectively in his arms. "What you think, Lou. John, Norman?"

"No, let's give this one a new spirit too. I know," she said after looking out the window reflectively at the blue, white-streaked sky. "Joseph Wheeler Stevenson! He's a little one, the general did pretty well for a small one, don't you know."

"James Taylor and Joseph Wheeler, huh?" Solon took the sounds and meanings of the names in. "Jim and Joe. You know that's what they'll get called, Lou. Yes, those are good names for a strong team. Good," Solon said. Lou smiled and slightly nodded her head, looking first at Jim, then at Joe.

After a quiet time of appreciation and visualizing what might be possible of these two miracles, Solon said, looking up from Jim into Lou's eyes, "What about their Indian names, wife?" His eyes twinkled and a near smile warmed his face.

Lou looked questioningly at him as if to say, "Shall we?"

Solon said, "From everything Mama Bear has told me and what I know about the Cherokee, I think we ought to. Their granddaddy, your father, was half, and Miss Nancy is half—what does that make you?" He went on without waiting for her answer. "Mr. Fields has gone on so about Robin Hood and 'borderland' people, his stock he says—pirates, outlaws from the crown—rebels all, the right kind!" he paused, realizing he was beginning a sermon. "Lou, they're good stock, Anglo-Saxon English and your Principal people. Let's start 'em off good with names that mean something. Hey, girl, they're ours, tarnation!" His energy was a blend of joy and recognition.

Lou didn't respond for a few moments. Her mind and heart were both struck by the thoughtfulness and wisdom of this orphan boy from the ridge a few hollows west. A soldier for so long, now God's agent for over ten years, her husband was a gift, a precious gift, and she savored that blessing. "Well, husband, we sure can. Yes, we should." Smiling at Joe she said, "Any suggestions?"

"They're twins, right?" Solon creativity was engaged. He continued, "Together they'll be for a long time. Together they were born. Nature offers your people the inspiration for naming, right?" Lou nodded, refraining from intruding on his ideas. "Well let's think about that, nature, what goes together—what things in nature are partners, share in life?" He'd got the process going, but it was now stalled. He looked perplexed, as if searching his memory for what to do, what to suggest.

"Animals? Birds?" Lou entered this process. "Sky, moon, stars, sun? No, that does not feel right, we're of the ground, land folk." Lou had stalled now. Solon was inspired again.

"Trees, Lou, that's it!" Solon's excitement startled Jim, and he began to stir. His father paused from the conversation and gently rocked him. "It's OK, boy. It's OK," he said quietly and gently to his firstborn. The baby quickly calmed and resumed his napping. Lou watched and chuckled to herself.

"Well," she said after a moment. "There's chestnut, oak, cedar—but Mama is Lonesome Cedar ... there's sycamore, pecan, elm, hickory, poplar, pine," she paused, thinking about more. "Maple, dogwood, beech, birch, ash, hackberry ... which ones you like? Which two strike you as being right?" Lou was pleased with all the names she'd been able to offer.

"Which ones you favor?" Solon passed the process back to her.

"Well, I'm partial to the useful ones, pretty is OK, but, well ..." She returned to reflection and then said, "Hickory."

"What about 'Old Hickory'? He pretty well betrayed your people, didn't he?" Solon said. "You'd think it'd be right to give one of our boys the name they gave Andy Jackson?"

"Hickory sure came long before General Andrew Jackson," Lou responded sarcastically. "Besides, the Principal People ended up calling him 'Chicken Snake'!"

"What grows with Hickory?" Solon said, both as an inquiry and as a prod to his thinking.

"Oak," Lou answered. She smiled at him with a sense of accomplishment.

He returned her acknowledgement with, "Yes, Hickory and Oak."

Lou said, "Tall Hickory and White Oak. Good wood and acorns and hickory nuts are good to eat."

Solon stood. With Jim in his arms, he softly sat on the bed's edge. Securing the bundle in his left arm, he put his right behind Lou's head on her top pillow and held her right shoulder. "James Taylor Stevenson—Tall Hickory—and Joseph Wheeler Stevenson—White Oak—say hello to your mama and daddy." Both laughed just hard enough that both babies fussed and Jim cried.

Chapter 23

On New Battlegrounds

"General, don't let down any of the people. Remember all of our citizens, sir," advised Professor W. H. Councill, the most important African-American leader in north Alabama and president of Alabama Normal College in Huntsville, Alabama. A leading Republican, Councill, like most practical leaders, accepted the shifting of power after Rutherford B. Hayes and the GOP abandoned black empowerment in the old Confederacy. Allies were needed in all sorts of camps to keep some of the blood-purchased rights African-Americans had pursued for over a decade.

Joseph Wheeler, one-time career soldier, now forty-four-year-old planter/lawyer and Democratic candidate for the US Congress representing the Eighth District of north Alabama, shook hands with the dignified and well-spoken professor.

Joseph Wheeler was given the opportunity to be an agent of reconciliation and renewal for his region and nation. The "calling" of clergy is but one way of being. Others are called to be for life or against it in a huge variety of ways. Joseph Wheeler was about being and doing that which he saw as right and good. As with everyone, he wasn't always successful or his path straight, but he was faithful to his call.

It was past time to look forward, not backward. The ordeal of national civil war and the hard time afterward certainly informed the future—1876 onward—but new vision was needed if Alabama, the South, and the nation could achieve "... a new birth of freedom; and that this government of the people, by the people, and for the people shall not perish from the earth." Abraham Lincoln had presided over the terrible ordeal of war. He kept faith with the ideal of one nation and the goals of the Declaration of Independence. Had he embraced the moral imperative of the abolishing of slavery for political expediency? It signified little. He and the Union Army's supremacy made it happen.

Lincoln, the low-born backwoods Kentucky native become substantial Illinois corporate lawyer and politician, had advised the victorious Union commanders in the field at the defeat of the South. He counseled them to "let them up easy." Lincoln was killed, and the unfortunate Andrew Johnson couldn't carry out the "malice toward none" his champion and predecessor had envisioned. President Grant governed for eight years, and the harsh reconstruction policies of revenge on the white South gradually gave way to a compromise of federal hands-off with the Compromise of '76. Blacks and poor whites were thrown to the pleasures of a new/old aristocracy. It was an uneasy and conflicted era.

"Professor Councill, I hope I can do justice to all my neighbors," the general answered. His words were those of a politician, but his sincerity was true.

Eight-year-old Joseph Wheeler, Jr. (Joseph) pulled his father's other hand. "Papa, can I drive the buggy home?" It was a short drive from Courtland to Pond Spring, the Wheeler's home. The Courtland campaign rally was winding down.

"Yes, Son, but we have more people to talk with. Go get me some of that lemonade, would you please, sir?" the father said with sweetness and amplified decorum. A miniature of his father, Joseph ran smiling over to his big sister, twelve-year-old Annie.

"Come on Annie, father wants some lemonade. Let's get some, too." Joseph and Annie had an atypical big sister/little brother relationship; they were partners in sibling politics. Lucy, the oldest, was number one in all things. The two middle ones could barely, together, touch her influence in that position. Four-year-old Carrie, the youngest, and Lucy, the oldest, had special places in the family. The two middle ones, since sister Ella had died at age two, were hard pressed to maintain equality of status. They tried mightily, together. Annie liked Joseph much more than her female competitors. She had the rough and tumble way more fitted for a boy's play. She and Joseph thrived.

Their mother was home. This pregnancy was proving to be a difficult one. She had already delivered eight children during her thirty-eight-year life. This baby was due in four months. Cataba, twenty years a slave and now nearly twenty years a free person employed by her former mistress, served as Mrs. Wheeler's good right hand. She was tending the baby, Carrie, and mother. The Wheeler household's domestic ruler had laid down the law to her "Miss Da-nella" about this pregnancy. Her do's and don'ts were severe—and mostly don'ts. The general had mildly tried to come to his petite wife's rescue after one of Cataba's burst of law-giving a few weeks ago.

"General, sir, we've lost two—two little precious ones," she exclaimed, "and I'm not burying no more. No sir, I sure ain't."

The general had no protest to this wisdom and power.

The Joseph Wheeler family of Pond Spring Place, Lawrence County, near Courtland, Alabama, had evolved into a busy, happy tribe, overcoming the loss of two children with resigned acceptance and measured grief. Investing Mrs. Wheeler's inheritance in the New Orleans business her husband had managed right after the war had proved to be a sound judgment. They had realized a good profit when it was sold. The general's operation of Colonel Jones's vast farming/business operation had made money in spite of the fickle economy. The money realized had been largely put into improvements for the farm, the Memphis and Charleston Railroad, and the building of a less-than-ostentatious home. "Pond Spring's" main house was one hundred yards south of the railroad. A new stop had been designated "Wheeler." The rehabilitated railroad had been a success. The general and his lady were significant stockholders. He was a board member and attorney for the profitable, growing railroad.

"Pond Spring," Joseph and Daniella's plantation, procured by her father from her husband's family by the hardest after years of haggling, became the center of an agricultural and transportation community along the Tennessee River in Lawrence County, Alabama. Some two thousand acres would be served by cotton gins, stores, depots, churches, schools—all developed by or because of Pond Spring and the Wheeler's guidance. Eventually the estate would include eighteen thousand acres in several plantations located in three states: Alabama, Tennessee, and Mississippi.

The siren of politics had sung its alluring tune, and the planter/lawyer's odyssey had taken a new direction. He ventured into the stormy sea of American politics. Alabama's political life had roughly come through the turmoil of Civil War and Reconstruction and now stood at a crossroads. The domination of the carpetbagger, scalawag, and black freeman was weakened and vulnerable. New political alignments were taking shape: the re-enfranchised court-house boys, fire eaters, brigadiers, silk hat, and planter aristocracy: the "Bourbons"; the re-enfranchised long-standing independent Jacksonian yeoman farmer, small business, hill country, anti-Montgomery, Richmond, Washington: the "Wool Hats, the long-standing independents; younger "New South" boomers from various old families, both wealthy and otherwise, who saw prosperity as fore-most; the weakening Republicans favored by Washington patronage, made up of the politically active blacks and immigrant Unionist white citizens; and a new growing progressive agrarian contingency who sought an alliance of the latter groups against the "big mules"—Bourbons—"Lords of the Lost Cause and the Land."

The Bourbons thought the others, who they termed "the Radicals," were spawns of Satan set to destroy their social and eco-nomic garden. Into this skirmish—soon to be war—rode the former chief of cavalry of the Army of Tennessee, "Fightin' Joe" Wheeler. Never a rabid ideologue, Joseph Wheeler, while loyal to his adopted class, took the lead in moderating the reactionary qualities of the

Bourbons. He took the grievances and ideals of the Independents seriously and pragmatically reckoned with the aspirations of the exploited rural whites and "New South" pro-business pushers of the emerging gilded age. Not an active and enlightened reformer on race issues, he, never the less, dealt with the plight of the abandoned black countrymen with less rock-rib discrimination than most white Southern politicians. Bitterness and hatred were not aspects of his character in war or peace, but work and accomplishment were.

As the underachiever in cavalry tactics at West Point had done twenty-five years earlier, the political novice applied himself and mastered this new trade with the same determination and success. The sitting congressman, ex-Colonel William M. Lowe, wounded Confederate veteran of Bull Run and native Huntsville lawyer, had united the Independents—a sizeable segment of the black diminishing electorate and Agrarians—to get elected in the first post-Reconstruction election of 1878. He was a bright, credentialed, effective forty-year politician whose star was rising. His dreams were of an alliance of "little mules" to out-number and out-pull the big mules. His hopes were that such a working team would govern and carry him to the U.S. Senate. "Fightin' Joe" entered the field against Col. Lowe.

After a rambunctious campaign and election, the Democratic candidate was declared the winner by a margin of 43 votes out of a total of 24,773 votes cast. Ex-General Wheeler went to Washington and Congressman Lowe went to court. The court returned the seat to Lowe after the general had served ten months of the eleven-month session of congress. Tuberculosis struck down the newly declared Congressman and emerging progressive leader in October 1882. The general went to the huge Huntsville funeral. The next year he won the seat handily, as he was honored to do in the following eight congressional elections.

A second son, Thomas Harrison Wheeler, was born in March 1881. Cataba, Miss Daniella, and the six children kept the home fires burning while the general was at the nation's capitol. They all met the congressman at the new "Wheeler Station" on the Memphis and Charleston Railroad. The feisty new congressman took to the new field of national governance as the young cavalryman had—with zest, creativity, and long hours. Among his enduring contribution to the nation was his vision of the significance of the Muscle Shoals region and of the Tennessee River and the whole valley drained by the Tennessee. Over the years he secured finances for improvements and publicity on the untapped potential of the shoals of the Tennessee. A progressive thinker and diligent toiler for his district and region, Congressman Wheeler extensively researched the background and necessity of the legislation he proposed. He worked diligently for a weather service for the gulf coast in order to help that region to better endure the faithful and destructive storm seasons. In the 1890s he became chair of the powerful Ways and Means Committee. In his subterranean office in the Capitol he became an expert on the nation's tax structure. The economic issues of the national life and the government's primary role—tariffs—were the responsibility of his committee. A low-tariff Democrat, his powerful

Republican opponents sought high tariffs. The struggle was decades long, and the Republicans held sway.

The increasingly wizened, pert but shy and austere representative of the people became one of the most informed and diligent members of Congress. Never a Beau Brummel in civilian attire, the "Honorable Member from Alabama" briskly navigated the Capitol with his big hat in hand or on his head, his lengthening and steadily whitening beard whisked back by his fast pace of walking, his arms filled with books, and his coat and vest pockets jammed with papers of state. "Fightin' Joe's" natural gait was "advance at a trot."

In world affairs, American trade and influence was pushing the nation toward the status of being a world leader. It was a troubling development for the revolutionary democracy—the first to successfully rebel against the British Empire. Would the United States become another powerful nation—an empire?

Congressman Wheeler promoted his position in the emerging world power when, in 1897, he guided a $50,000 appropriation from the public treasury to the relief of the hungry in war-ravaged Cuba. Early on he was a fervent proponent of "Cuba Libre." Helping provide attention, preaching American principles of democratic freedom, and expressing loathing for the cruel bullying of the failing Spanish Empire, he would soon provide more than words and money to the cause of Cuban independence. He'd strap on the horse soldier's spurs. He would be sixty-two years old when he followed the dance music of Mars yet another time in his life.

He was in the president's office on the morning the Washington papers carried the story of the sinking of the "Maine" in Havana harbor. "Fightin' Joe" was the first to volunteer.

Chapter 24

❧

Politics and Religion

T he day after the twins' thirteenth birthday, Solon took
them to see Mr. D. C. Sherrill in Dellrose. The next
Saturday, a rainy December day, found them leaving home
at 5:30 a.m. to begin their new jobs at the Sherrill-Stone Store. It was
a fifteen-minute ride, and Solon took them every Saturday in the
work wagon teamed by Nash and Monty (for Nashville and
Montgomery). During the four months of school, October to
March, they had regular chores before and after. Joe was always the
most physical. He busted tough, rough-cut hickory and oak logs—
about eighteen inches tall—with a double-edged axe, providing for
the fuel needs of the cook stove and fireplaces. He also hauled the
chunk-coal from the pile to the forge for his mother's work. Jim
tended the chickens: fifteen docile mixed hens and one mean Rhode
Island Red rooster, "Chanticleer." He "mothered," "bossed," and
"dispatched" the nesting chickens—the layers, fryers, and roasters.
His efforts kept the table supplied with eggs and meat. His second-
ary task was the grooming, clipping, and braiding of the manes of the
mules and horses. He took care of the coats, manes, and tails, and his

mother watched their hooves and health. His gentle touch calmed even the most skittish animal.

Solon thought the town job would help the boys broaden their learning. Lou agreed. It did.

Jim worked in the office helping Mr. Sherill and the chief clerk, Mr. Flountroy, with posting accounts, checking invoices, copying orders, and doing the general helper chores of a business of many departments. He learned enough about clerking to wait on customers during the hectic harvest seasons. Joe spent his work hours between the grocery, men's fine clothing, and work clothing department. A stock boy in grocery, Joe was also an apprentice salesman in the clothing areas. He soon learned to love the visits, and appreciate the style, of the several drummers who called on the store selling their "line," especially the men's fine clothing. His favorite drummer was Mr. Morris from Neely-Harwell in Nashville. A snappy dresser and genuinely kind person, Mr. Morris offered Joe the character of a businessperson plus traveling man that was positive and an appropriate model for an aspiring "comer."

He soon thought of himself as well versed in men's fancy attire, favoring fine wool Brooks Brothers suits especially ordered from New York for winter season. He fancied Haspel and Company of New Orleans's popular summer linen suits in white and buff for late spring and summer. The summer heat even wilted those suits of fine cotton. He learned to fit suits, shirts, shoes, and hats. The fedora was becoming popular. The Derby and skimmer were the hats most favored by the younger men. The classic large-brimmed, high crowned slouch hat in black and brown sold the most. It was a farmer's headwear. In shoes the work brogans moved well after harvest time—October

through December. For Sunday-go-to meeting, the Nashville-manu-
factured Johnson-Murphy shoes sold the best, in black for the older
men and brown for the younger. Mr. Washburn, head floor walker
for clothing, gave Joe a lesson in how to get his less-than-well-
scrubbed men's shoes customers to use the "sizing sock." He
explained that, otherwise, the unwashed feet and occasional dirty
socks of many customers would soil the shoes. Joe became very adept
at this ruse.

That early fall, 1892, their mother's longtime interest in politics
and women's suffrage took a more active part in all their lives. She
took them to Nashville to hear "The Boy Orator of the Platte," the
thirty-six-year-old congressman from Nebraska, William Jennings
Bryan. Bryan, nominated a few months earlier for president by the
Democrats, was the new giant-slayer-designate for farmers, laborers,
and small business folk. He lived up to his calling and smote, chest
and thigh, the moneyed robber barons of monopolies, tight money,
and high tariffs—and the high-faluting power broker's hired hands,
the Republican party. Lou had read much about Bryan and his
lawyer wife, Mary. In 1892, at the age of thirty-one, Bryan had
entered Congress. Reelected in '94, by 1896 he had become a nation-
ally recognized leader of the progressive liberal wing of the
Democrats. His "Cross of Gold" speech at the convention created a
truly spontaneous nomination. This powerful plea for economic justice and agrarian reform kicked off his run for the White House as

the youngest candidate ever. The "Panic of '93" had wrecked the national economy, with farmers, workers, and small business people buried under the crumbled ruins. Times were bad, the worst in bustling, growing America in over fifty years. Hundreds of thousands were jobless. Farm prices were rock bottom, and costs were sky-high.

Conservative Democrat President Grover Cleveland followed the spendthrift conservative Republican Benjamin Harrison. Harrison and the GOP-lead Congress had spent the US Treasury surplus accumulated by Cleveland in his first term, 1884-1888, and the vaults were dry. Cleveland was left with the mess. He couldn't get Congress to pass the needed legislation that might have overcome the situation and restored the economy. More than a campaign, Bryan had mounted a crusade to reform the excesses of the moneyed barons who manipulated the national economy with the able assistance of Congress for the profit of the few. "Free-Silver" was the battle cry of those who wanted to increase and make credit easier in the national economy. Gold and silver as available money—along with regulating the few huge business trusts and monopolies and fighting for lower tariff costs—were the foundation planks of Bryan's platform.

The "Gold Bugs" nominated the high-tariff Ohio governor and former congressman William McKinley to continue the conservative, reactionary policies of big business and keep the big mules in power. It was city versus country; big business versus small business and labor; the wealthy versus everybody else; the Northeast versus the rest of the USA; and the status quo versus change. Bryan's campaign would be comprised of more than 600 speeches and 18,000 miles traveled across twenty-seven states during the three-month campaign. He became the first presidential candidate to actively campaign nationwide on the behalf of his aspirations, ideas, and principles. McKinley stayed home in Ohio and spoke from his "front porch." When the votes were counted, McKinley edged Bryan by 600,000 votes. Bryan would receive more votes losing than Cleveland had received winning in 1892. The McKinley crowd, financed by big business, out-spent the Democratic effort ten to one. A slight shift of less than a few thousand votes in six states would have elected Bryan.

Solon had shown Lou a newspaper piece in August. They were both stirred by Bryan's words.

"There are two ideas of government … there are those who believe that if you will only legislate to make the well-to-do prosperous, their prosperity will leak through to those below. The democratic idea, however, has been that if you legislate to make the masses prosperous, their prosperity will find its way up through every class which rests on them."

Bryan had met Mary Baird when he was a student at Illinois College (Jacksonville). He graduated as valedictorian in 1881 and went to law school in Chicago. Returning to Jacksonville, he opened his law practice and courted Miss Mary. He and Mary married in 1884. They had a boy and two girls. While having babies and making a family, college graduate Mary was tutored by William in the law. She was carrying their second child, William Jennings Bryan Jr., when she passed the bar in 1888.

When Lou read of Bryan's ideas and his wife, she saw something she knew to be good. She longed for improvement in the place of women in society—from voting to economic influence. It was time to do more about it than to send small donations, write letters, and yearn for a better world.

"My fellow citizens, friends, and neighbors, let us citizens of the beautiful and fortunate state of Tennessee welcome the 'Great Commoner'—the able voice for democracy and justice, the warrior for prosperity, the builder of a brighter future for our great nation— the honorable William Jennings Bryan!" This rousing introduction was exclaimed by Robert L. Taylor—"Our Bob." Only a few years older than Bryan, Taylor had already served two terms as Tennessee's governor. He had been renominated in the summer for another round in the governor's chair, and he and Bryan were campaigning together. The nearly seven thousand attendees—laborers in overalls, young men in dapper attire, farmers in brogans and ill-fitting suits, a sprinkling of wealthy progressive "big mules," women, the young and old, shop owners and craftsmen whose places were closed for the day—clapped, cheered, stomped, and bellowed "Bry-an, Bry-an, Bry-an" when Bryan stepped forward. They had come to the Volunteer State's capitol city to be with "Mr. Will." The champion was with his patrons. Lou looked at Solon, her eyes smiling, as they joined the clapping. Solon let out a "Rebel yell." The sixteen-year-old twins were having a grand time joining in the ruckus, cutting up and trying to out shout one another. Joe won the contest. All across the littered building site for the Tennessee Centennial Exposition on Nashville's West End—just west of Vanderbilt University—the joyous multitude embracing their political savior. They feverishly awaited a latter-day miracle of economic and political loaves and fishes.

"Mrs. Bryan, I'm Mary Louise Stevenson. Pleased to meet you," Lou said as thirty-two-year-old, petite Mary Baird Bryan extended her gloved hand. They stood in the lobby of the Maxwell House three hours after the Bryan rally.

"Is it Mary Louise or just Mary, ma'am?" responded the candidate's partner in life and work. Her manner was warm and sincere. Lou liked her immediately.

"Well, Mrs. Bryan, it's actually Lou," said forty-eight-year-old Lou with a reserved smile.

"Then Mrs. Stevenson, please call me Mary, and if you permit I'll call you Lou," instructed the confident small woman.

"Yes, Mrs. Bryan—Mary—I'd be pleased," Lou granted. They stood chatting for a minute. Mary Bryan was small, pretty, and petite; Lou was tall, thin and plain.

The crowd in the ornate lobby had pretty well thinned, and those left were hovering with Mr. Bryan and Bob Taylor. Solon had an animated conversation underway with the governor and would-be president, each taking a turn talking while the others nodded their heads. Taylor, the cigar smoker, took care to blow his wicked-smelling

Cuban away from Bryan, the teetotaler. Solon shared with them the misery and struggle he saw in his annual four-month preaching season in Tennessee, Alabama, and Mississippi.

"The times and people need a better deal," he told them.

"Lou, let's find a table in the restaurant and have some coffee. I've never been fond of tea you know, coffee suits me best," Mrs. Bryan told Lou. "Oh, and this new rage—Maxwell House Coffee—has me intrigued," Mary asserted with the skill of a natural politician. The two spent nearly two hours talking at a neat, white table-clothed table in the ornate hotel café. Then Lou and Solon went with the Bryans down the six blocks to Union Station by trolley to get the northbound to Louisville. When Lou had gone with Mrs. Bryan to the café the twins were allowed to ramble around sightseeing for a few hours. The twins were instructed to meet Lou and Solon there at six for their trip home. Each was given a fifty-cent piece by their father with the admonition to "not waste it."

The boys thought the whole occasion—the ride up on the L & N, the trolley from the station to just west of Vanderbilt University, the festive rally at the exposition site, exploring the grand hotel while the adults did what adults do, and now a few hours on the town—a great adventure indeed. They went straight down the north side of the Capitol Hill to Sulphur Dell. Finding a way into the empty baseball park, they pantomimed pitching and hitting on the same ground of their baseball team, the Nashville "Volunteers." The "Vols" were on the road that Saturday playing a consistent rival, the Memphis "Chickasaws." The Vols were given good coverage in the *Nashville Banner*, and the boys were faithful fans with Uncle Alex, tracking their team's fortunes, good and bad. Jim dreamed of being a speedy shortstop, and Joe thought of himself as a wicked left-handed pitcher. The day was balmy and they had a wonderful outing. Lou found and spent time with her new friend and heroine, and Solon stood with national and local politicians and gave them his two cents worth. The twins had had an opportunity to explore a larger, fascinating world. It was a very big day for the Stevensons.

Joe favored his mother in appearance—dark, lean, and tall with an easily tanned complexion. He inherited his father's intensity and internal power. Jim favored his Uncle Alex—fair and short, but without his stockiness. His skin would easily burn in the sun. Jim carried his mother's internal grace. He also shared his Uncle Alex's artistic qualities, while Joe had his mother's mechanical gifts. Jim was witty, chatty, and outgoing. Joe spoke his mind when required, but didn't fancy having a crowd hear him. The twins represented another generation of heart and hands, poet and craftsman, sky and earth. The best of friends, they were a matched team in spirit, if not style.

Joe had gotten mad at Jim often over the last few months. During their just-completed visit to Nashville, Jim had not been able to keep up with Joe as they explored the Capitol Building, Maxwell House Hotel, City Hall, Sulphur Dell Park, and the train depot. He coughed badly and had a hard time catching his breath. They had stopped often until the cough ended and Jim's strength returned so that they could continue their adventure. As young children, the twins had offered the family very different characteristics. Joe was the plunger and Jim the floater.

After returning from the Nashville excursion, the routine of farm and store life continued. Jim had taken to finding opportunities to talk about Mr. Bryan and the evil McKinley-Hanna crowd. The tyranny of the bankers and industrialists and the major points of the presidential campaign of 1896 were expounded by Jim one afternoon at the Sherrill-Stone Store.

"Those Republicans will drive us common folk before them like the slaves of Egypt," Jim heatedly preached to some customers, the parents and children of the Marks and Harwell families, one early October Saturday.

"James, could I see you for a moment here please," Mr. Washburn, the grocery's chief clerk said, peering over the rack of work shoes. His demeanor was not friendly. "Son, you do not discuss politics or religion in a place of business. Never. Do you understand? We get all kinds of customers here: rich, powerful, Populist, Democrats, and even occasionally a Republican from the colored folk and ridge people. All sorts, son, and you shall not inflict your opinions on those two subjects. You understand?"

Jim, taken aback by the dressing down, could only respond, "Yes sir, I do."

BRYAN FOR JUSTICE IN 1896

The '96 Crusade Comes to Tennessee

Chapter 25
August 1886

Changes

"Amen." Over sixty attendees moved slowly from the hot mid-afternoon sun of August 1886. The deep brown loam was fragrant over the new grave. Encircled by green grass, it appeared as a scar on nature. A mature mound beside the new one looked in place, not raw like the new one.

Lou's arms rested protectively over her sons' shoulders, Jim on the right and Joe on her left. Jim's sobs were deep, his face red and wet, his nine-year-old body heaving to restore his steady breath. Joe's mouth was tight, his eyes fixed on the ground before them. He looked like he dared anything to be in their path.

Alex walked beside them. Tears were drying on his stricken face. His ordinary talkativeness and good cheer was absent. Grief and loss occupied him this day. Turning from his feelings, he said, philosophically, "End of an era, Sister. The descendent of the pirate and Sherwood Forest outlaw is gone. Mighty sad ..." His words trailed off, and he hugged the three as they walked.

Solon, Reverend Hawkins—the Methodist—and Brother Scott—the Campbellite—stood for a time at the fresh grave. Solon looked at each in turn and shook their hands.

He said, "Much obliged. Mr. Fields didn't give y'all much slack about religion that's for certain. Today with your kind words you've shown me Jesus summons all sorts for his work." He didn't smile with his back-sided compliment, but his tone and eyes relayed his appreciation and regard.

"Well said, Brother Stevenson, yes mighty right," the Methodist acknowledged with his own off-center response.

The Church of Christ preacher, not to be outdone by a Universalist and a Methodist, added, "Solon, Miss Lou, Mr. John L., and Miss Bear have been the best of neighbors. I'll leave it to the Lord to sort out the goats from the sheep."

All smiled and went quiet for a few moments, letting the humor fade and letting out the feelings only preachers knew when they stood over a fresh grave: hope and wonder, edged by fear. Solon had conducted the service for John Longstreet Fields (1798-1886) with quiet dignity and solemn significance. Now, with the words said, his eyes teared up and chill bumps came up even on the near 100-degree day. He swallowed hard and nodded his head, put on his hat, and walked away from the two. Lou, Alex, and the boys were over near Bee Spring Church. Nancy had just taken the buggy home to get ready for the callers. He walked away from the graveyard and church to the woods. He walked fifteen feet into the cooler shade of hackberry, hickory, cedar, and gum trees. Taking his bearings, he walked twenty more, took off his hat, pulled his clean bandana out of his right back pants pocket, and wiped his face of sweat, taking in the cotton clothes' smell of lye soap and sunshine.

Placing the handkerchief across his mouth, his thumb resting on his nose, he cried hard. "Damn, old man, I'll miss you," he muttered into the wet cloth.

Mama Bear's death three years before had left John L. lost. He moved through life, but his love of it had died with his bent, withered Cherokee maiden. He occupied space but was hollow. Lou and Solon worried mightily at first, but as time passed they accepted his loneliness as his to have. The twins could enliven him from time to time and he'd come back to life, but not to stay.

When word got out of the ancient's death, the neighbors had brought enough food to feed five times the number of folk who called—and there were lots of folks. Lou and Nancy busied themselves with sending callers home with ample amounts of the bounty evoked by death. There was plenty left, though, and Lou said, "Mama, the pigs need it. I know it's a waste, I guess, but my we can't store it, and the flies already are aggravating enough." She paused with that decision made. "See if the boys are out of their good clothes, would you?" she asked of her mother.

"Yes, Sister," answered Nancy, and she wiped her hands on her apron and went out into the hall in her search for Jim and Joe. She found them on the edge of the yard under the big pecan's shade with their father. Solon and Jim were in the wicker bench Lou had put out for them to take the evening breezes. Joe was up two branches of the tree. Jim sat beside his father, head down, hands in his lap. Nancy paused for a minute at the porch edge, taking in the scene.

"Boys, get in here and change your clothes, goodness!" she called across the yard. Joe with agility descended his perch, and Jim leaned over to his father. Solon's right arm came down from the bench back and he held Jim for a moment.

"Go on James, Miss Nancy and your mother …" His swollen face and red eyes looked up at his father as if life had no hope. Solon smiled slightly, "James, it will be all right. Your Grand John L. is with Mama Bear and God. They'll always be with us too, here." He gently patted his chest, then his son's.

"Yes, Daddy, I know," Jim answered, but not as if it were true. Solon held him then in both arms.

"Come on Jim," Joe, standing beside the bench, said quietly and with encouragement. Jim pulled away from Solon, and the two boys walked slowly up towards their grandmother.

At the family's Thanksgiving dinner, Joe T. and Mary made an announcement. J.N. had invited, urged them, to come live with him. His wagon shop had prospered enough in his first ten years for him to find a wife—and two years ago a house. Joe T. had been getting feebler than his age should have made him, and Mary was hard pressed to care for and to watch him. "Senile," Grand John T. had called him a year ago during one of his rare feisty episodes. That was too harsh. Joe T. was just tired and soul-scared.

J.N.'s wife, Elizabeth, had lost her father, Rufus Sherrill, when he was killed at Stone's River with Cheatham's division, the 8th Tennessee Infantry. Her mother died in 1879 when she was seventeen. She had no other close family. Her great uncle, Mr. D. C. Sherrill at Sherrill-Stone's, had seen to it that she'd gotten to attend and graduate from Martin College in Pulaski, Class of '80. Coming to Fayetteville school that fall, she'd taught primary school for a while. J.N. saw her walking to and from school and took a fancy to her. She was a tall, thin, auburn-haired girl with a sharp tongue. He courted hard and she relented. Solon married them in the spring of '82 at the same spot in the Stevenson's yard where Lou and Solon had taken their vows. Dr. Stone had told them after three years of trying that they'd not have any children. J.N. had survived mumps that first year back from New Orleans. Dr. Stone said that was probably the reason.

"I want a family, J.N.," Elizabeth had said out loud to her husband one morning when she served him his breakfast. J.N.'s pride and hurt would not allow him to respond to her intense declaration. "I lost Father and then Mother, been without a family of my own until you," she pressed her case and offered J.N. a surprise. "Let's get Mr. Joe and Miss Mary to live with us. I like them both very much. They've been good to me. I put up with rowdy younguns all day. Be nice to have grown-ups around our house," she said as she took her place at their table.

J.N., whose eyes had been locked on his cooling eggs and ham, cowered. He kept his silence for a few moments before responding to his wife's appeal. Elizabeth's eyes were fixed on top of J.N.'s head.

"Our house is big enough for four," he thought. "Mama could help with the house. Daddy could go to the shop with me. I need to be with him more. He could help, too." But what sealed his acceptance and approval was his wife's explanation of wanting a family. He was her family, and it was right and proper that his family be her family.

"Miss Eliza, that is one fine idea. Yes, madam, a splendid idea." He rose, moved to behind her chair, and wrapped his arms around her. She turned her reddish-brown head back and they gave one another an upside-down kiss.

"J.N. Mayberry and Company," South Franklin Avenue, Fayetteville, Tennessee, became a place for Joe T. to piddle, help his son some, and keep up with the happenings close and far. Joe T. sauntered down to Mr. N. O. Wallace, Jr. at the *Observer* office every few days to read the numerous big city papers that the newspaper received every day. Then, in decent weather, he'd go to the courthouse lawn "liar's bench," whittle with the other codgers, and settle the county and world affairs.

Back in Dellrose, Lou, the twins, and Grandmother Nancy carried on in an emptier house. Nancy gradually took on her mother's role in the family. The twins teased her and she cherished them in silent strength. Lou, after a while, allowed her, in mind and heart, to become the family's "Beloved Woman." Solon liked her more and more. Out of Mama Bear's shadow, Lonesome Cedar assumed her place as the matriarch of the family. He appreciated her quiet, intense ways. Seemed she was at other places in her mind often, yet that only intrigued her son-in-law. When she was drawn out by Solon's questions and conversations, her take on things was most interesting to him: detached, honest, wise.

Changes had occurred. There were fewer chairs at the Stevenson table, fewer voices in the house, but life held its gifts: two emerging young men and Solon's satisfaction with his work on the road and refreshing time at home. Alex and Lou carried on with the farm. Nancy tended the house and garden. When help was needed, a black family down the hill was hired. Life was devoid of drama. That was quite all right with most all of them, except the twins.

"Sir, are you certain? That's too far to jump, sir!" Captain W. G. Spencer, U.S. Army Corps of Engineers, challenged the small, fifty-ish man wearing a white cotton linen suit, white string tie, big Panama hat, and old beat-up cavalry boots. The host and guide ignored the career Army builder, braced himself, and jumped the distance of at least four feet to the riverbank. In a run, he tried to hop up on the debris-covered, reddish-brown slug. His left foot stuck, and he struggled forward up the bank. His boots and hat stayed on.

"The rope, Captain!" called Congressman Joseph Wheeler to his boating companion, bobbing in the Tennessee River, as he turned back toward the river.

The master of Pond Spring—planter, lawyer, and businessman— was serving his third term as representative of north Alabama's Eighth District in the US Congress. After a winter of convincing, the secretary of war, William C. Endicott, had sent the engineer home with the congressman in early August after the recess of the first session of the forty-ninth Congress. Three weeks later, after countless hours on horseback up and down the stretch of Tennessee River from Whitesburg up river just south of Huntsville to down river, or upriver again, west of the shoals at Tuscumbia, the two had taken measurements, made observation notes, and drawn sketches of the ornery heartland waterway.

Every generation since white habitation of the Tennessee Valley, dreamers have shaken their heads and said, "This big stream has got to be improved for navigation. Look at New Orleans, Memphis, and St. Louis on the Mississippi and Louisville, Cincinnati and Pittsburgh on the Ohio. Even Nashville on the unambitious Cumberland has prospered because of a useable river."

Joseph Wheeler was the latest to lament the wide, unruly river that split his property. The wild river brought annual spring floods and frustration along its banks. The whirling, churning low shoals at Florence, Alabama blocked the easy navigation of the fickle river that stretched from the creeks of the Appalachian Mountains in Virginia, making a wide arch southeast to Tuscumbia, then back northwest to

Paducah, Kentucky and the Ohio River. The Tennessee was one of Mother Nature's truly uncontrolled children. The number who had dreamed of civilizing her was legion. The cavalryman turned politician and planter had the fever.

With Grover Cleveland in the White House, the first Democrat in the White House since befuddled James Buchanan (1857-61) and five Republican chief executives, the Southern Democrats had someone to listen to them, seriously, at the head of the executive branch of government. Presidential influence, patronage, even with the recent civil service reform, was still important.

Cleveland had two former Rebels in his cabinet—Mississippi's Lucius Q. C. Lamar as interior secretary and Attorney General August H. Garland of Arkansas. Lamar had borne arms while Garland had served in both houses of the Confederate Congress. A Democratic president and House of Representatives was new and significant for the "Solid (Democratic) South." A Southern leader, more interested in the horizon than the road traveled, carried weight in Washington. Congressman Wheeler was on a political vidette.

"Captain, I've waded, swum, and ridden dozens of different mounts across this big creek and sure don't mind getting my boots wet," Wheeler said with a smile as they negotiated their way through a tangled thicket away from the boat.

Near Rogersville on Second Creek, the two walked through a river bottom towards the little town. They'd secured the rowboat for the night, tethered to a root-washed old snarled willow.

"Father, Captain!" Annie called as they walked into the village. She was in the phaeton beside Homer, the family's driver. The team was hitched in front of the post office at the designated meeting place. "Where have you all been? We've been here for hours," she chided, though it had been only a half-hour wait. She knew her father well. He'd invariably get involved and forget the time. Older sister, twenty-year-old Lucy, and youngest daughter, Carrie Peyton, just nine on August 8, came out of the store next to the post office just as the water-splashed, muddy duo neared Annie, Homer, and the wagon.

"Goodness, Annie, they swim from the river?" Lucy said with a false concern on her face. She and Annie both laughed after a perfectly timed pause.

Carrie smiled briefly, then realized the joke. "Don't make fun, sister," she said as she ran to hug her father. Homer smiled as he stared at the matched bays' rumps.

"I was just telling the captain here that it was not far from here in October '63 that the boys and I crossed just ahead of some blue-clad pursuers. Come to mention it, they wore uniforms the very color of our gallant Yankee here," Wheeler said and then offered a whimsical smile through his long gray beard.

"Yes, Poppa, that was when you met Mother, right?" Carrie said with warmth. She possessed the adoration that most younger children hold for older fathers. "Poppa" returned the regard.

"Rightly so dear," her father answered, releasing their embrace. He took her hand, and the two walked smiling to the carriage, father with muddy trousers and boots, daughter with muddy dress.

Chapter 26

Through High Places and Valleys

S olon received an invitation to help break ground for the new Cincinnati church building just after the election. Lou and the boys went with him for the week's adventure during the third week of December 1896. It was a good chance for them to help get over Bryan's defeat by McKinley.

Cincinnati was a strange and wonderful fairyland for the boys and quite a spectacle for Lou. Nashville was fine, but Cincinnati had a feel—old, European, settled, and bustling. It was magnificent. Large ornate buildings, some eight, ten stories high, the majestic Roblein Bridge connecting Cincinnati with Covington, Kentucky, the new exotic Moorish Wise Temple and the beautiful fountain, all nestled along the dark, brown, swift Ohio River with an expansive ridge as the backdrop from east to west. The local boosters said it was like the seven hills of ancient Rome. The sounds were fun to hear and confusing to understand—languages, machinery, trains, steamboats, wagoneers, peddlers, street musicians, and more. There was even a funny dressed foreigner entertaining outside the hotel. "Gypsy," Jim thought, "with a trained monkey and trick dog." The monkey was named "Georgie" and the dog "Dickie."

Taking a nice sixth floor room facing the river at the magnificent Netherland Hotel with its grand lobby mirrors, the Stevensons of Tennessee were captured by the busy, smelly, noisy, and colorful "Queen City of the West." Sounds, sights, and the smells of cooking hops, stockyards, the river, manure, bakeries, eateries, meat plants, rot, spoilage, and coal fires all blended in the cold December air to wash over and invade them.

The steamboat traffic, freight and passenger, carried no end of fascination for the twins and Lou. The boys and Lou watched the activities from their room and then ventured to the muddy, fishy-smelling riverfront to explore the steamboats that had pulled in. New foods were discovered in the wonderful German eateries that dotted the area. The boys loved the strudel, and Lou favored the dark, bittersweet, and seedy rye bread, fresh baked, with real butter. She even sipped a bit of Solon's favorite beer, Hedepol, touted as Cincinnati's finest German lager brew out of many. Baseball season was just past, but the boys found Redlegs Park and imagined playing in a real game there. They kidded about how good they'd do. Finally Jim said, "Well, Joe, maybe we can see a game, anyway."

"Someday, yes, someday we'll see Cincinnati whipping Anson's Chicago 'Orphans,'" Joe responded.

"Love saved humanity—men, women and children. Love saved you and me," Solon intoned to the just over one hundred adults and some three-dozen children standing on the dried grass of a building site on Plum Street, Cincinnati, Ohio. It was a bright winter Sunday morning. It was cold, but the sun shined brilliantly. The cooking of Sunday meals from the neighborhood provided a fragrant atmosphere for the proceedings. Dr. Ulysses S. Milburn presided over the groundbreaking. Dr. Isaac Morgan Atwood of Crane Theological School at Tufts University, Boston, gave the key address.

Solon had been asked to read scripture and offer a prayer. Standing behind the lectern, which was sitting on a dark red rug on the smooth fresh soil, he read from Romans:

Who shall separate us from the love of Christ? Shall tribulation, or distress, or persecution, or famine, or nakedness, or peril, or sword?

As it is written, "For thy sake we killed all the day long; we are accounted as sheep for the slaughter."

Nay, in all things we are more than conquerors, through him that loved us.

For I am persuaded that neither death, nor life, nor angels, nor principalities, nor powers, nor things present nor things to come.

Nor height, nor depth, nor any other creature, shall be able to separate us from the love of God, which is in Christ Jesus our Lord.

Solon looked out on the faces of the people as he ended the holy words. Some were prosperous looking, well fed and well dressed. Others appeared less so—plain suits and dresses. All had their best on for the event, and the children were well scrubbed and rosy-cheeked. They smiled in affirmation of his choice of words, the foundation of their Universalist faith.

He said, after a moment of surveying the outdoor congregation, "Let us pray. Mother and father God into thy grace we have been called. May our efforts in sharing your gospel of love be untiring and our mission blessed. Guide us by thy spirit in reforming the nation and ministering through you, thy abundant, saving grace. Amen." Retrieving his old beaten Bible, he took one of the several chairs that held the officiants.

Lou's attention had been lovingly fixed on her husband of twenty-five years. She thought how she had not really seen her husband in the pulpit that often during all that time. His preaching was across several states and not too often at home. He quoted Jesus about "a prophet in his own home" when they had talked about that. She had responsibilities on the farm, and he had carried out his work away from home, alone. Solon was not truly handsome, rather more intense, dignified, with an expressive, full face that was quick to smile as well as frown. His dark hair had grayed and thinned. The moustache, which had been on his face for over forty years, was full and around the corners of his mouth; it was near silver-white. His carriage was comfortably erect, and his good suit fit him well. Joe had taken over dressing him, or at least getting his clothes to fit better since he'd started selling fine men's clothing. Solon protected his old-fashioned, boiled, banded white shirts from Joe's fashion influence.

The father told the son it was right for his calling, his business. Solon was a man—an image—in black, white, and silver gray. Lou realized after his brief part of the service how he fit his life and how life fit him. She had not thought of that before, and it made her feel good. She always knew she loved him, but now she realized how profoundly she admired him.

On the L & N southbound, while rumbling between Louisville and Elizabethton, Kentucky, the boys asleep on each side of a snoring, sleeping Solon, Lou, sitting across the seat, saw a picture that caused her eyes to moisten and her throat to tighten. She smiled through the tears out the train window toward the luminous full moon and said to herself, "Nothing can separate …" She noted Joe's swarthy flesh tone and Joe's paleness in the light through the window as they traveled southward. The faithful full moon provided illumination along the darkened countryside until it was joined by the morning star as the train rolled slowly to stop in Pulaski. Home was thirty miles away, and Alex was waiting in the new Sunday carriage.

"Come on Joe, slow down, will ya?" Jim wheezed as the sixteen-year-old dropped, coughing violently on the limestone wall along side the road. He was extremely red-faced and gasping for breath when his twin brother retraced the twenty feet between them. Joe was filled with zest, and Jim was well on his way to being a very sick teen who may or may not see adulthood. Dr. Stone had delivered the judgment in the winter: consumption. Solon and Lou knew there was little that could be done, but they determined to do what they could. They could send him to Murfreesboro to the sanatorium, but he'd hate it there. Dr. Stone offered them his ideas on how to combat tuberculosis. Solon and Lou followed his guidance. Strict attention to sanitary conditions, good, abundant, thoroughly cooked food from the canned goods made by Nancy Bird in winter, and vegetables from the garden in summer. All cooking and drinking water was boiled, and there was to be cleaning and disinfecting of all things possible. The Stevenson family restructured their way of life. Nancy Bird occupied the position of primary care giver for her grandson, reading everything Dr. Stone could provide her on the disease and how to treat it. Aunt Mary was relief nurse. Alex assumed an enhanced status as uncle and companion. Jim's father, Solon, stayed home more, limiting his mission work to January through spring. Brother Joe, with gauze mask, read to him, and they discussed what was read and everything they could come up with was talked about. Lou operated even more as the no-nonsense chief of operations of household and livelihood. The big things were discussed with her husband, but she was the director in chief of family life. Everybody knew and accepted that. She had earned her status as "Beloved Woman."

Within six months the family had evolved into a well-run care facility as well as an operating farm. Jim's condition stabilized, and the nursing system was perfected. He lost more weight and coughed too often, yet the rhythms of living he and his family had developed proved adequate, if not a curing treatment. Joe and Uncle Alex's roles were critical to Jim's mental and spiritual health as surely as the women folks' efforts were vital to his physical condition. Solon and Lou talked every night about his day's activities, attitudes, and accomplishments. They both were cheered by the love and attention Alex gave Jim, and by Joe's faithful brotherliness to his younger twin brother.

"Play them again, Uncle A. 'The General' and 'To the Standard,'" Jim pleaded with his forty-seven-year-old bachelor uncle. His nephew, twin son of his twin sister, looked thirteen, not his true seventeen. Pale and fair, his resemblance to Alex was as pronounced as Joe's was to his mother. Jim had always adored his Uncle Alex, and in his illness and confinement the two had become close. They were as mentor and apprentice to one another. Alex kept him still and fascinated with stories of Lou, Solon, and his Civil War adventures. He did not sanitize the dirt and gore, and Jim loved the whole story, asking questions on the details. He got his uncle to play for him the standard cavalry calls of the Army of Tennessee. Uncle Alex said there were nearly thirty different calls in the US Cavalry Bugle Manual of 1841, but only six or eight were used in battle: "Forward," "Halt,"

"To the Left," "To the Right," "About," "Rally on the Chief," "Trot," "Gallop," "Commence Firing," and "Disperse."

"Joe, the noise in skirmishes is awful: shot, shouting, horses making a ruckus, screaming wounded and dying, clashes of metal, and troops and mounts—well, just all sorts of noisy commotion. Horse soldiers can't hear shouted orders clearly twenty feet away, much less one hundred yards or more. The bugle becomes the officers' clear voice, carrying his orders clear and loud about the den of hell. A well-commanded cavalry troop is something to behold, and the bugle gives them the what and when for their actions."

Alex's old bull bugle horn was well worn but had a sound that carried mighty well, piercing Jim's bedroom walls. Folks at the barn or nearby fields could hear it. Jim would watch out his window towards the stock lot as Uncle Alex "ordered" the farm's trained older mules and horses to several actions. It was always amazing to Jim how the younger lots of untrained animals followed the lead of the older seasoned ones in reacting to the bugle calls. It was like "follow the leader" that the twins had played as small children.

In October, Jim had gotten a Sears and Roebuck catalog in secret. Using some money his grandmother had loaned him, he ordered his brother Joe a beautiful brass "regulation" cavalry bugle, according to the sales pitch in the catalog. Jim was scared that it would not arrive in time for Christmas. It came only three days before the day.

On Christmas morning, Jim said to Joe when he opened the present, "Jim, you're going to learn to play it for me, OK? Uncle A. said he'd teach you. It ain't that hard."

Jim didn't add that his wounded lungs couldn't conquer the instrument's requirements. Joe knew, though, and seemed delighted by the gift and Jim's plans for him. By July 4, Joe was able to give the family a feeble bugle concert. Jim beamed with joy, his ashen face becoming nearly a healthy pink. Joe was accomplished by the following Christmas.

Uncle Alex was surprised by his teaching success and Joe's abilities. His eyes twinkled as he allowed, "Well Joe, it ain't as sweet as my bugle horn, but it's mighty sweet. Your daddy and the general would have kept you busy like they did me." He smiled wide, "Yes, mighty fine."

Thin, ashen, and severely weakened after nearly two years of struggle, Jim's body became an inadequate vessel for his spirit. Hemorrhaging in early March, he fought gallantly for breath and life. He did not win. He was unconscious in a blood-soaked bed when Dr. Stone arrived in the middle of the night. Joe had ridden like a pony express rider the three miles to Dellrose and fetched him.

"Folks, you've done mighty good by that boy," the doctor said, standing in the hall outside Jim's room with Solon and Lou after seeing Jim and giving him laudanum. Nancy Bird and Joe were inside tending the stricken nineteen-year-old as he slept.

All the family, tears running down their faces, stood around the bed. Dr. Stone listened for Jim's breath and heartbeat with his ear on the covered bloody nightshirt. He heard no sound. The sun rose and struck the wall through the bedroom's door as the doctor looked up to Lou. No words were necessary. They all saw his look and knew.

"Through the valley of the shadow …" Solon said to himself, his heart bleeding into his soul.

After the burying at Bee Springs, five miles west of the place, the family came home. It was a cold March day. After changing funeral clothes for her work clothes, Lou came into the kitchen where Solon, Dr. Burrus, and Brother Cortner sat in quiet conversation. Dr. Burrus had responded to Solon's wire and come from Camp Springs, Alabama, to conduct the funeral along with Brother Cortner, the Methodist preacher at Dellrose.

Nancy Bird busied herself with kitchen doings, and Alex greeted neighbors in the front yard while Joe carried into the dining room the gifts of food brought in accordance with timeless custom. Alex was gatekeeper, so only family and preachers were inside the house.

"You all be still. I'm going to check on that new jack colt," Lou told them as she came into the kitchen in her work clothes and went directly to the back porch. She didn't go to the barn, instead she walked to the edge of the woods out to the west side of the house, some fifty yards, crossing the rock wall that bordered the house's yard. In a grouping of cedars, she found a three-foot high limestone outcropping and sat down.

After gazing back at her house, stock barn, shed, wash house, smoke house, fields, and garden patch, she looked up at the slate blue sky, seeking to find a cloud. There was the shadow of one down toward the river stretching north to over where she had left her Jim:

the Bee Springs Church and graveyard. Taking off her hat and placing it on the ground at her side, she placed both hands on her face and sobbed. At first it was controlled, but then she gave out deep gut-wrenching crying. It took a few minutes for her to get the terrible grief under control. As she stood, she wiped her face with a big blue and white bandana. Then she leaned over, grabbed her hat, and put it on. Turning to the gray, ageless, moss-stained stone she said, "I share my pain with you old one, I can't carry it all." She turned and went back to the living.

Solon had wrapped up good and gone and sat on the front porch steps. He looked out across the yard down the brown gravel drive lined with hickory, oak, and chestnut trees. He thought, "Even the place grieves." Then his thoughts returned to the wake in the big room of his house the night before. Solon had stood before the polished, finely finished cherry casket. Placing his hand on the smooth cool lid, he surprised himself with the thought that came into his mind: "My goodness, Joe, and Alex did a fine piece of work on this." He chastised his inner self for that thought. It was as if he couldn't let into his heart the meaning of the occasion. He knew lots of folks buried their children, but he was not finding anything like acceptance. His spirit felt as if it was horsewhipped, and his sixty-five-year-old body ached from head to heel. "I'll get through this," he told himself, "but it'll take a lot of doing." Then he remembered more about standing numb at the bier. Joseph Wheeler Stevenson, his surviving son, had come up to him, discretely taken his hand without shame, and then stood silently with him at the beautiful/ugly casket of his brother for nearly half an hour.

Chapter 27

Unorthodoxy in the Piney Woods

Brother Stevenson, the postmaster brought this letter for you a few days ago," Miss Worth said as Solon walked into her boarding house just south of the New Orleans and Northeastern Depot (N.O. & N. E.) in muddy Laurel, Mississippi.

"Miss Mary, much obliged," he acknowledged as he began to move to her desk in the wide hall of the ten-room boarding house. But first he cleaned his boots vigorously on the front door floor mat. Not satisfied with the job, he said, "Excuse me ma'am," and went back out on the wide porch and used the boot scraper and his pocketknife to rid his worn boots of Piney Woods winter clay. With the job completed to his satisfaction, he returned inside. Smiling as he removed his hat for the second time, he took the letter from the prim, properly attired woman in her mid sixties. She was a contemporary of his, it would seem. Solon had been impressed by his hostess when he'd come into town over three weeks ago.

Several of the folks he had come to see in Jones County had met him in Laurel when he arrived. He'd made arrangements with Miss Mary then and was assured of a room after his time around the county. Several unorthodox religious folk—isolated Universalists—and he had worked up a preaching schedule for his time in the area in hopes of starting a church. Shed Sholers and Andrew Herrington down Ellisville way had been in touch with Dr. Burrus and Solon about getting a "no-hell" preacher to bring the faith of a "larger hope" to Jones County. The *Herald* editor, Dr. Burrus, had given Solon the names of five subscribers with Jones County addresses, and Solon had kept up correspondence with three families he'd met when he passed that way before. Solon was out of Laurel on a rented mount within three hours of his arrival in Laurel. Shed, Andrew, and Solon rode to visit those folk and arrange for some meetings at Pleasant Ridge, Ovett, Curtis, and Ellisville.

Miss Mary communicated a sincerity and interest in the person she was talking with, whether rough millwright, would-be sophisticate, fast-talking drummer, or taciturn stranger. That genuineness was a rare gift Solon had learned to appreciate during his years of meeting and dealing with all sorts of folk. He liked this woman. She had style and grace.

"Beautiful Christmas tree, Miss Mary," Solon complimented his hostess as he began to walk with letter in hand to the small writing desk halfway down the hall.

"Thank you. Christmas is but five days away, and we must be festive, don't you know." Solon nodded in answer and salute. He looked at the letter curiously as he walked the fifteen feet to the mahogany desk. Lou would have wired if there was an emergency. He'd received a few letters from her over the years of his traveling. They were not numerous and usually were her musings or wonderings about the boys, stock, crops, and such.

Taking a deep, deep breath as he settled into the wonderful fitting chair, he sighed and let out an equally deep breath. The livery had not had much to choose from in riding horses. He'd chosen a big ten-year-old, gray white, wide-backed mare, "Ghost." Ghost was an easy ride, but he had traversed near two hundred miles all around the "Free State of Jones"—Jones County in south Mississippi. "Ghost would have been a fine mount if I were thirty," he thought. "But I'm not thirty. What is it now, sixty-five?" he added in reflection and wonderment.

He opened the letter from Lou.

December 15, 1897

Dearest Solon,

I write you with a heavy heart. There is nothing out of the ordinary here except my deep, deep hurt from our dear son's departing us. I know there is an All-Wise Dispensation, but how it hurts. I haven't really shown my deepest feelings. That is not me, but this is the hardest work I've ever done, husband. I fully know how you have been hurt by Jim's death and I know it has been long enough that I should be worried about those new foals due in spring and getting Joe ready to go away to college in September. I have plenty of time for that, I know, but it is so dif-

ficult for me not to dwell on his brother. That day we named them …

I had to go for a walk in the cold air across the ridge towards the river for a while. This is written Sunday night. I started this letter Saturday afternoon and thought about throwing it in the fire but didn't.

Solon stared at, without seeing, the needlepoint magnolia in a large black enamel frame on the wall above the desk.

Lou had never really been this expressive, and her husband's eyes teared as his grief was rekindled by her voiced pain. He swallowed several times, pulled his spectacles off, and wiped his eyes and face with his handkerchief. He then sat stark-still with his hand across his mouth in his "milking" gesture, as Lou called it. His face was hard, his teeth clenched, and his jaw locked. He held that position for many moments before shaking himself out of the hatred of a dark, mean place. He went there when he remembered when he had two living sons. He returned to Lou's letter half mad and half hurt with tears wetting his tired face.

I'm not pleased that I have not been able to move on as I should, dear husband, but I know I will. We will.

I've gotten Joe a beautiful new leather trunk ordered by Mr. Washburn with his initials stamped in gold above the lock. Are you sure about him going all the way to Ohio for school? I know Buchtel is your choice, but what about Sawanee? Kirby-Smith heads it and General Polk—I mean Bishop Polk—founded it before the war. The "University of the South" is such a grand name, too. It's less than a hundred miles, and Akron is over eight hundred!

Solon was pleased that Lou's writing about Jim had relieved some of her hurt, and that she was now reckoning with Joe's future.

Yes, I know of Buchtel's Universalist connection and your Cincinnati fellow being there. That is important, I know. We will go see him during the school year, though. We will, you understand!

Travel safe, dear one. See you the 23rd.

My heart,
Lou

Solon's tears were gone. He was just anxious to get home, but his train north wasn't until 7 p.m., nearly three hours away.

He was hungry. The Herringtons, down towards Ellisville, had fed him breakfast before daybreak, but he'd missed dinner, lost in the Piney Woods after forgetting the directions given him. It was overcast, and he had a hard time reckoning the winter sun in the tall, tall pines. Some were upwards of a 125 feet tall. The virgin yellow pine was thick at the tops, but there was lots of clearing in the shade of the great trees. Daydreaming as Ghost walked, Solon had missed the marked tree for the turn at a crossroads called Buttermilk Crossing. He had noticed this daydreaming happened every once in awhile nowadays. It bothered him some, but as he'd gotten absent-minded he'd also acquired a sense of less urgency.

"Hungry," he thought as he rose and turned towards Miss Mary.

"Excuse me, ma'am. Reckon there's somewhere I can get some vittles?" he asked.

"Why, our Miss Peggy down the block across from the depot and up the hill a bit has wonderful meals. With all the busyness around the mill these last few months, the workers come all hours it seems. She'll be happy to accommodate you."

"Much obliged, ma'am! You say up west from the depot?"

"Oh, Brother Stevenson, you'll smell the cooking before you get there. Just follow your nose," she smiled, not like someone who'd tried to be funny, but rather as someone who was being quite reasonable and accurate.

He found the place by the good smell, just as she had said. It was just past the corner where the old deer stand once stood, as he learned later from Miss Peggy.

"Come in, hon, come right in," the stout redhead said as Solon opened the door to the good-sized board and batten building with a wide front porch. Gilded gold letters on the plate glass front window read, "Laurel Canteen." Solon was a bit startled by the familiar greeting. The fortyish woman's smile and sparkling green eyes quickly assured him that he was merely one of the many "hons" that frequented Miss Peggy's eatery.

Three men in deep conversation stood up from a table covered with a white tablecloth. They moved towards Solon.

"Well done, Miss Peggy, as always," the taller one said as they took their hats from the hat rack by the door. The shortest one said matter-of-factly to Solon, "I recommend the potato soup. Fit for Queen Victoria's table. Yes sir, try the soup."

Miss Peggy's face turned nearly as red as her hair. "Mr. Silas, you do go on. Now you all get back to work," she responded. "Nice having customers with money to spread around this place. I had four new mechanics for Eastman-Gardiner from Milwaukee in just yesterday."

"Yes ma'am, George here says we're nearly back to full operation," Silas Gardiner said.

George S. Gardiner joined in the exchange. "Yes, Miss Peggy, we are doing just fine. Most all the men are all back to work and we're recruiting up in Iowa and even out in Washington as well as elsewhere. Silas here has been on the road most of the fall with father talking to potential workers one day and investors the next," George S. Gardiner said as he led the three towards the door. He patted his brother's back and gave him a brother's teasing smile. Lauren Eastmen, the third, silent diner, laughed out loud at the pair's interaction.

"Fine gentlemen, those three," Miss Peggy said as she motioned Solon to a table along the wall. As she walked by the vacated table of the three who had just left, she picked up a neat stack of two-bit pieces.

"Here we are, hon, will this suit?" the gregarious hostess said as she paused at a small two-person table neatly laid out with good dishes and utensils on a gingham tablecloth. "Coffee, then?" she asked.

"Yes ma'am, coffee is fine," Solon answered.

"The first earnings from their mill went to the mayor and city for a new schoolhouse. It was $600." Peggy was regaling Solon about the good civil standing of the Gardiner brothers as he finished his meal.

Solon had ordered the soup and enjoyed it mightily. After two more helpings and more coffee, he sat satisfied and warm. His hostess had given him a bit of local history each time she brought Solon more soup and coffee.

Originally from Clinton, Iowa, two brothers, George S. and Silas W. Gardiner, and their brother-in-law, Lauren C. Eastman, established Eastman-Gardiner and Company in 1891. Lauren, the vice-president, worked back in Clinton and throughout the Midwest and Northeast to secure financing. He also made contacts for sale of the long-leaf yellow pine lumber. Silas was treasurer. George, the president, was in charge of the operators, supervising the set up and production of a huge modern lumber mill business that would produce 300,000 board feet of lumber a day. They'd recruited a whole crew of millwrights from other timber areas of the country to execute the plans for the mill. Folks from all over south and central Mississippi, west Florida, and southwest Alabama had also been attracted by the mill jobs.

Then the depression of 1893 had hit hard. The United States economy faltered, sputtered, and nearly died. Hundreds of banks and businesses closed, and thousands of workers were without jobs. This was the United States' hardest economic depression since Van Buren's administration in 1837. Eastman-Gardiner and Company, a huge new lumber mill operation in Laurel, Mississippi, felt the effects of a very sick economy. After only two years the company faced extinction and hundreds of workers on the rails and back trails were abandoning the Piney Woods.

Silas Gardiner and Lauren Eastman went out and beat the bushes for financial resources. At the mill, George S. Gardiner called a meeting of the company's millwrights and mill hands. He told them the situation. It was bad, real bad, but he said the company was sticking if the workers would stick. He offered enough pay to cover the essential living expenses for all who would continue to work. He told them that the new storage facilities were finished, and the lumber could be stored until times got better. The paymaster would keep a record of all wages due, to be payable when business got better. A raise would be forthcoming then. Only a few turned down this act of faith. For seven months everyone involved in the company lived close to the bone, hoping sales would revive and good times would come around again. Gradually, they did come.

Workers were urged to use their withheld earnings to build homes. They did. Lauren C. Eastman laid out the expansion of the city of Laurel.

Within twenty years Laurel milled and shipped more long-leaf yellow pine lumber than anywhere else in the world. The Piney Woods was the third largest supplier of superior pine lumber for buildings on Broadway, America's Main Streets, country lanes, and foreign climes for nearly half a century.

Borderland Scotch-Irish immigrants from Georgia, Alabama, Tennessee, and places unknown settled in the southeast section of Mississippi by the early nineteenth century. The land was heavily timbered with great stands of virgin yellow pine. Oak, willows, cypress, bay, gum, and other tree varieties were present in the low valley areas, but on the high ground the pines occupied hundreds of thousands of acres across the clay ridges. All were drained by the Pascagoula, Chickasawhay, and Leaf Rivers watersheds. The land under and between the great forests was sandy, swampy, and poor for farming. Tangled into impenetrable masses of laurel, scuppernong, and honeysuckle vines there was poison ivy and snakes. The people struggled along on small homesteads growing a little cotton, hunting, growing simple food crops, and extracting turpentine for the naval stores markets at the ports of Mobile, Biloxi, and New Orleans. When the Choctaw land, located just north—two-thirds of the land within the states' boundaries—was opened in the late 1830s, the area's small population became even smaller and really didn't grow again until Reconstruction, years after the Civil War.

In the Piney Woods, panthers, wild hogs, and bears menaced the scrubby, mongrel-bred cattle, chickens, goats, oxen, mules, and horses that helped the settlers wrestle out a meager living around the swampy areas under the shade and in the shadows of the great woods. Called "smutty skins" from constantly cooking over open fires kindled with smoky pine knots and cones, the pioneers of Jones County were survivors. These folks, a long way from anywhere, had nothing in common with the plantations and aristocratic power structure hundreds of miles away in all directions.

Black Americans, slave or free, were few in number. Those few who were in the Piney Woods lived much like their neighbors—hard and isolated.

These borderland folk, black and white visionaries, Midwestern timbermen, and a stray Choctaw or two, would change the culture and economic status of a seven-county area within two decades. The area emerged from backwoods frontier to an example of New South prosperity, possessing homes, schools, churches, civic institutions, hotels, hospitals, and transportation. Laurel, Mississippi, in the "Free State of Jones," was a generator of that transformation. The Northern capitalists came after the railroads opened southeast Mississippi's virgin forests to vast commercial potential. The Gardiners, Eastmans, and Rogers (cousins of the two families), founders of Laurel's greatest commercial enterprise, different from other investors, planted roots and helped lead a progressive community. They paid African-American employees a higher wage than possible elsewhere in the South and established good schools that made it possible for black citizens to create one of the first African-American middle class communities in the South. This was in a time of reactionary, Bourbon rule in Mississippi, with an atmosphere made toxic by rabid racists such as the Vardemans and Bilbos.

"So those folks, those 'Universalists' treated you OK, hon?" Miss Peggy had taken a nearby table and she talked while Solon listened, sipping his coffee and overcoming a big piece of chocolate cake.

"Yes, ma'am, they surely did," Solon answered.

"Sure is amazing to find folks who, well, let's just say see things contrary to the way most folks do," Solon confessed as he put his fork down.

"Oh, it ain't that amazing, Brother Stevenson, not the way I see it. Lots of folks don't always see things the same, no matter where you're from or where you're at. Mr. Orange came to my place one day and showed me that church paper," the cheery eatery owner-operator allowed.

"I liked what he said and read to me. You take my neighbor out near my sister in Soso—Mr. Frank, Mr. Frank Mauldin. He's ..." she paused to make sure her place was empty. It was and had been for quite a while. "Well, he's near a socialist! Backed General Weaver in '92. Told anybody that would listen about those, d-a-m plutocrats robbing and oppressing most everybody." She stopped talking and smiled, waiting for her diner's response.

"Well, well," was all Solon could muster.

"Yes, sir, voted Populist in '92 and been rabble-rousing for socialism ever since. You know what that is?"

"Yes, I do, ma'am," Solon looked thoughtful, his mind thinking of Lou and his conversation not long back about the mess of robber baron government.

"Old man Owens down the way from him thinks he's titched," she said matter-of-factly.

"Well, well, does he?"

Solon slept most all the way home, waking only to change trains in Meridian and Birmingham.

In the middle of February 1898 a message boy with a telegram ran up the street beside Ervin's boarding house onto the front porch of C. D. Sherrill's. A passing farmer, Mr. Graham, went out to the boy. He read the telegram. Then he shouted several times.

"They Sunk the Maine! Spanish in Havana sunk the Maine!" Lou heard the racket and came to the door as the twelve-year-old black boy stood in the middle of the road, winded and holding his knees. Mr. Graham stood beside the boy, looking dumbstruck.

"They killed our sailors," he sputtered. Lou got to her buggy just as Joe jogged up from towards the billiard parlor.

"Mama, is it true?"

Joe had been set to begin at the University of the South in Sewanee come fall. He didn't. His education would be in a different setting from the beautiful campus fifty miles east.

Chapter 28

A Late Calling

"Solon, you're sixty-eight years old! I'll be danged if you'll go traipsing off to that god-forsaken place. Besides, it ain't nothing but another rich man's war. It's sugar this time. The 'power brokers' are at it again, lusting for more. Last time it was cotton and before that Indian land. Next it'll be something—what? Hell, maybe oil. How in tarnation can some folk throw away lives on such greedy foolishness? I'll never know!" Lou was as mad outwardly as she had been in a mighty long time. She got up her steam again. "You, Solon, have preached about the folly and madness of war since forever. This Spanish mess is surely folly. Mr. And Mrs. Bryan are active in the Anti-Imperialist League. They know. They know, Solon. Mark Twain has even spoken all over about the sham of our country becoming an empire. McKinley is making some headway with those Spaniards to make things right for the Cubans. No, no, Solon, please."

Solon sat in the swing hanging from the fifty-foot ash tree on the backside of their house. Lou was beside him. They had been taking in the April weather as the sun set over towards Bryson. When Solon told her of his intentions to go to Chickamauga to get the general to take him as a chaplain to Cuba, Lou had stomped both her feet down on the worn, grassless spot under the swing, bringing the gentle swinging and their pleasant time to a violent halt. Her eyes flashed on the side of his face. He looked forward, frozen with his mouth fixed and his eyes staring out across the barn to the pale orange and robin-shell blue sunset. He kept his silence for a few moments, allowing Lou's anger to hang in the gracious spring air. Energy spent is weakened energy, he knew.

"I suppose so Lou, but ... well, I'm going. You've read, like me, about those crimes that tyrant Weyler and his Spanish lords have visited on those poor people. Concentration camps, Lou ... whole towns, thousand of people rounded up and moved away to fenced in 'stock pens.' Lou, Jackson, Van Buren, and Scott did that to your Cherokees! Your "trash Southern aristocracy" did it to the coloreds! The Cubans been fighting for thirty years—all colors, all sorts—to rid themselves of the Dons. I showed you the newspaper articles. Now its time to do something. Yes, McKinley will have to do something, but it can only be by force.

"Lou, the general has been outspoken in his respect of that Jose Marti and his struggle down there. He was with him just a few weeks ago in New York." Solon's words had taken on an unhurried, reasoned, and steady tone. "The current *Universalist Leader* says it's our duty to liberate the Cubans from the atrocities of Spanish misrule." Lou's gaze stayed fixed, her defense was formidable. Solon continued after checking her eyes to see if there was an opening head on. There wasn't. He tried the flank.

"Lou, Mr. Bryan has just gotten an appointment as a colonel in the Nebraska regiment. He's the latest one who changed his mind, and Mark Twain now says we gotta help the Cubans and do something about the Spanish evil. He sees it different now after the Maine. Lou, there haven't been many revolutions lead by poets—this Marti is a poet, a writer. His ideals about the rights of humans and the acceptance of all sorts of people are something. Something new—all people in spite of color, station ... it's what I've been trying to get folks to understand and make happen. Don't you see Lou, he and his are trying to become ... become, well, free ... and together? Together." He let that word stand alone for a moment or two. He looked at Lou's dark, hard eyes and knew his efforts at turning Lou's offense had stalled. His eyes turned to the front and took in the darkening blue sky. Lou made no spoken response, but she saw his retreat. Solon's arguments had been repulsed.

Dread and fear weighed heavy on her spirit, but that only strengthened her position. She then turned to the front too, as if seeking to find help in the horizon for her thoughts and actions, or to figure out his next move and be ready for it.

"Lou," Solon began again with a new tactic, "you and Alex had to come to find us and avenge your father and brother in '63. Remember? I understand that." He paused, organized his thoughts, and said, "I'd like you to understand something about me. When I was six, a bully twice my size, maybe twelve, took it on himself to trouble me, bully me. He jabbed my stomach and ... well, I spent half a Saturday morning in Fayetteville trying to avoid the hellion. I ducked into alleys, crossed the square, but he always showed back up. He pulled his mean stuff three times while I hung around the square waiting for my daddy, who was somewhere doing his business. Fourth time he started jabbing, I flew into him. I fought him like my life depended on it. It was the first time I unleashed the 'Wolf.' He hurt me mighty bad, tore my shirt, and I had a busted lip, but after our fight he ran off. I can't abide unseemly arrogant bullies, just can't. Might be why I was a fool and fought my heart out with the general. I felt like I was fighting those bullies coming into our homes." He paused, thinking about how that was a big part of the truth about that hell of four years. "I can't do no 'rassling or shooting anymore. Heck, sometimes it takes a second try to get my legs to go. I know I'm not a strapping eighteen-year-old, but I'm a preacher, and those boys, well, I might be able to do some good for them while they take care of a real bad bully who is hurting people bad."

"Oh, Solon, no, no," Lou said, knowing her pleading was to little avail. Solon had blocked her, stopped her offense and turning the struggle.

"Remember that heathen smug fool chaplain in that barn, Lou, remember? He tried to bully you and me with his self-righteous arrogance and mean-spirited judgment. Remember, Lou?"

Chill bumps rose on Lou. Her heart did a pitty-pat, "Yes, dear, I remember." Her defenses crumbled. No one had won the argument, but she knew right then that she could only declare a truce.

"No, no, not both of you. I just won't have it!" Lou's anger had been provoked for the second time in two days. Joe announced at the Sunday dinner table his intention to join the army heading for Cuba.

"Mother, I'm nineteen years old. Nineteen, Mama! I can go without your permission. Daddy said I couldn't go too, but I'm going." Joe's resolve was sure, but his dread of his mother's displeasure and protest was substantial. Lou glared at him across the table, then at her husband at the other end of it. The others in the family kept their silence. Only Alex watched Lou's face.

"Joe Wheeler Stevenson, you know what your granddaddy and grandmother would say? They tried to keep me and your Uncle Alex from that hell thirty-five years ago. Don't be a fool. War ain't a play time!" Lou's tears began rolling down her cheeks—big plentiful tears without voice.

The next morning after chores Lou saddled up a three-year-old big gray mule, "Moon." Pausing at her flower garden on the front edge of the front yard, she gathered purple iris, some hollyhock, and edge-trimmed marigolds. She rode over to Bee Springs Church. At Grand John L., Mama Bear, Nancy Bird, and Jim's resting places, each in turn, beginning with her boy, Lou touched her family's head stones. She placed a few of each of the colorful flowers on the ground at the base of the four granite monuments that recorded her loved ones.

"Folks," she said quietly aloud, looking first at the deep blue beautiful cloudless sky over the top of a grove of pecan trees and then to the four green grass covered mounds. "I need y'all's help. They're both going. Abide with them and bring them home to me." She wiped her nose with a bandana from her work coat pocket. Tears seeped from her sad, forlorn, and hollowed brown eyes.

On the way home, her spirit was chilled by fear and dread. She gradually became a bit resolved and knew what she had to endure. When she came to Bryson a whirl of brown activity caught the edge of her vision and she heard squawking and shrieking birds. Focusing toward a big live oak up the hillside, she witnessed a pair of mockingbird's fluttering, singing frantically, and swooping at a good-sized chicken hawk who was making a small circle above the tree. Lou pulled Moon to a stop and sat for a few minutes until the contest was settled. She saw two brave, undersized, and overmatched survivors keeping the much larger and dangerous flying predator from their tree.

"Yes, you two little ones don't know your not supposed to be able to do that, do you? No, you sure don't," she said quietly, watching the couple as they defended theirs with all their might. After a short fierce fight, the beaten, cowering hawk soared away, leaving with a pitiful squawk. Lou slapped Moon's reigns gently and rode on over the gentle ridge to home. Her tears stopped after about five miles when she turned up the drive to her place.

The three—parents and son—were at the Fayetteville depot at 7:30 a.m. two weeks later, waiting for the train to Dechard and then to Chattanooga. Alex had wanted desperately to go with Lou, but she talked him into staying and tending the place. He wasn't happy about his assignment but accepted Lou's entreaty and took them to the station. He got wet-eyed and left them after hugging each one.

He waited up the hill from the depot out of sight till the train pulled out. He made a slow carriage ride home to Dellrose.

They'd be there by a little after noon. Lou had packed some ham biscuits. Joe had his brass trumpet that Jim had given him the Christmas before he died in a small valise with a few underclothes and shaving items. Solon had his journal and old Bible in an old beat-up black satchel. His small suitcase was stowed above their seats. Lou had her handbag. Inside was a souvenir from her war.

It was an old knife. She hadn't looked at it in years. Kept in her cedar chest since the move from the Sequatchie, it had responded to the old concoction Mama Bear had told her about. The old wool rag made from one of Solon's worn out suits had burnished the silver till the heirloom had shined like a new silver dollar. Lou, at sunrise, had sat on her rock near the house in the cedar thicket with it after she was satisfied with its renewal. Tears rolled patiently down her face as she held it in her old soft clean handkerchief. The cool metal brought forth warmth in her heart.

"Honor," Fightin' Joe's daddy had told the Augusta watch shop owner to engrave on the going-away present. As she thought of that gifting nearly half a century past, her old grief was awakened. The hurt for her murdered daddy and big brother a lifetime ago was refreshed. She was surprised at herself when she found some sympathy for those unknown Yankees in that Georgia thicket. They were people, and unfortunately for them they just happened to have had to pay Life a debt that their kind had made to her kind.

The pocketknife was wrapped and lay in a new, once-washed, bright, ironed yellow bandana when Lou packed for their pilgrimage. When Custer had met the consequences of his foolhardy arrogance, the papers had gone on about the color yellow as a symbol of the cavalry. Lou's mind went quiet and joyful when she remembered Solon's old war worn kepi with badly faded yellow band in the bottom of their old oak wardrobe. She saw again in her memories the discolored yellow-green piping on the general's tunic that day so long ago along the Tennessee at Courtland.

Chapter 29

Getting to Another War

T he Stevensons missed the general by two days. He had been sent from Camp Thomas (Chickamauga Battlefield, ten miles south of Chattanooga, Tennessee) to Tampa, Florida. The newly commissioned major general of the United States Volunteers was on his way to Tampa to take over command of the 2,900-member cavalry division of the V Corps. They were destined for Cuba. Veteran cavalry units were in his new command. They came from cavalry stationed in posts, mostly in the West and Southwest. A third of his troopers were "Buffalo Soldiers" of the 9th and 10th cavalry. These Black troops were thought by the paper pushers in Washington to be better able to endure the death dealing summer heat of tropical Cuba. They weren't.

The most conspicuous of Wheeler's V Corps cavalry were the "Rough Riders," officially, the 1st Volunteer Cavalry. The recently resigned assistant secretary of the Navy, Theodore Roosevelt, the future president, was a published naval historian, former Dakota rancher, New York state senator, and commissioner of New York City police. He had raised the "Rough Riders" and pushed for their inclusion in the military. He shied from command of the unit because of his lack of military experience. Roosevelt's role in the approaching war was significant. His actions while his boss, Secretary of the Navy John Long was away from Washington, placed the US Navy warships in strategic positions in the Gulf of Mexico, Phillipines waters, and east Atlantic coastal shipping lanes. They were set for offensive action. The newly modernized US Navy, posed for hostilities with previously developed plans for their primary role in the conflict, was equal to or better than any seagoing fighting force in the world. If war came, it was intended to be a joint naval and army effort.

The sinking of the USS Maine, a battleship of the line, in Havana Bay, February 15, 1898, was the final straw of US and Spanish tension and struggle over the issue of Cuban independence. Off and on, rebellions by Cubans determined to rid Cuba of Spanish rule with the establishment of a free and independent nation had been going on since 1868. President William McKinley had resisted war cries for most of his administration. He had worked for a peaceful solution, with Spain giving Cuba greater independence. He'd made some progress. The sinking of the Maine had brought a demand for war from across the nation and halls of Congress. He listened to the voice of the people.

On April 19, Congress passed a joint resolution "... for the recognition of the independence of the people of Cuba ... direct the president of the United States to use the land and naval forces of the United States to carry these resolutions into effect."

The U.S. Army had counted 27,146 soldiers as of April 1, 1898. This tiny force was spread from the Atlantic to Pacific coasts. The Indian Wars were over. No large-scale war training had been undertaken in decades because of small numbers and the lack of any real need for such training given the mission of the Army. By August 1, 1898, the Army numbered 272,046: 56,012 regulars and 216,034 volunteers.

Congressman Joseph Wheeler, from Alabama's Eighth Congressional District, West Point graduate, class of 1859, six-year veteran of the United States Army (1854-1861), and four-year veteran of the Confederate States of America Army (1861-65), was one of the first to volunteer. He, Matthew C. Butler, and Fitzhugh Lee, all Confederate generals, were appointed major generals. The Civil War was more over now than anytime in the years since 1865. "Fightin' Joe" was critical to that reconciliation in his volunteering for US service.

"Sir, you can't go through," the sergeant of the guard informed Solon in a strong voice. "This is a military reservation, not a holiday lark. It might look like an amusement park, but it ain't! You people have no idea what's what." The lean, crisp, sunburned private said to the Stevensons in disgust.

"Soldier, I need to see General Wheeler. It's important." Solon tried to persuade the guard to relent and let him, Lou, and Joe in.

"Sorry, I have my orders, sir."

Solon, exasperated, looked away from the dutiful soldier's face. He gazed away from the sentry towards the tops of the huge palm trees that filled the sunny sky and puffed his breath out in frustration. He turned and looked at Lou. His eyes were filled with anger, but he was an old soldier and knew what the sergeant meant.

"A message then, son?" Lou said, joining in the impasse. She was standing a step back and left of Solon and Joe and stepped up to the sentry as she addressed him.

"Ma'am I can't be leaving my post to deliver civilian notes," the impatient career soldier informed the three. He didn't add that his volunteer army courier was off somewhere out of the heat. The situation was messed up enough.

"General Wheeler will want to see us, Sergeant," Lou tried again.

"General Wheeler? Did you say General Wheeler, madam?" came a clear, high voice from behind the three.

Lou turned toward the voice, her gaze followed by Joe and Solon's.

"Sir," snapped the sentry, saluting the smallish, fit man in a new khaki uniform with bright yellow trim. He wore a new brown campaign hat with the left brim turned up and pinned to the crown with crossed sword insignia, highly polished shoes with knee-high brown leggings, and a white bandana with blue polka dots as a loose cravat around his neck. The sun flickered off the small gold-rimmed spectacles that rested on his red nose. A brushy moustache like Solon's, only dark brown not nearly white, topped his big toothy smile.

"Madam, sir, son, I'm Lieutenant Colonel Roosevelt of the 1st Volunteer Cavalry," sang the man to the visitors. "General Wheeler is our cavalry's field commander and I'm on my way to let him know we're here. We just arrived from Texas. May I be of service?" the confident young officer said.

"We have to see the general, Colonel," Lou answered.

"Southern, madam? Delightful accent, delightful," smiled the stranger. "My dear mother is a proud Georgian. Yes, delightful." Roosevelt twittered, "We had a resident Rebel in my home during the War of Southern Rebellion, Madam—my mother!" Roosevelt laughed robustly and his eyes twinkled with good friendly humor.

A thought had come to Lou while confronting the sergeant, and now she acted on what she thought. Always one to keep her business to herself and not broadcast it to others, she was concerned about the nature of their mission and what to tell or not tell this stranger. Acting without caution, she reached into her handbag and pulled out a small object wrapped in a bright yellow handkerchief.

Roosevelt continued, "Madam, maybe you'll allow me to take a message. General Shafter has cracked down on civilians in camp. Difficult for us to do our necessary preparations with all the confusion of supplies, transport, foul-ups, and this rather challenging weather. Many of the boys are sick. We can't have our good citizens plighted by our malady. Yes, madam. But I certainly can get a message to the general on you folks' behalf. Be delighted madam, delighted," he said pleased with his solution.

Joe thought, "What a dude. He's too cheerful by half." He felt an equal measure of fascination and irritation as he experienced the first cavalry officer he had ever seen for real.

Solon was not taken in by the bombast of this Lieutenant Colonel Roosevelt. He just saw a shave-tail with lieutenant colonel boards on his collar and was once again bemused by the ways of the military and the world. He knew, as Lou knew, who Roosevelt was. They'd read of his exploits as police commissioner in New York City. A grandstander for sure, both had agreed with his raids on the awful sweatshops. They cheered his aggressiveness in helping attack the child labor outrages but were perplexed by his equal energy in disrupting labor unions and reform groups who were trying to change the oppression of the workplace. Do "good" acts cancel out "bad" ones? They'd spent many hours on that query. Solon supported the positive and Lou the negative.

Lou quickly scribbled a note on a piece of paper with a stubby pencil offered by the colonel. She wrote, "General, sir, we're at the Tampa Hotel, room 317. Lou." She folded the note and gave it to Roosevelt with the knotted yellow handkerchief.

The young politician/soldier bowed as he held his hat brim. "My pleasure, Southern lady," he said warmly. He turned and was off on his mission.

"Lieutenant, I need to see the general," Lieutenant Colonel Roosevelt informed the young, very slight man at a campaign desk under an old twisted palm tree a few minutes later. Roosevelt knew that the young officer was General Wheeler's adjutant. They had met in Washington before the war at a West Point affair at which Roosevelt had spoken. A canvas screened army tent stood buttoned-up twenty feet to the rear of the desk. The area had the neat precision of regular Army. The ground had been cleared of all leaves and refuse. Even the few coconut-sized rocks were lined into a parameter.

Jumping up and snapping to attention, the younger officer said, " Sir, the general is not here, sir."

The colonel returned his salute. "Drats, when will he be back?" Roosevelt asked.

"Sir, I don't rightly know," the lieutenant responded.

"Well, I've got to get to the quartermaster. This supply situation is outrageous, outrageous," Roosevelt fumed. "We've just arrived and can't make heads or tails of this place."

"Yes sir, the general is continuously about that concern with General Shafter," the adjutant said.

"Very good, bully, yes, very good, excellent," Roosevelt cheered. "Here, Lieutenant," he handed the small handkerchief wrapped object and note to the young man. "An elderly gentleman—clergy by dress—a lady, and young man wish to see the general. See that he gets this," Roosevelt said. "Sure hope its not some complaint out of one of the boys' town activities," he reflected seriously.

"It may be a while before the general is back in this area, sir. I'll see the general gets this when I take him the morning report and paperwork within the hour."

"Capital, Lieutenant, yes. Not quite sure about all the mystery here. Yes, but I certainly don't want our boys acting reckless with the local citizenry. They might have told me the nature of their business. Could be they're like my Dutch country people in New York State— they keep their business close, yes, yes, close." Roosevelt reasoned out loud as the perplexed, young, short officer stood straight, stretching all his 5-foot 5-inch frame and 110 pounds. The sun cleared the palm and shone directly on the two. Beads of steamy perspiration rolled down both men's faces into their tight collars. It was another brutal south Florida tropical day.

"Yes sir, I'll see that the general gets this, sir, immediately," smiled the young officer.

Roosevelt wheeled and said as he walked with fast steps, "Very well, very well." On his second step the sandy ground held his foot and he had to push and pull his way through the soft footing, losing his military bearing. The general's aide took note of the soaked-through uniform back of the two-month-old lieutenant colonel.

As a West Point graduate, class of 1895, First Lieutenant Joseph Wheeler Jr. was quickly learning about volunteer soldiers—some were good, some bad. Working as his father's adjutant offered him a post-graduate course in the real Army's mystique. He chuckled to himself when he remembered that he was trained at the military academy as an artillery officer. Protecting his father against all the silliness folks brought to him and shuffling papers rather than sending shot against the enemy was a different function, sure enough. He preferred the offensive operation that he was trained for rather than the defensive maneuvering required in this job.

He lay on the bed in his drawers and undershirt. The ornate bed's coverlet was pulled down, and the once-crisp sheets were damp from his fitful sleep. The ceiling fan moved the air. It was some relief from the muggy, stifling atmosphere over Tampa in the early summer of 1898. Joe Wheeler's attempt at rest had some success but was not a complete accomplishment even though the Tampa Hotel was renowned for its comfort and grandeur. It was sure more comfortable than the sand and swamp of camp. The reality of his task and its importance was a heavy burden for him.

"It is beyond imagining," he said to himself as he rummaged in his awakening. Dreams had invaded his sleep: scenes of unnamed farm fields, woods, muddy trails mixed with rain, smoke, bloodied crawling men, and riderless horses confused his unconscious world. His dreams offered old odors of burnt gunpowder, manure, blood, salt pork, and honeysuckle. He was in a modern exquisite hotel, but he was also young and back at war in his dreams. "Fightin' Joe" was there again, and so was the Irishman—Cleburne. And his idea—that idea.

"Pat, you were right," the mostly asleep Wheeler mumbled. Behind Joe's consciousness, his inner world took him to the Civil War and a reunion with Patrick R. Cleburne, fellow officer and colleague in numerous conflicts. Cleburne was killed at Franklin, one of six Confederate general casualties in that desperate, failed advance against Thomas's force. Cleburne, Irish veteran of the British Army and Arkansas businessman and lawyer, had proven to be one of the best Confederate field officers.

"Pat, we did it at Ringgold Gap after they pushed the boys off Missionary Ridge, didn't we? We held Tunnel Hill too, saved the Army that day. Sherman, Thomas, Grant—we stopped 'em cold, your division and my cavalry.

"You were right ... the coloreds. They're here Pat. I'm commanding them and the 9th and 10th cavalry are the best in the regular Army. You wanted us to free and recruit the slaves in '64 ... I fought you. Raised all manner of opposition to it. Thought it crazy and unimaginable. Yes, Pat, they are good, and we might just have stopped Sherman on his way to the sea if they'd been in my command. What would we have been with thousands of colored in our ranks? I was so young. It was so different." He shook off the disturbing visitation, returning to the now.

"I'm sure not twenty-five. Maybe I'm wiser now at sixty-two!" he mumbled to himself as he reached for his pocket watch on the side table. "1:18." As he turned back and looked at the ceiling, his mind went to work. "What a mess this war is, and I'm in the smack dab middle of it." He'd spent three twenty-hour days trying to get some system set up for his corps cavalry. He'd seen to his various units and tried mightily to do right by them. Joe Jr. had demanded he leave their tent in the camp and rest, and had escorted him to this room—even pulling off his boots. When he'd settled the fatigued general, the junior officer Wheeler had "ordered" his command officer father to bath and bed.

The general's thoughts wandered and struggled. "So few horses meant a dismounted cavalry. Well, maybe that can be overcome since jungle-like conditions face my boys. We're going to be facing the best of the kingdom of Spain, and they know the ground. I'm not sure about Dr. Woods much—the 1st Volunteer Cavalry! That young socialite 'damn' Republican cowboy Roosevelt is a 'forward charge' type. That can be good and that can be bad. Fouled up supplies ... Army serving at the pleasure of the Navy ... no mounts ... outdated weapons, little smokeless ammunition ..."

When they'd arrived the first time at headquarters at the hotel several weeks earlier, there had been no small share of benevolent smiles and a few smirks as the two small men entered. They were versions of the same physique—one old, wizened, bald, whiskered, 5-foot 5-inch gentleman dressed years out of date, and the young one clad in simple civilian attire. General Wheeler's quick walk was duplicated by Lieutenant Wheeler. They looked out of place in the assorted uniforms—National Guard, regular Army, Navy, wool and canvas, and dandy hangers-on.

When the general came down from his room, the son smiled at the father as the elder quickly stepped to his chair. "Father, I've reviewed the reports. Most are worthless, and the others are discouraging. There's a note and strange package here from Colonel Roosevelt's." Joe Jr. handed the items to his father. The general took them and sat down in the chair on the other side of the parlor. He read the note and felt the bundled handkerchief.

He'd not been in contact with the Stevensons in years. Their lives had been filled with time separate from his. He untied the bandana and his heart smiled when he felt the cool silver of his childhood gift from Father in his hand. "Well, I swear!" was his choked response as he blinked eyes moistened by memories of Spring Place, Miss Vann, lace curtains, good whiskey, stinking poultice, and Lou's rough but gentle hands tending his foot and his life. "I swear," was his attempt to restrain his strong unexpected feelings. He got up and went directly to the magnificent lobby stairs without a word to his son. As he moved, he stuffed the note in his coat pocket and clutched the yellow bundle in his left hand. He sprinted to another reunion upstairs in room 317.

Chapter 30

"Cuba Libre," 1898

Lou sipped her frosty root beer. It was a brutally hot day in Dellrose, Lincoln County, Tennessee, fifteen miles west of the county seat of Fayetteville. The soda parlor in the drug store of the Sherrill-Stone Company, an expansive two-story dry goods, grocery, hardware, and drug store, offered cool treats that would help with the heat and humidity. The *Fayetteville Observer*, the weekly county newspaper, had come in on the 11 a.m. freight wagon. Lou was at the loading dock to meet the wagon. She took the paper back to her booth.

Oblivious of the fan's whirl were the busy, heated clerks and customers, twenty feet away in the dry goods department of the store. Lou adjusted her round silver wire glasses, lifting her head so as to use the bifocals' lower half. Focusing on the folded paper, she read the lead story across the top fold:

Special Report to *The Observer* from *The New York Herald* by Richard Harding Davis.

June 28 – Los Guasimas, Cuba.

"Rousing Victory. Rough Riders Rout Spanish Regulars. Wheeler's V Corp Cavalry Clear Road to Santiago"

Theodore Roosevelt, late assistant Navy secretary, police commissioner of New York City, Dakota Territory rancher, and his volunteer "Rough Riders," joined by regular U.S. cavalry troops, fought jungle and Imperial Spanish might at a ridge called Las Guasimas at sunrise June 24. This location is eleven miles from the U.S. Army landing site on the beaches at Daiquiri. Las Guasimas is just west of Siboney, a small village on the road from Daiquiri to Santiago. The outnumbered liberation forces, fighting uphill against intense rifle volleys and artillery, pushed the soldiers of Imperial Spain off this critical ridge northwest of the American landing site. Enemy batteries were posed to rain shot and shell on the thousands of landed and landing warriors of the V Corp.

Fewer than 1,200 soldiers—two hundred and forty-four troopers of the 1st Regular Cavalry and 220 of the 10th Colored Cavalry, Leonard Wood and Theodore Roosevelt's "Rough Riders" (1st Volunteer Cavalry), 530 strong aided by several hundred Cuba Libre soldiers, executed a difficult offensive engagement against over 2,000 entrenched Spanish infantry and artillery. The Spanish were arrayed in three successive lines along Las Guasimas Ridge. To their backs and a mile west of their position was the small village of La Rodonda.

Major General Joseph "Fightin" Joe' Wheeler (US Volunteers), a sixty-two-year-old former Confederate major general in the War of Rebellion and currently Eighth District Congressman from north Alabama, commanded the V Corp Cavalry. He personally directed this technically "maverick" mission. The standing order from V Corp Commander, Major General William R. Shafter, was that Wheeler's and his cavalry, the first ashore, were to entrench inland of the beach and cover the landing operation. The horse troopers were to watch and not engage.

Alerted to the dangerous position of the Spanish, they were to do more than watch and wait. Cuba Libre General Demetrio Castillo Duany reported to General Wheeler the disposition of the entrenched Spaniards with artillery on the heights of Las Guasimas. This ridge runs roughly parallel to the landing beaches three miles to the northwest. General Castillo advised General Wheeler of the Spanish plan to bombard and attack the landing Americans.

General Wheeler, with three of his staff, did a personal reconnaissance of the Spanish positions to confirm this information. The feisty cavalry veteran saw nothing special in the ride deep into enemy territory. He called it, "Just a little vedette." Good readers, "vedette" is an old cavalry word meaning "a mounted scout forward of position to observe and report enemy movements." His personal scouting mission validated the threat reported by General Castillo.

Taking a sip of her root beer, Lou chuckled and said to herself, "Lordy, General, you ain't twenty-eight anymore. But what else could we expect outta you." Pulling her handkerchief from her cuff, she patted her forehead and cheeks. The heat in the Elk River Valley was intense this summer morning. Returning to the newspaper story, she found her place and read.

He held a council of war with his officers and the order was given: "Move on the enemy positions at 0600, the next day, June 24. Aroused at 3 a.m. and after a breakfast of hard-tack and bacon, washed down with black coffee, the troopers checked their equipment and formed ranks. The weather was oppressive even before daybreak, but morale soared. America's finest had come to do freedom's work with good cheer.

Two columns of some 500 men moved out at 6 a.m. as dismounted cavalry (foot soldiers).

This looks like only the first of such dismounted deployments for these horse soldiers. Only a few horses and mules for the artillery pieces and officers' mounts were brought on the hasty and poorly planned expedition. The War Department was very neglectful of the situation and needs of this operation, but our brave young men did wonderfully despite all the difficulties.

The terrain restricted a unified line of ground movement; thus, the Rough Riders and the Regulars struck at different ends of the Spanish entrenchment. Each segment made slow, destructive progress. Both American elements encountered strong resistance with increasing casualties. Nine regiments of regular US infantry 2nd Division had moved up behind the cavalry attack, a mile back in support. General Wheeler ordered General Henry W. Lawton and his command to come forward. Almost immediately after that order the Spanish retreated west. At this break of will and effort, the dismounted cavalry attack became a Spanish rout with the infantry joining in the victory.

General Wheeler, hearing and seeing the troopers advance of the Spanish positions, shouted as he did a little jump, "Come on, come on Boys. We've got the d——d Yankees on the run!"

- RHD -

Lou laughed out loud when she read the general's quote. "That old bantam is the child of the young bantam," she said to herself. "I'll be, I'll be …" Recovering from Davis's report of the general's antics, Lou turned the folded paper over to read the lower half, below the fold, fearful of any casualties report with Joe's name. Her eyes went instantly to a boxed story on the right side. The headlines read, "Tennessee Trooper Stevenson Saves Horses and Mules." Startled, Lou knocked her root beer off the table onto the store's dark brown, oil-soaked oak floor. The heavy mug bounced on the floor but didn't break. Half of her drink spread over the worn grooved floor. A stock boy, working on a low shelf of men's toiletries, jumped up from his stool.

"No bother, Miss Lou. I'll take care of that. Let me get you a clean mug and more root beer."

"Son, that's fine, don't bother," Lou said, disoriented and flustered.

"No bother, no bother at all," the thirteen-year-old, chubby teenager said as he went about his responsibilities with a full-faced smile.

Lou returned to the paper.

Tennessee Trooper Saves Horses and Mules. Ten-Foot Waves Terrify US Cavalry Mounts. Daiquiri Landing Accomplished with Difficulty.

Special to *The Observer* by Charles Berryhill, special correspondent in Cuba for *The Nashville American.*

Daiquiri, Cuba – June 24, 1898.

A chaotic spectacle characterized the landing of 17,000 American soldiers of liberation twenty miles east of Santiago Bay. The most troublesome feature was the heavy swells, ten-foot waves. Two troopers drown in the operation. Scores of mules and horses were thrown overboard as getting the boats alongside the short pier was impossible. Disoriented, some of these noble, martial animals swam in circles until exhausted and drowning. More swam away from shore out into the sea.

Corporal J. W. Stevenson of Dellrose, Tennessee, bugler and aide to Major General Wheeler, had the clarity of thought to use the time-honored method for directing cavalry mounts—he blew a clear call "To Horse." The noble steeds turned and swam back to the shore of the fouled landing.

Lou hurriedly found a dime in her change purse and put it on the glass-topped table. She folded the paper and put it under her arm. Grabbing her bonnet, she was up and out the store's door. In the hot, sunny, heavy air, she went to the horse and buggy and was off to the Western Union at the depot across Dellrose Creek.

General Wheeler at Santiago

"During one of the most active engagements of the Cuban campaign during the Spanish-American War, General Wheeler started on the two-mile journey to the front in an ambulance (suffering from yellow fever). About halfway to the front, he met some litters bearing wounded. The veteran (Wheeler), against the protest of the surgeons, immediately ordered his horse, and after personally assisting the wounded

into the ambulance, mounted and rode onward. The men
burst into frantic cheers, which followed the General all
along the line." – Correspondence, *New York Tribune*.)

Into the thick of the fight he went, pallid and sick and wan,
    Borne in an ambulance to the front, a ghostly wisp
        of a man;
  But the fighting soul of a fighting man, approved in
        the long ago,
  Went to the front in that ambulance and the body of
        Fighting Joe.

Out from the front they were coming back, smitten of
        Spanish shells—
  Wounded boys from the Vermont hills and the
        Alabama dells;
  "Put them into this ambulance: I'll ride to the front,"
        he said:
  And he climbed to the saddle and rode right on, that
        little old ex-Confed.

From end to end of the long blue ranks rose up the
        ringing cheers,
  And many a powder-blackened face furrowed with
        sodden tears,
  As with flashing eyes and gleaming sword, and hair and
        beard of snow,
Into the hell of shot and shell road little old Fighting Joe!

  Sick with fever and racked with pain, he could not
        stay away,

For he heard the song of the yester-years in
the deep-mouthed
cannon's bay—
He heard in the calling song of the guns there was work for
him to do,
Where his country's best blood splashed and flowed 'round
the old Red, White and Blue.

Fevered body and hero heart! This Union's heart to you
Beats out in love and reverence—and to each dear boy
in blue
Who stood or fell mid the shot and shell, and cheered in the
face of the foe,
As, wan and white, to the heart of the fight rode little old
Fighting Joe!

—James Lindsay Gordon in the *New York Tribune*

Fightin' Joe, Solon, & TR

Epilogue

❦

"Taps, day is done ..."

It was a cold, clear, crisp winter day on the gentle brown banks above the Potomac. The sun helped the cold crowd, but no one was comfortable in spite of the sun's valiant efforts. The setting served as a beautiful backdrop for the somber duty attended by hundreds of bundled folks. Politicians were fronted by President Theodore Roosevelt, a former subordinate. Senators from dozens of states and Congressmen from twenty score districts across America stood behind the family. The generals of the U.S. Army, active and retired, formed a blue and gold clad detail behind the politicians. Completing the square were old comrades, those who had worn blue and tan in days not a decade earlier and blue, gray and butternut over forty years ago.

When the clergy—an active duty U.S. Army chaplain full colonel and an elderly civilian preacher concluded the service—a bugler in the active military unit assigned to burial detail began the tribute. He stood at the side of the clergy.

Taps

Day is done, gone the sun...

All is well, safely rest

God is nigh...

The first few notes of "Butterfield's Lullaby" rose above the congregation of blood, memory, and honor as another sound resonated from up towards the Curtis-Lee mansion. There were two other bugles, far off, joining in the mystical call that signaled the horse soldiers' advance into eternity.

Solon's tears began hot but chilled as they covered his cheeks. Bowing his head, he smiled down on the simple army-issue casket when he recognized the strain of a duet. He thought, "Alex and Joe have done it. The general would be much obliged."

Standing with Senator Bob Taylor of Tennessee and a few rows behind the general's children—Lucy, Annie, Joseph, and Carrie—Lou heard the distant tribute. As she listened, her eyes fixed on her husband's bowed gray head, tears came from her eyes and a smile to her lips. The stiff breeze and the chilling tears made her face feel like it had when she had been soaked crossing the Tennessee following Fightin' Joe Wheeler's troopers in her farrier wagon forty-three years ago.

The four pilgrims from Tennessee, all veterans of war and peace, sinners and saved, caught the overnight to Chattanooga at six. They left from Union Station on their way home.

Afterword

A portion of the proceeds from the sale of *The Mockingbird's Ballad* will be contributed to the restoration of the Joe Wheeler home at Pond Spring, near Courtland, Alabama, in Lawrence County. It is estimated that 95% of the contents of the Wheeler residence date from the period between the 1860s and the early twentieth century—artifacts, clothing, furniture, fixtures, records, uniforms, weapons, equipment, correspondence, etc. A $9.2 million project is planned.

The State of Alabama Historical Commission is in the process of restoring Pond Spring. Renowned experts and craftspeople are working with professional staff, scholars, and volunteers to present Pond Spring to the public (grounds, eleven buildings, cemeteries, and a visitor/educational center) as the finest living museum west of Williamsburg and east of San Simion. Visitors and researchers will be able to walk through time to an era that buried one culture and birthed another, the time between 1850 and 1900.

Who knows, "Fightin' Joe's" spirit might greet you at the gate and invite you for a walk in the garden or to take supper with him,

Miss Daniella, and the children. You could press him to tell you about his and the boys' "Ride 'Round Rosecrans" in 1862, or the taking of San Juan Hill and Kettle Hill in 1898. Don't be disappointed if he'd rather talk about what promise the Tennessee Valley and waterways hold for Southern renewal and America's greatness. He's like that.

Miss Annie Early Wheeler (1868-1955) was the Wheelers' second daughter, and she faithfully maintained her family's possessions and Pond Spring. Today it is a collection of remarkable historical and cultural significance. Her fifty-seven years of involvement with the American Red Cross (in three wars: as a nurse with Clara Barton in the Spanish-American War, Cuba, and the Philippines; in France during World War I; and her energized World War II stateside efforts when she was over seventy years old) make up no small part of the Pond Springs story and treasure trove.

There are a variety of ways people can become involved in saving and restoring Pond Spring.

Visit the Joe Wheeler Home at Pond Spring.

Twenty-three miles west on Interstate 65 (Exit 340) on AL Hwy. 20 (Alt. US 72), seventeen miles west of Decatur, Alabama, twenty-six miles east of Muscle Shoals. Nearby are historic Wheeler Dam of TVA, Joe Wheeler Wildlife Preserve, Wheeler Lake, and Joe Wheeler State Park.

Thursday, Friday, and Saturday hours: 9 a.m.–4 p.m.

Sunday hours: 1 p.m.–5 p.m.

Groups are scheduled any day of the week.

For information call 256-637-8513.

E-mail: www.wheelerplantation.org

Help save and restore Pond Spring.

Tax deductible contributions may be made to:

Friends of the Joseph Wheeler Foundation

Pond Spring

12280 AL Hwy. 20

Hillsboro, AL 35643

Volunteer

This project offers a wide variety of opportunities for hands-on participation in the life of Pond Spring; restoration assistance, helping with educational programs, being a guide, helping with archives, etc. Contact Pond Spring for additional information.

Resources

W"e all stand on others' shoulders," a wise one observed. Among those on whose shoulders I stand in this work are ...

- John P. Dyer, *From Shiloh to San Juan: The Life of "Fightin' Joe" Wheeler*. 1961. The lone authority.
- E. F. Williams and J. J. Fox, they reprinted in one volume W. C. Dodson's *Campaigns of Wheeler and His Cavalry 1862–65* and *The Santiago Campaign—Cuba 1898, 1899*. This work was compiled from General Wheeler's unpublished memories and interviews by W. C. Dodson in 1899 for the Wheeler's Confederate Cavalry Association.
- Albert A. Nofi, *A Civil War Treasury*, 1992. A very helpful resource, easily accessible.
- Donald Cartwell, *The Civil War Book of Lists*, 2001. A most useful quick reference work.

- Philip Katcher, *The Complete Civil War*, 1992. This is an excellent fact file of the campaigns, weapons, tactics, armies, and personalities of the great conflict.
- David S. Heidler and Jeanne T. Heidler, *The Encyclopedia of the American Civil War: A Political, Social and Military History*, 2000. This is a remarkable work of 1,600 essays. It strives to be a "comprehensive source" for a boundless subject, and it gets mighty close.

Civil War research is a vast reservoir of information. The quality of that material varies greatly. Several "giants" in the field provide wonderful insight and analysis ... Bruce Catton, Shelby Foote, William C. Davis, and James McPherson.

The short war with Spain in 1898 represents a milestone in United States history and America's sense of nationhood. The United States involvement in world affairs was changed forever. George Washington's admonition of "no foreign entanglements" was ignored. The USA entered the international stage, went about unique empire building, and became a member of the world's elite group of "great powers." The why and how of that change needs more attention.

Useful references are ...

- Albert A. Nofi. *The Spanish-American War, 1898*, 1996. This very accessible work is a source of extensive information from personalities to units. Analysis is not its objective, but there is some—which helps.
- Donald M Goldstein and Katherine V. Dillon, *The Spanish-American War: The Story and Photographs*, 1998. A very good resource. The graphics are most intriguing.
- Stan Cohen, *Images of the Spanish-American War: April-August 1898*, 1997. This is a rich and expansive resource.

Two special references required noting . . .
- Russell E. Miller, *The Larger Hope*, 2 vol., 1979, 1985. A remarkable history and resource for the unorthodox and mostly unnoticed liberal faith.
- Marc McCutcheon, *Everyday Life in the 1800s*, 1993. An indispensable help for writers, students, and historians.

The Author

A sixth-generation Tennessean, Doak M. Mansfield and his kin have hunted, farmed, preached, fought, and taught school across the Sequatchie and Tennessee Valleys for over two centuries. Born in Fayetteville on November 28, 1948, he was reared in rural Lincoln County (Dellrose, Yukon, and Mary's Grove) and attended its public schools: Carmargo, Taft, and Central High. He began working when he was in high school at age thirteen at Kirkland Grocery, a nearby country store.

Able to finance a college education through work-study programs and National Defense Loans, he left his share-cropper/factory worker home in 1966 for Martin (Methodist) College in Pulaski, Tennessee. He graduated from Martin in 1968 with an Associate of Arts degree. He then attended Austin Peay State University in Clarksville, Tennessee, graduating in 1970 with a major in history (Bachelor of Science) and teacher certification. Mansfield taught public school in Cowan, Tennessee, for a year before returning to Martin College as dean of admissions and director of housing.

Entering the ministry in 1973, he attended Wesley Theological Seminary in Washington, DC, while serving as pastor of Sudley United Methodist Church adjacent to the Manassas (Bull Run) Battlefield in Prince William County in northern Virginia, 1973-75. He became a Unitarian Universalist minister in 1975 and served the Heritage UU Church (originally the First Universalist Society) in Cincinnati, Ohio, for ten years, 1975-85. He earned his Master of Divinity degree from United Theological Seminary in Dayton, Ohio, in 1977.

During his Cincinnati ministry, he served as part-time staff chaplain at the Bethesda Hospital, as a U.S. Army reserve chaplain, and in various community service activities in the Mt. Washington, Anderson Township, and greater Cincinnati communities.

In 1985, Mansfield became minister of the Unitarian Universalist Church of Huntsville, Alabama, and retired from that position in 2000. He earned a Doctor of Ministry degree from the Graduate Theological Foundation, South Bend, Indiana, in 1996.

He now devotes most of his time to writing, occasional preaching, tending to house and cat (Opie), and practicing unconventional ministry.

This is his first novel. He lives in the Piney Woods of Jones County near Laurel, Mississippi, with his wife, Peggy F. Owens-Mansfield. He is the father of two grown sons—John Amos Mansfield of Hattiesburg, Mississippi, and James Adam Mansfield of Cincinnati, Ohio—and is the son of Margaret J. Maddox Mansfield and the late John H. Mansfield.